ONCE A MONTH

Also by Kelvin L. Reed

Rookie Year: Journey of a First-Year Teacher

Midnight Sunshine

President Pro Tem

Guilt by Association

ONCE A MONTH

A NOVEL BY

KELVIN L. REED

Copyright © 2015 Kelvin L. Reed

ISBN 978-0-9667631-1-9

Library of Congress Control Number: 2014960366

This is a work of fiction. All of the characters, conversations
and events contained therein are imaginary. Any similarity to
real persons, living or dead, is coincidental and not intended
by the author.

Peralta Publishing Company, Las Vegas, NV

Printed by CreateSpace, an Amazon.com company

Cover design by Graphichubs

www.kelvinlreed.com

This book is dedicated to my beloved wife, Marieta,
and to my dear, departed brother, Gregory

ONE: THE PROPOSAL

"Tony, I want to talk to you."

"Can it wait? I want to finish grading these papers before I turn in."

"This is important."

Anthony Monroe, called "Tony" since he was a little boy, frowned, conveying slight annoyance. He didn't like being disturbed when working in his small office, located on the second floor of the home he shared with his wife and their two children. The modest two-story Colonial house was one of hundreds in Hyde Park, a diverse, middle class neighborhood in the southern part of Boston.

Rose Monroe, standing in the doorway, put her hands on her hips. "Dang, the third week of September and already you're grading papers? But like I said, this is important."

"Uh-oh." Tony moaned. He sat back in his wheeled, high back padded chair and spoke with playful caution. "When you say 'this is important' it's going to cost something." He gestured with his right hand, beckoning Rose to enter. While not welcoming the interruption, he appreciated that she and the children had been generous, ceding the office as *his* work area. To show she had garnered his full attention, he capped his red felt-tip pen and dropped it onto the desk, which held a desktop computer and a stack of eleventh grade history quizzes he had almost finished correcting.

He watched with resignation. His wife of fourteen years entered the room and casually inspected the two identical chairs on her side of his desk. After a slight pause she plopped into the one on the right. The dark brown curtains, tan walls, and soft glow of the desk lamp, which augmented the brightness of the overhead light—its own full potential cut in half by a dimmer switch—complimented her pretty, medium brown face.

"In a way 'cost' is what I want to talk about," she answered, "and it's not going to cost us anything." She lowered her head and stared at her bedroom slippers and the carpet, which was slightly darker than the walls. "I know we've had a million talks about how to get out from under what seems like a mountain of debt, and I admit this whole thing is mostly my fault."

"Don't blame yourself, baby," Tony retorted. "We're a team. We're both to blame." He always made that declaration, although both knew Rose was by far the big spender in the family. Further assuring her of his love in spite of this, Tony stretched one of his long legs under the desk and ran his socked foot over Rose's leg, covered by cotton pajama bottoms. He felt warm with satisfaction when she returned his affectionate gesture by kicking off her slippers and likewise rubbing his leg with her foot.

Rose abruptly put her feet under her chair and got down to business. "Anyway, you know Cam is my best friend," she opened, "and she's been hurting so bad lately."

"Poor little rich girl," Tony moaned.

"Now that's not fair," Rose protested. "It's not her fault she's been unlucky in love and keeps choosing jerks who use her."

"She can't buy love."

"Are you going to listen or not?"

Tony nodded. "I'm sorry, hon. You know I'm very fond of Cam too, because you and the kids love her and because she has a good heart." He shook his finger. "I hope you haven't asked her for any more money." His normally mellifluous baritone voice grew low and stern. "We agreed we have to figure out how to get out of this mess without ask—"

"No, honey," Rose interrupted. "I didn't ask her for anything." She lowered her head again and played with the bottom button of her long-sleeved pajama top. "But Cam has been so full of hurt and resentment these days. I've never seen her so lost."

"Poor thing."

Rose stood and put her hands on her hips again. "Now you're being mean. That's not right. Cam's my best friend."

"I'm sorry," Tony said. "I'm just teasing." He rose to his six feet, four inch height, ten inches taller than Rose, and gently tugged on her hand, prompting her to sit. He returned to his chair. "I know she's been dealt some low cards from time to time." He ran his fingers over his clean shaven face, several shades darker than Rose's, then caressed her leg again with his foot. "Honestly, I wish there was something we could do."

Rose took a deep breath. "Actually, there is."

"Really?" Tony asked. "What can we do to help a woman who's a multimillionaire?"

"Cam says money isn't everything."

"People who got money coming out the ying-yang always say that."

Rose took another deep breath. "Well, to tell you the truth, it's not really what *we* can do to help. Mostly it's what *you* can do."

Tony blinked several times. "Me? What can I do? Like you said, she's *your* best friend."

Rose nodded in agreement, then lifted Tony's hand and kissed it. "We have a good marriage. Don't we, dear?"

"I would say so."

"Fourteen years—not without ups and downs, of course—and two beautiful children."

Tony took a deep breath and waited, hoping Rose would get to the point, but she didn't. Instead, she stared at a custom-made calendar frame hanging on the wall above a bookshelf. A photo taken the previous year of her, Tony, and their then eleven year old boy-girl twins loomed over the word "September." Tony attempted to prod her by squeezing her hand. "What is it, Rose?"

She squeezed his hand in return, then released it. "We've always said nothing would ever come between us, right?"

Tony shook his head. "Never, baby, but what does all this have to do with our financial mess—definitely one of those downs you mentioned—and Cam?"

Rose stood and paced back and forth. "Well, Cam...I mean Cam and I...I mean, there's something that would help everyone out." She opened her arms and dropped them at her side. "Cam is very attractive, don't you agree?"

Tony nodded. Attractive wouldn't begin to describe her. Cam was what his British colleague at school would call a "right looker." Just the same, Tony had always chosen to be nonchalant about Cam's beauty so there would never be any misunderstanding about his intentions from Cam or Rose. "I suppose she is," he replied, sounding almost bored. "You told me she even did some modeling years ago before she started—and later sold—her company, making her rich." The computer monitor on his desk went to sleep and faded to black. Tony glanced at it and returned his attention to Rose. "Just tell me what's going on."

"I don't know how to say it."

"Just say it, honey."

Rose pushed her thick, shoulder length hair away from her face. "Cam will give us ten thousand dollars; ten thousand dollars a month for—"

"No!" Tony snapped, gritting his teeth. He stood again. "Damn it. We already talked about this and we agreed. No more loans from Cam. It took us almost a year to pay back the ten grand you borrowed from her before—without consulting me, I might add."

"But this time it's not a loan."

"The Monroes don't ask for nor accept charity."

"It's not charity either."

Tony scratched his head, covered by a thick dusting of very closely cropped hair and wondered: *What the hell's going on?* "Then what is it?" he inquired, with his tone indicating a hint of exasperation.

Rose pointed. "Sit down." Tony did. So did she. "What I've been trying to tell you is...well, Cam is lonely and in pain, and she's always been very fond of you too. She thinks you're the sweetest, most considerate man she's ever met—and I completely concur."

"Thank you both," Tony said. "But what—"

"So she wants you to spend the night."

"Spend the night?"

Rose closed her eyes. "With her. She wants you to make love to her."

Tony leaned forward. "What?"

Rose shrugged. "And I said okay."

"You what?" Tony grabbed the arms of his chair and squeezed them. "So my own wife is pimping me out?"

"It's not like that, honey."

"What have you two been smoking?"

"You said you'd hear me out."

"No I didn't," Tony countered. "And even if I did, it wouldn't matter because I didn't know you were going to suggest something so ridiculous."

Rose clutched the wooden arms of her chair as if she were going to stand but instead let go and remained seated. "Will you please listen to me?"

Tony sat back in his chair and folded his long, muscular arms across his chest. "Go ahead." He couldn't believe the conversation taking place.

Rose resumed running her foot across Tony's leg, covered by blue jeans. "I don't have to tell you we're in quite a mess. The two mortgages for this house, the kids' tuition, the orthodontist bills, the car payments, credit cards, you know." Tony simply nodded. "Unless we get our hands on some serious cash very soon we're going to be, as you would say, up Shit Creek without a paddle."

"I know," Tony said. "It doesn't look good."

"Well," Rose continued. "For years Cam's been saying how much she wishes she could find a man like you: handsome, intelligent, tall, considerate, honest, and black—and a great lover carrying a big gun." She wiggled her meticulously pruned eyebrows.

Tony scowled. "Jesus, Rose. What have you been telling people about me?"

"Not people, hon," Rose replied, "but I may have mentioned something to Cam once or twice over the many years of our friendship."

Tony put his hand over his face and shook his head. "You women. Always treating us men like we're just a piece of meat." He chuckled, forcing an appearance of dimples on each cheek. "I'm not just another pretty face, you know."

Rose smiled. "True, but to make a long story short, Cam doesn't want to be out there in the dating scene for a while, so she's offered to give us ten thousand dollars a month for twelve months. That's one hundred twenty thousand dollars, if you, um, well, come to her house once a month for one year and...and you know, make her feel better." She paused and waited. Tony said nothing. "This would be a win-win deal for everybody. We keep the wolf away from our front door and Cam gets something she needs." She paused again. Tony still said nothing. "Well, what do you think?"

Tony grabbed the mouse of his computer and turned off the machine. "No," he grunted before stuffing a one inch pile of school papers into a folder with "Boston Public School Department" printed on the cover. Indignation welled up in his throat like the taste of expired cough syrup. How would Rose feel if he announced he had given some man permission to sleep with—have sex with her for money? "No," he said again. "Hell no," he added for emphasis. He left the papers on the desk and slowly stepped around it, heading for the door.

Rose bounded out of her chair and cut him off. "Tony, there's no other way. You're thirty-nine and I'm thirty-seven."

"I know how old we are. So what?"

"We can't start over at our age," Rose declared. "You know we can't get any more credit. If you don't do this, we're going to lose our home and probably one of the cars. The kids are going to have to leave the private school they've been attending since kindergarten and go to a public school here in Boston. They'll be humiliated. We'll all be humiliated."

Tony listened. After years of marriage he no longer noticed the softened R's in Rose's words from her Boston accent, which surfaced prominently when she became excited. "We brought this on ourselves."

Rose rested her head on Tony's chest, partially obscuring the "Alexander Hamilton High School" lettering of his sweatshirt, and whined like a child. "You're absolutely right. We brought this on ourselves, especially me, but we can't let Zoë and Adam suffer for our mistakes, can we?"

Tony spoke without making eye contact with Rose. "So rather than pray about it and trust God as we agreed, the answer is to enter a pact with the devil and have me cheat on you?"

"It's not cheating if I consent to it," Rose insisted, "and I'm willing to make this sacrifice for our family, especially for our children, even though you know sharing you even once will just about kill me." She lowered her voice to almost a whisper. "I admit I've put on a few pounds and our love life has been less than stellar lately. I know you've been frustrated in more ways than one— and that's been my fault as well. So this would be something for you, too. I mean, what man in his right mind wouldn't want to spend a few nights with someone like Cam?"

Tony put his large hands on Rose's shoulders and eased her backward at arm's length. "Maybe a man who loves his wife and goes to church with his family every Sunday and takes his marriage vows seriously?"

Rose put her head back on Tony's chest. After waiting for a few seconds she spoke tenderly. "Please, honey," she whispered. "Don't decide right now. Think it over. Sleep on it." She hugged him. "It's nearly ten o'clock. You have to get up at five. Let's go to bed."

Tony sighed with frustrated longing. Years earlier Rose's eyes burned with desire when she breathlessly whispered, "Let's go to bed." These days "go to bed" meant "go to sleep." He glanced at the clock hanging on the wall near the door, the clock for which she had paid over four hundred dollars, a fraction of the price for the one she had bought for their bedroom. Several seconds passed before he finally replied. "I can't believe I'm saying this, but okay, I'll think about it. That's all."

Rose tilted her head, puckered her lips and gave Tony three kisses in quick secession. "That's all I ask, honey."

TWO: CAM WAITS

Cam Spencer had received a text message telling her to expect an important telephone call after nine o'clock in the evening. Clad in silk pajamas, she sat on the plush sofa in her living room accompanied by half a dozen magazines. Elvira, her Siberian cat, lay next to her. Cam sighed while anxiously rat-a-tat-tatting her index and middle finger against the tire of a Jaguar sedan advertised in her magazine. To ascertain the exact time, she checked the cable box that rested on a shelf under her television. The TV, with its sixty-inch screen, sat on an oak wood stand with a marble top, nestled between a pair of china cabinets. The cabinets, seven feet tall but only three feet wide, were filled with valuable china from her many travels.

At her previous inspection the yellow bars on the cable box formed the numbers 9:10. Now they read 9:12.

Cam tried to focus on the periodical in her lap as well as the TV documentary featuring the history of Halloween in America. She shook her head with disapproval at the models in the fashion magazine. They were almost all white and looked like emaciated stick figures; just one of the reasons she had gotten out of that line of work. Cam flipped the magazine upside down and closed her green eyes, recalling her years in the fashion business.

She began modeling as a senior in high school but lasted only two years, having tired of being repeatedly advised to diet in order to lower her size four dress size. Next, while in her junior year at UCLA, she started her own company, called Otra Cosa, Spanish for "Something Else," as a school project; part of her double major in business and fashion design. She designed and sold clothing and accessories for wealthy women of color. It had not taken her long to realize she had tapped into a neglected niche. Within a year Cam had more work than she could handle. While most of her classmates had scurried pell-mell in a panic trying to find jobs at graduation, Cam had to hire someone to cope with sales volume.

She initially intended only to design and sell but eventually branched out into manufacturing, filling Internet orders, licensing the Otra Cosa brand, and opening retail stores in New York, Boston and Los Angeles. Her success notwithstanding, after eleven years she had simply grown weary of the rat race and sold every aspect of the business but retained the right to design under her own name. Her experience in the business prompted her to reach two conclusions. First: she would never be taken seriously among the beauty-fashion industry bigwigs. Second: most of the beauty-fashion industry bigwigs were racist and full of shit.

Cam opened her eyes and reached for the spill-proof cup of chamomile tea on the end table and took a sip, then placed the cup back on the table. She scratched Elvira on the head and behind the ears. The loyal feline responded with soft purrs. "Isabella and Lakshmi have gone home for the day to their families," Cam whispered with her own naturally sultry purr, "so once again, it's just us single ladies tonight, darling."

Elvira meowed.

Cam yawned and covered her full lips with her right hand. Although she enjoyed her five thousand square feet Colonial-style home in Weston, Massachusetts, she felt lonely and depressed in the evening after her housekeeper and personal assistant left for the day. Those feelings were joined by sexual tension. A year had passed since she had shared her bed with her ex-husband. She lacked nothing when it came to offers for dates but after the fiasco of her marriage, she had the good sense to recognize she was in no emotional condition to form any kind of serious union with a man. Her therapist, whom she saw once a week, agreed.

Cam sighed from loneliness. Weston offered a comfortable life for families but little in the social life department. It was a small town of only about seventeen square miles with a population consisting of less than thirteen thousand people, over ninety percent white. To its credit, Weston boasted one of the lowest crime rates and the highest per capita income level in the state. Cam felt safe in Weston. Three years earlier she had left Boston—only twelve miles away and where her parents still resided—and had moved into the five-bedroom property that sat on one and a half acres of land. After years of dividing her time between Boston and New York, she had settled into the quiet, domestic life of a suburbanite.

Her fellow Westoners generally treated their beautiful, single, five feet, ten inch tall neighbor with curiosity and friendliness—the men more than the women. The former found her quite exotic looking, with her light brown face, almond-shaped eyes, curvaceous figure, 36D natural breasts, and dark hair flowing down to the middle of her back in long, shiny S-curls. Even at thirty-four, when she entered a crowded room people gasped and stared. Her heritage from her African American-Philippine father and Mexican-Irish-Paiute-Shoshone mother intrigued and attracted them. The staid engineers, doctors, orthodontists, high-priced attorneys and business owners in the affluent suburb were also intrigued by the relative aloofness of their neighbor; a reputed former model turned business owner turned venture capitalist.

Cam reopened her magazine and scoffed at the beaming size zero blonde with her arms extended, wearing a red dress while showing off a full-length sable coat. "Yuck," she groaned. Cam hated wearing fur and felt proud that during her short career as a model she had never sported one—not that fur was in high demand for a woman posing in a bikini on the beaches of Mexico or Hawaii. "What do you think, Elvira?" she asked. Elvira responded with a loud meow. "Oh don't fret, dear" Cam assured her. "I'm sure she's not wearing anyone you know."

The TV program reminded Cam that Halloween was only one week away; she would have to call Zoë and Adam so they could get to work decorating the exterior of the house. In her zip code it was considered the height of bad manners not to adorn one's home with elaborate decorations for Halloween as well as Christmas. Cam felt obligated to make a positive showing to her wealthy neighbors, many whose homes were worth double, triple, even ten times that of her two million dollar abode she had purchased for 1.5 million in a hurried short sale.

Cam tossed her magazine to the end of the sofa and took two gulps of tea before reaching for another magazine. A loud commercial appeared, itemizing the alleged major shortcomings of a state political candidate. Cam grabbed a remote control but the device adjusted the recessed lighting ten feet above her head, not the TV. She returned it next to her half-full cup and waved her hand over the six remotes, aligned on the table like parked cars—one for the stereo, the ceiling fan, the lights, the room thermostat, the security system and the TV—and grabbed the latter to lower the sound. After doing so, the telephone rang. Cam felt her heartbeat accelerate as she grabbed the receiver on the second ring. "Hello?"

"Good evening, Camellia. How's my little cupcake?"

Cam grimaced and mentally slapped herself for not checking the caller ID before answering. "Vincent, what do you want?"

The man on the other end of the line snickered. "Now Camellia, is that any way to talk to your beloved husband?"

"*Ex*-husband, and the biggest mistake I ever made in my life," Cam said. "The biggest mistake by far," she added, pounding her fist into the sofa, causing Elvira to jump to the hardwood floor and scamper into the kitchen. She hated it when he called her by her full first name. At least he said it right. Most people said kah-MEEL-ee-yah when it was pronounced kah-MEEL-yah. That's why she had simply started introducing herself as "Cam" back in junior high school.

"Oh, you hurt me so deeply when you say such things, my dear," Vincent moaned. His regal voice projected the benefits of an expensive private school education and privileged rearing. "After all we meant to each—"

"What do you want, Vincent?"

"Well," Vincent replied, "besides wanting to know how you're doing, I wanted to give you the first chance to invest in a little business opportunity of mine. It's an invention that's going to revolutionize the telecommunications industry. I just need a little—"

"No, thank you," Cam replied, breathing heavy with indignation. Obviously, the bastard had heard of her successful venture partially financing a low-budget, independent movie that had become a surprise hit the previous year; even garnering two Sundance Film Festival Award nominations. Her percentage of the profits would pay her substantial dividends for some time. "I sunk enough cash into your stupid ideas during the thirteen months we were married to last me a lifetime. I'm not throwing good money after bad. And besides..." She paused to switch the receiver to her other ear. "...what happened to the final settlement I gave you?"

"Well, what can I say, love?" Vincent replied. "One hundred twenty-five grand just doesn't go as far as it used to."

Cam sighed. "You mean the horses at Suffolk Downs just don't run as fast as they used to."

"My, oh my," Vincent gushed in a mocking tone. "What do you think of me?"

"Or," Cam answered, "spending on your pretty boyfriends doesn't go as far as it used to."

"Camellia, my dear," Vincent said, "if you keep talking like that you're going to hurt my feelings." His voice became low and cold. "And I know you don't want to do that."

Cam took a deep breath. "I'm hanging up now."

"Before you do, sweetheart, there's something you should know."

Cam hated herself for being curious, but asked anyway. "What is it? That you've conned some other unsuspecting woman out of her hard earned money?"

"No, my angel," Vincent replied. "A woman—a publisher—called me last week. Said her company is interested in giving me a sizeable advance for my memoirs;

you know, providing details about my life with the great, internationally renowned designer, Cam Spencer."

Cam balled up her fist. "Vincent, don't forget the terms of our divorce," she whispered. "You so much as breathe one word about the details of our ill-advised marriage and you'll owe me double what I gave you. So you better not open your mouth for anything other than sucking you-know-what, or I'll have your lazy, down-low, worthless ass in court so fast it'll make your head spin."

"Camellia darling," Vincent said, his voice syrupy sweet again. "Of course I would never betray you, but you know how things are nowadays with anonymous sources and all that? Those publishing houses have a whole stable full of lawyers to protect them. Anything can happen."

"You better see to it that anything *doesn't* happen," Cam demanded, "or you'll find out the hard way which one of us still has friends in New York." She looked at the cable box clock. "I'm hanging up. Please don't call me again." She pushed a button on the receiver, ending the call. Not sure of what to do next, she covered her mouth with her hand and let out a muffled scream.

Afterward, barefoot and seething with fury, Cam stomped into the adjacent formal dining room, causing the motion sensor to automatically turn on the lights. She marched past the dining table, which seated twelve, and stepped behind the bar into a three-walled space the size of a closet. After pouring herself a glass of wine, she sat at the dining table and stared at the grandfather clock in the corner rather than sit in one of three chairs opposite the bar. How could she have been so blind, marrying that man?

They had met in New York at an art gallery three years earlier when she was thirty-one and he was twenty-five. Vincent Moreau had oozed charm and sophistication well beyond his years. He had attended Columbia University, he had told her. His family was very wealthy and owned a thriving export-import business, he had revealed. With sad, puppy dog eyes he had professed his worry that women would be interested in his family's money rather than in him. Therefore, as an African American male he had always been attracted to somewhat affluent, beautiful, older women of color.

Cam had fallen for the handsome, suave, six feet tall Adonis almost immediately. Everything he had told her was true. However, he had left out a few facts: his parents had disinherited him for being a rogue, he had been expelled from Columbia after being caught selling stolen exams—and he actively engaged in sex with men.

The ringing telephone brought Cam back to the present, causing her heartbeat to race again. She walked back into the living room and picked up the receiver. After checking the caller ID information and sighing with relief, she pressed the button to address the caller. "Hey there, Rose."

"Hey there yourself," her friend replied. "I'm sorry it took a little longer to get back to you than I planned."

Cam decided not to mention her conversation with Vincent or her excitement about Rose's call. "Oh, it's no big deal. How've you been?"

"Fine," Rose said. "I know it's getting late so I won't keep you long. A month ago I told you I approached Tony about, you know."

"And he said no."

"Actually, he said 'Hell no.' But that was then."

"Really?" Cam asked, trying not to show her enthusiasm. "You mean he's changed his mind?"

"In a word, yes," Rose said. "It took some doing but I've worked on him, and we got a couple of angry final demand-for-payment letters, so he's come around."

Cam silently jumped up and down, which enticed Elvira to appear and dance with her. "So when do we meet to go over the terms, so to speak? Informally, of course."

"Well," Rose answered, "how about this Thursday evening? I'll arrange for Zoë and Adam to spend some time with my parents."

Cam thought for a few seconds. She didn't want to sound too eager. "How about the day after? Dinner at my place at seven?"

"I'll check with Tony," Rose replied, "but I'm sure we can make it."

Cam calmed herself. "As we agreed, we'll draw up a general agreement, but no lawyers."

"Except Tony," Rose interjected, her voice clearly expressing exasperation.

"Now don't be like that, doll," Cam softly commanded, employing a term of endearment her father still used. "If the man didn't want to take the bar and become a lawyer, that's cool. I think it's admirable that he felt called to teach. You ought to be proud of him."

"Pride doesn't pay the bills," Rose insisted, "but we can debate that one another time. So the day after tomorrow, your place."

"It's a date."

Rose lowered her voice. "One more thing: Remember, not to mention anything to Tony about all the details."

Cam took a deep breath and smiled as she remembered their conversation a month earlier. "Of course not. He doesn't have to know."

THREE: NEGOTIATIONS

Three days before Halloween, Tony sat in Cam's living room watching the Boston Celtics struggle to hold their fourth quarter, five-point lead against the younger, faster, Indiana Pacers. A lifetime Celtics fan, he sympathized with their plight. He had been on the winning and losing side of such competitions when he had played basketball in college at UMass-Boston. Tony felt quite comfortable in his jeans and a Massachusetts School of Law sweatshirt. He also felt very satisfied after digesting a delicious chicken fettuccine alfredo dinner prepared by Cam's now absent housekeeper. He had been tempted to indulge in the meal even more but he maintained an athletic physique by resisting such temptation and exercising five times a week.

The conversation in the adjacent dining area, however, made Tony somewhat uncomfortable. He listened to Cam and Rose sitting at the dining table, each armed with a tablet, politely arguing over him as though he were an automobile. They had been negotiating for around fifteen minutes. Tony could see the profiles of both women. It marked the first time he had witnessed the two best friends show signs of disagreement. He tried to focus on the NBA combatants, but the discussion a few feet away was almost impossible to ignore.

"Ten thousand in cash whether you're satisfied with the results or not," Rose demanded. She wore jeans and a thick, long-sleeved blouse.

Ouch, Tony thought. He expected a little more confidence from his own wife.

"But don't worry," Rose added. "You're going to be more than satisfied."

Tony folded his arms across his broad chest and leaned back. That's better. He wondered how Cam would cough up ten grand every month under the radar but imagined rich people knew how to hide and produce their money without arousing too much suspicion.

"But no payment until after the concert is over," Cam retorted. "I don't want the musician falling asleep at the piano."

The Celtics center slam dunked the ball over the outstretched arms of two defenders. Tony stood and stretched out his own arms. "Take that!" he exclaimed, then returned to his seat. He didn't know whether to feel a bit insulted over Cam's remark or not. He hoped both the game and the ladies' fussing would be over soon so he and Rose could go home. He didn't like how Rose's demeanor changed sometimes when she visited Cam out in the burbs surrounded by rich white folks. His wife always inspected every inch of her immediate vicinity and became filled with envy at every new piece of furniture or landscaping improvement or other evidence of Cam's affluence.

Tony remembered when Cam had bought a new all wheel drive, BMW sports utility vehicle last fall "for the snow." Rose couldn't wait to get home so she could jump on the Internet and ascertain the price of her best friend's acquisition. Admittedly, the $105,000 price tag made them both gasp.

He listened further to the discussion taking place in the dining area.

"Not that it's any of my business," Cam said, "but what are you going to tell the kids?"

Rose snickered and shrugged. "The truth."

"Shut up!" Cam shrieked, her voice evincing levity.

Rose continued. "Sure. The truth: Daddy's got a new part-time job that will take him away from home late."

"Okay," Cam said. "Now about protection..."

Tony tried to stay with the game but the conversation in the next room proved more captivating.

"I'm listening," Rose answered.

"I know Tony's had a vasectomy," Cam said, "so I'm not worried about getting pregnant." She paused to take a sip of her tea. "Since I can assume you two aren't going to sleep in separate beds for the next year, I recommend that all three of us get a battery of tests for all known STDs, so we know we're starting with a clean slate."

"Makes sense," Rose replied. "You got somewhere in mind?"

"Yeah," Cam answered. "I know a real discreet doctor in Boston. She's top notch. Does this all the time for models after they've had two much to snort or drink at some wild party and woke up with some schmuck whose name they can't even remember. I'll text you her number and address. Just go sometime during the next week or so and give your names as Mr. and Mrs. John Smith. She'll give you an ID number and you can call for the results in a couple of days." She pointed at herself. "Of course, I'll pay for everything."

Tony didn't care much for getting a needle stuck in his arm. He didn't like needles. He turned his attention back to the game but continued listening to Rose, the most important woman in his life, and Cam, a trusted family friend and the godmother to his children, discuss what he still considered to be a very bizarre proposition. It was like being a witness to an avant-garde performance. On top of that, their negotiations shifted in tone and content. Sometimes they would agree on an issue immediately.

"Any one of us can choose to end this thing at any time."

"No problem."

Sometimes they would argue over some small detail.

"He'll come see you after dinner..."

"Before."

"After."

Sometimes without warning, they would switch to talking about something that had nothing to do with the arrangement.

"Rose, what is that sweet color on your nails?"

Then they would get back to business. Sometimes the discussion made him grimace.

"Look, Cam, he mounts you once. That's it."

"Hell no. For ten grand it's over when I say it's over."

"Well, just make sure he takes a shower. I don't want my husband coming home with sticky dicky."

Tony frowned. How had Rose allowed Cam to talk her into this?

"God Almighty, Cam. When did you get that beautiful watch? That must have set you back a few grand."

Tony frowned. Rose had provided the answer to his question.

After nearly fifteen more minutes Cam shrugged. "I think we're about done," she concluded. "Just a couple more things. You said Tony would be out 'late.' I'd like him to spend the night." She lowered her head. "You know, leave in the morning after the sun comes up."

Tony could hear the sadness and loneliness in Cam's voice. He couldn't help but feel sorry for her.

"Fine," Rose said. "But remember, it's not a date. I'm loaning him to you for money."

Tony winced. Apparently Rose couldn't help but relish a moment in which Cam had to beg, for a change. Tony stared at the TV, hoping the game would provide him with a place to hide but no such luck. The screen grew dark and the sound became almost mute; a movie trailer was building suspense for a currently playing horror movie. The silence made Tony squirm with uneasiness.

"One last thing," Cam said. "When do we start?"

Rose stood. "How about something like the third Friday of the month? We can always adjust the date if necessary." Rose turned to Tony. "That okay with you, honey?"

Still seated, Tony nodded. Just get me out of here, he thought.

Cam stood and pushed in her chair. "I'll type this up and get it to you in a day or two."

Rose nodded. "Okay, is there anything you want to add, Tony?"

Tony fought the urge to laugh. Now she was asking? "Yeah," he answered, his voice somber. "Once this thing gets started, I don't want any of us talking about it."

"Of course not," Rose replied. "This is a very personal and private matter."

"I mean even among ourselves," Tony said. He stood and faced Rose, who remained seated. "You and I don't talk about it." He pointed at Rose and Cam. "You two don't talk about it." He pointed at Cam, then himself. "And outside of the, um, concert, you and I don't talk about it."

Rose looked at Cam, then at Tony and shrugged. "Okay, honey. We said all along this isn't going to change our friendship or our marriage but if that's how you want it—"

"That's how I want it."

An awkward silence ensued for a few seconds. The grandfather clock in the corner of the dining area began to chime softly, indicating ten o'clock had arrived. Rose smiled and pointed. "I love that clock. We better get going. It's getting late." She stood and stretched. "That cheesecake sure was good. I'm going to run to the powder room before we go." With that, she sauntered down the well-lit hall.

Tony watched Rose, remembering when she was twenty pounds lighter. Too much cheesecake over the past couple of years, he lamented, had turned his beautiful bride into a—

"So how'd our boys do tonight?"

Tony turned and smiled at Cam, who entered the living room. She stopped about three feet away from him and pointed at the TV with her thumb. "The Celts win or lose?"

"They won," Tony replied, "but ugly. They'll have to do better than that."

Cam glanced at the hallway where Rose had just traversed and took a step closer. "Tony, I'm sorry if all this makes you uncomfortable. I know you're doing this because you're in a fix." She displayed a sad smile. "I'll try to make it as painless as possible."

Tony laughed. "Thanks, I appreciate that." He made eye contact with Cam. He had learned to ignore her attractiveness and view her as a dear friend of the family; practically a sister to his wife. Now, he struggled to allow himself to appreciate her dazzling beauty again. And yes indeed, she was beautiful. She had tied her hair back, which accented her naturally high cheekbones and sexy, pouty lips. He could see the outlines of her ample bosom pushing through the powder blue silk blouse she wore. Her dark, form-fitting pants showed off her curves, especially her shapely thighs. "I-I'm honored, Cam," he whispered. "Someday you'll meet someone who deserves a wonderful woman like you." He took her hands in his. "In the meantime I'll make this..." He paused and squeezed her hands. "I'll make this meaningful for you."

Cam rushed into his arms and hugged him. "Thank you." She tilted her head and gazed into his eyes while maintaining their embrace. She touched his face with her hands and gently pressed her lips against his, then opened her mouth to speak but the sound of the bathroom door down the hall being opened caused her to release him. The two backpedaled to opposite ends of the sofa like a pair of guilty teenagers.

Tony moseyed over to Rose in the hallway and handed her a mid-length leather jacket. "Ready to go?"

Rose nodded. "Hm-hmm. How was your game?"

"We won."

"Good. Let's go to my parents, pick up the kids and get home."

The three strolled toward the door in their usual fashion: Tony in front while the two women chatted. A brisk wind greeted Tony when he opened the front door. "It's all yours, pal," he said to the huge, plastic skeleton taped to the outside of the door. Cam flipped on the outside lights and Tony inspected the decorations garnishing the porch. "I'll be glad when Halloween is over," he said, calling out over his shoulder, "but I admit the kids did a nice job yesterday."

"They really did," Cam agreed.

Tony watched thousands of brown leaves crisscrossing each other on the ground. Two weeks before, the leaves had adorned trees in dazzling displays of red, yellow and orange. Now the half naked trees shivered against a brisk wind. The temperature had plummeted twenty degrees into the lower forties since the start of their visit at seven. Tony paused at the top of the stairs. He turned and waved to Cam, now standing at the threshold waving back. He wanted to avoid staring at the outline of her nipples—the cold air caused them to push against her blouse—so he whipped out the remote to his late model Cadillac SUV, unlocked the door and held the passenger door open for Rose. After the couple had been securely seated in the automobile, he eased down the wide driveway.

Cautious about "driving while black" in Weston, he cruised along the dark, tree lined residential street at twenty-five miles per hour. He glanced at the multitude of bright stars in the moonless sky and considered what reassuring words he could offer Rose; something about how much he loved her and how the one-year arrangement would never change that. God Almighty in heaven. How had it come to this? How had—

Rose poked his shoulder with her index finger. "Did you check out that new marble countertop Cam had installed for her center island? I bet it cost a fortune."

Oh yes, now he remembered.

FOUR: THE THIRD FRIDAY MORNING

"**M**om, are you alright?"
Rose blinked and refocused on her daughter. "Of course, sweetheart."

Zoë sighed, showing signs of exasperation. The twelve-year-old girl placed her backpack on the center island in the kitchen. The open floor plan provided clear view of the television in the great room but no one paid any attention to the commercial about a Christmas sale. "You were saying something about Thanksgiving being less than a week away but you stopped mid-sentence." She ran her fingers through her short, curly hair.

"That's the second time this morning, Mom," Adam said. "You did the same thing earlier when you were talking to me." Zoë's twin brother laid his backpack next to his sister's and opened the refrigerator door to return a carton of orange juice.

Rose smiled and placed her hand on Zoë's broad shoulder. "I'm fine, dear. I just lost my train of thought. It happens." She visually surveyed the child who had entered the world five minutes before her brother. At five-six, she was already the same height as Rose. No doubt the lanky girl would be tall, like her father.

Adam, who already stood an inch taller than Rose, approached her. "To be honest, Mom, me and Zoë have noticed that—"

"Zoë and *I*," Rose insisted. "For fifteen thousand each, you'd think I wouldn't have to remind you." She playfully pulled her son's ear.

Adam chuckled. "Zoë and *I* have noticed that you've been...I don't know..." He glanced at Zoë, then continued. "A little preoccupied lately."

Zoë positioned herself next to her brother. "Yeah, Mom. You know, we're not kids anymore. You can talk to us if something's on your mind."

Adam nodded. "That's right."

Rose smiled again and inspected the only children she would ever have. Both had her medium brown, unblemished complexion. Both flashed enthusiastic smiles revealing teeth covered by stainless steel braces. Both were clad in a blue blazer, white shirt and red tie. Adam wore blue trousers while Zoë wore a blue skirt.

Apparently, Rose surmised, this kind of verbal exchange among "friends" was encouraged at Boston International Academy among rich, white children and their teachers—or parents. However, the twins weren't at school. She didn't want her children picking up bad habits from their classmates. It was enough their voices sounded more like the white children at the Academy than the black children at church. "Everything's fine," she answered.

"Is it...you know," Adam said, "our tuition?"

Rose's smile disappeared. "Of course not." She heard someone honking the horn in front of the house and pointed at the backpacks, relieved to end the conversation. "That's Mrs. Chen. Now get your things. She's nice enough to drive you to school every day with Jia-Li. The least you can do is be ready."

The two seventh graders shrugged at each other, then quickly kissed their mother and rushed to grab their backpacks lying on the floor under the center island. Within a few seconds they had scampered through the great room and out the front door. Zoë snaked half of herself back into the house to pick up a black case containing a rented flute, then dashed back outside, racing to catch up with her brother.

Rose glanced at her watch and noted the seven o'clock time. Mrs. Chen picked up the twins at the same time every day. She would drop her own daughter, as well as Adam and Zoë, at the front door of the Academy fifteen minutes later; classes started at seven thirty. Rose liked Mrs. Chen, a stay-at-home mother married to a highly paid cardiac surgeon. Rose wished she too could afford to remain home and look after the family's needs. Instead, she would have to spend another day as the customer service supervisor for Emerald's, a high end department store.

The ringing telephone brought her attention back to the kitchen. She turned and grimaced. A ringing telephone these days often meant a bill collector. She hadn't been totally honest with Adam: They *were* behind with their school tuition. Rose lifted the receiver hanging on the wall, checked the caller ID and breathed a sigh of relief. It was Tony; no doubt he had just arrived at work. "Hello, hon," she said, trying to sound cheerful.

"Hello, baby," Tony opened. "Is your morning off to a good start?"

Rose nodded. "It's been just fine. How about you?"

"So far, so good," Tony answered. A long pause followed. He broke the silence. "The kids get off to school okay?"

"They just left," Rose answered. "You know we could set our watch by Mrs. Chen."

"That's for sure," Tony said. After another awkward pause, he spoke slowly. "Look, baby, we don't have to do this."

Rose frowned. She would have to be strong for both of them. "There's no other way."

"There's always another way."

Rose took a deep breath. "You already know what that smug ass heifer at the school told me. If we don't come up with some serious bank by the end of the month our babies are going to be suspended."

"Why don't you let me call the school and—"

"And do what, Tony?" Rose remonstrated, raising her voice. "Beg those privileged white folks? No." She realized she was getting angry but couldn't help herself. "Zoë told me one boy missed school for two weeks and came back with some story about a sick relative in Mexico, but every kid at school knew he got suspended because his parents fell behind on his tuition. He's not looked at the same."

There was another pause before Tony again broke the silence. "I-I just don't know if this is the right thing to do."

"It's the best thing among a long list of poor alternatives," Rose countered. "We've talked about this how many times?" She checked the clock again. "I have a bunch of things to do before getting to work." She knew the way she had said "work" evinced resentment, but she couldn't seem to hold the feeling back. "Remember I'm closing tonight, so my mom is going to pick up the kids and keep them for a while. The house will be empty when you come home. Will you be okay for dinner?"

"Yeah," Tony said. "Well, I'll see you, um, tomorrow morning. I love you."

"I love you, too," Rose replied. "Nothing's ever going to change that." She pressed the button to end the call and sat down on a stool in front of the kitchen bar. She had errands to run but an oppressive rush of anger and melancholy descended on her like darkness at dusk. She stared at the calendar hanging on the wall as she inhaled and exhaled slowly. Today was the day. The third Friday in November. The first day of the twelve. She knew later in the evening, while she utilized her most syrupy sweet voice, obsequiously addressing some rich old biddy who wanted to return merchandise a spoiled grandchild had damaged, her husband would be having sex with her best friend.

Rose looked at her hand and realized she still held the telephone receiver. She placed it on the counter and grabbed the television remote to check the current weather. Instead of the toothy, shapely blonde who had been recently reporting the weather—the station seemed to be changing its image—a commercial ran. Rose watched the man on the commercial. She knew him. His very presence had tormented her for several years. Every time she saw him she felt twinges of longing and anger. She turned up the volume; might as well torment herself further.

"Hello," the man on the forty-two-inch flat screen began. He was filmed from his head to his waist. "I'm Phil Masters." The image widened. The handsome, well-dressed man was now surrounded by four dozen professionally dressed adults in a huge indoor showroom filled with brand new automobiles. He continued. "We at Masters Motors want to wish you and yours a happy Thanksgiving..."

Rose gritted her teeth and muted the sound. Smug bastard, she thought. *Wealthy*, smug bastard. Owned half a dozen car dealerships in the greater Boston metropolitan area. He and his family attended the same church as Rose's. His wife helped out at his dealerships from time to time but spent most of her hours taking care of their children or serving on the board of some charity or mingling with the wife of the governor—or shopping.

The commercial ended and Rose read the weather information at the bottom of the screen: current temperature, thirty-one, high of forty-five. Chilly outside but her face burned with envy. If she had played her cards right she would have been Mrs. Phillip Masters.

Phil Masters and Tony had been and continued to be good friends. Both had come from a working class background. Both had gone to undergrad at UMass, Boston. Both had attended the Massachusetts School of Law together. Both had courted her while in law school when she had attended UMass, Amherst working on her bachelor's in business management. She had chosen Tony because he had always earned higher grades than Phil so she had assumed Tony would go farther.

When Tony had announced his intention to become a public high school teacher rather than practice law, Rose had attempted to gently persuade him otherwise. Later she claimed if being a teacher would make him happy she would support his decision. Privately she had assumed after a year or two trying to teach the ill-mannered brats at a Boston Public School Tony would come to his senses. She further assumed he would eventually take the bar exam and his rightful place at some prestigious law firm whose partners were dying to see an African American male who didn't sport a blue jail uniform and a pair of handcuffs. She hadn't anticipated Tony would love teaching and want to make it his career for life. He didn't even bother to take the bar exam. "What's the point?" he had asked.

Rose turned off the TV and stormed up the stairs to the master bedroom. She walked to her dresser, opened the bottom drawer and retrieved a box that had once held her previous mobile telephone. She gently placed it on the bed and lifted the lid. First, she grabbed the envelope with the angry letter inside; one of many demand-for-payment missives. After fumbling with two more letters she just turned the box over and let the contents spill out onto the bed. They were all the same. Collection agencies, mostly representing jewelry stores and boutiques.

Because she managed the household finances—after all, she had the degree in business—she maintained two sets of books, so to speak: one she shared with Tony and one he knew nothing about. The pile on her bed represented the latter. Rose picked them up and dropped them back on the bed while recalling her husband's quip about the bar exam. "What's the point?" she asked and pointed at the papers. "Here's the damn point."

She looked at her watch and remembered she had several errands to run before starting work at one o'clock in the afternoon. She quickly stuffed the notices back into the box. As usual, she would take a short break and call about a half-hour before Tony got home to delete any messages from those nasty bill collectors. Those who had written the letters hidden in the box only had her mobile phone number. They would start calling in about an hour, the persistent little cockroaches.

Rose yawned and sauntered into the master bathroom. She stripped out of her pajamas, turned on the shower, and stopped to look at herself in the mirror, bringing a slight frown to her face. Formerly a cheerleader with a tight body pursued by two promising law school students, she admitted to herself she had put on a few pounds over the past couple of years, a situation that wouldn't have happened had she married the right man. Had she married Phil Masters instead of Tony Monroe, she would be in better shape in more ways than one. Phil Masters' wife had a female personal trainer who came to their fancy house in Wellesley four days a week. Phil Masters' wife drove a Porsche. Phil Masters' wife sported an impressive pair of brand new tits.

Rose shrugged and climbed into the shower. No need crying over spilled silicone, or was it saline these days?

*

At twelve thirty Rose drove on West Roxbury Parkway heading toward the upscale Chestnut Hill Mall in New-ton, Massachusetts, an affluent suburb seven miles from Boston. Traffic was generally busy but flowed well. The sun played hide-and-seek, occasionally darting behind a flotilla of scattered clouds. Her telephone had buzzed and rung several times that morning with text messages and calls. She had chatted with a couple of girlfriends but had not answered any calls with a "blocked sender" identity on the screen. She had other matters on her mind other than a few thousand dollars owed to compa-nies worth millions, such as her husband soon to be lying on top of her best friend.

Rose sighed. Tony had always been a wonderful lover: considerate, giving and romantic. She had always loved that about him. Also, he had not mentioned anything about her weight gain, bouts of depression or their di-minished sex life. Rose loved that about him even more. She knew their financial problems were mostly her fault but when she became depressed she didn't feel very pas-sionate. However, she would feel a compulsion to buy something nice for herself or her children. Now, thanks to her lack of self-control her best friend, who had every-thing, would have her beloved Tony, at least temporarily.

She wondered how the two would start, who would make the first move...probably Cam, who had confessed to Rose that she was ready to explode with loneliness and pent up sexual energy—and that was a couple of months ago.

Rose honked her horn at a truck driver who had cut in front of her without signaling. She hated not being able to put the thought of Tony and Cam out of her mind. She attempted to cull assistance in that endeavor by channel-surfing radio stations and turning up the volume. One station was already playing a Christmas song, an up tempo, doo wop version of "White Christmas." Rose, hummed loudly, trying to drown out her thoughts...

Tony and Cam in bed...Hugging...Kissing...Fucking.

At fourteen minutes before one o'clock Rose swerved her late model Jeep Grand Cherokee into the already crowded parking lot at the mall and searched for a parking spot. Fortunately, a male driver, clearly in a hurry, exited a space just fifty yards from a side door of the mall next to Emerald's. Rose parked, turned off the engine and jumped out of her vehicle. The sun had peeked out from behind a cloud but the chilly air stung her nose. The telephone rang again. She walked quickly, never breaking her stride while reading the screen. "Speak of the devil," Rose said aloud. She surveyed the caller ID information.

C Spencer.

FIVE: THE THIRD FRIDAY EVENING

Tony breathed a sigh of relief as he veered right onto Ramp 14, exiting a congested Highway 90, also known as the Massachusetts Turnpike, or just the Pike. He would reach Cam's house in five minutes or so. At nearly six o'clock in the evening post daylight saving time, the canopy in the sky had already transitioned from crystal blue to streetlight flooded black an hour earlier. Tony snaked his way through traffic, traveling northwest on Wellesley Street. Eventually he checked his rearview mirror and scowled. "Damn, just what I need," he hissed.

A Town of Weston police car coasted about four car lengths behind.

He slowed down and changed lanes less frequently while keeping a constant eye on the speedometer, careful to adhere to the forty-five miles per hour speed limit. After two minutes, however, he decided to take no chances. He signaled and turned into the three-fourths full parking lot of a shopping mall that hosted three dozen stores. The police car followed. Tony pulled into an area adjacent to an electronics superstore and parked several spots away from the cluster of other vehicles. He shifted his Cadillac into park and waited. The driver of the police car crawled past him before making a U-turn and exiting the lot.

"Maybe they weren't following me," Tony admitted aloud, "but better safe than sorry." He turned off the car engine and reached into the pocket of his suede leather jacket to retrieve the letter he had read three hours earlier, the one Rose had left on his dresser. He pushed a button to turn on the map light and read the letter for the third time.

Tony,

I appreciate what you're doing for our family. I've respected your wish not to talk about this whole situation, but because I've been friends with Cam for many years I just want to bring a few things to your attention. It's important that everything goes well tonight so that everything goes well for our family in the future.

Over the past year, Cam has expressed to me how terribly lonely she is. She's also told me many times that while she enjoys being in charge at work she wants to be with a man who lets her melt into his strong arms at home. She wants a man who can take charge, someone who's passionate, confident and assertive but attentive.

Tony chuckled. Now how many wives would take time out of her busy day to coach her husband on the best way to screw her best friend? He read further.

Like so many attractive women, Cam is insecure about her appearance and worries about aging. You can't tell her enough how beautiful she is. Finally, she's very self-conscious about her wealth (guilty even) and constantly worries that men are looking to fleece her. Of course, marrying that bum didn't help.

Tony shrugged. Vincent Moreau had been one in a long line of jerks Cam had attracted. She may have a head for business but her choice in men certainly left much to be desired—present company exempted, of course. He finished the letter.

When you come home we'll carry on like we always do. No mournful looks; no distance between us. We can talk about what to do with the money after the kids have gone to bed but we won't discuss how we came by it. I love you and nothing is ever going to change that.

Yours forever,

Rose

Tony folded the paper and stuffed it back into his jacket pocket. He didn't know what to make of Rose's letter. Truth be told, he did find the information she had provided to be helpful.

He checked for the return of the police cruiser and seeing none, started the car and continued on his journey. He eventually turned onto a much darker, sparsely populated residential street and tried to remember all the rules to which Cam and Rose had agreed: Payment in cash after the deed is done, rendezvous only at Cam's house, no sex after sunrise, no contact outside of the once-a-month agreement, etc. With only two blocks separating him from Cam's house he slowed down and stopped the car, yielding the right of way to a lumbering opossum obviously frightened by his headlights. While waiting he sighed again, still conflicted about the whole arrangement.

Rose had spoken the truth on the day she had first pitched the idea to him. For the past year and a half he had felt increased frustration over the precipitous decline in his and Rose's lovemaking; obviously oppressive money woes and sexual desire don't mix. As a result, he secretly welcomed this meeting with Cam. In fact, he had prepared for the event with ardent relish. For the past three weeks he had increased the intensity of his workouts and had reduced his caloric intake by nearly one-fourth. He had also viewed a couple of Internet websites featuring favorite sexual positions for women. He had eaten a very light dinner two hours before, and had spent more time than usual showering and shaving.

At around six-fifteen Tony pushed the doorbell button while standing under the double lights illuminating Cam's front porch. "I suppose it's show time," he whispered. He could feel his heart thumping in his chest like a base drum. He had spoken to or seen Cam literally scores of times over the years, but tonight he felt like a teenager on his first date. He watched the large mahogany front door, with its majestic arch top frame, being swung away from him toward the inside of the house, revealing Cam, who pushed the custom-fitted storm door open. With her thick, lazy curls combed so her long hair hung to one side of her smiling face, she looked amazingly beautiful and sexy.

"Hello, Tony."

Tony returned her smile. If he didn't know better, he'd swear she was blushing. "Hi there, Cam. Sorry I'm late. An accident on the Pike." He picked up his leather overnight bag and stepped inside. "It's chilly. In the mid forties. Ready or not, winter is on its way."

"I know," Cam replied over the soft jazz music playing in the background. "Everything is so brown. Even with Thanksgiving next week, November can be downright depressing."

"Well," Tony answered, "perhaps this will brighten your day a bit." He extended his right arm, which he had kept behind his back, and produced a single orange rose.

Cam beamed with delight. "Oh, that's so sweet!" She accepted the rose and examined it. "It's beautiful. It's perfect." She planted a kiss on Tony's cheek. "Thank you."

Tony smiled and slowly inspected his hostess from head to toe. "That flower isn't the only thing looking beautiful tonight."

"I get a rose and a compliment," Cam said. "Must be my lucky night."

"No," Tony replied. "Mine." He resisted the urge to reach for Cam. Instead, he opened the closet door and hung up his jacket, revealing his attire—a long sleeved, striped rugby shirt, jeans and sneakers. He glanced at the floor and noticed a brown paper sandwich bag with the word "Tony" written in black marker. In it, he assumed, were hundred dollar bills, one hundred of them. He would toss the money into his overnight satchel when he retrieved his jacket in the morning. He would not count it and neither he nor Cam would mention it. He closed the closet door, turned and sniffed the air. "I hope I didn't interrupt your dinner."

"No, silly," Cam replied. "I ate early, but I had Isabella prepare a light snack—you know, shrimp, crackers, cheese—in case you wanted something." She dashed into the kitchen and opened a cabinet. "And I've got some apple pie in case you're in the mood for something sweet."

Tony watched Cam swivel her hips as she negotiated the corners of the center aisle. *I'm in the mood for something sweet alright, but it's not apple pie*, he thought. "Thank you but you shouldn't have gone to any trouble on my account."

"It was no trouble at all," Cam replied. She placed her finger under the running faucet while filling a small glass vase two-thirds full. Finally, she snipped a small piece from the rose stem and placed the flower in the vase. "This is soooo pretty. You didn't have to do this."

Tony ambled into the kitchen and just stared at Cam. She was alluring in so many ways. She wore a form hugging pair of navy blue Capri slacks and a long-sleeved turquoise blouse; the plunging V neckline accentuated her considerable cleavage. Tony could feel himself getting aroused. Too soon, he thought, so he tried to focus on Cam's voice.

"It's perfect," Cam declared again. She gently placed the flower on the counter and clasped her hands together. "It's so pretty, Tony." She cupped her hand over her mouth. "I said that already. Didn't I? Um, how are Rose and the twins?"

"They're fine."

"How was work today? How are things at your high school?"

"Good, thank you."

Cam darted past Tony into the living room and pointed at the television remote. "I can turn off the music and turn on the TV if you want. Is there something on you'd like to watch?" She lowered her head and covered her face with both hands. "Oh my God! I must sound like a complete idiot."

Tony entered the living room and gently removed Cam's hands from her face. "You're just a bit nervous. That's all. I know exactly how you feel. I feel the same way."

Cam sighed. "You do?"

"Of course," Tony answered. "But listen." He squeezed Cam's hands and tenderly pulled her closer toward him. He couldn't believe how natural it felt to hold her in his arms. "It's like a first date, but we have an advantage."

Cam placed her forehead on Tony's chest. "We do?"

"Yes, we do," he asserted. He put his mouth next to Cam's ear and whispered. "Because we already know how it's going to end."

Cam softly punched him in the shoulder. "Oh you!" she said before joining him in a hearty laugh.

The ice successfully broken, the two sat side by side on the sofa. They nibbled the snacks Cam had placed on the coffee table and sipped wine and stared at the dancing flames of the gas fireplace. Elvira appeared and loitered near the couple, clearly hoping to be fed, but Cam shooed her away. Tony thoroughly enjoyed their conversation. Although he had known Cam for years, they had never spent any meaningful time alone. He couldn't help but peek at the woman's ample bosom, which bounced every time she laughed. He couldn't remember when he had felt so relaxed but excited at the same time. Occasionally one would touch the other on the arm or leg, adding to the sexual tension. After an hour they were interrupted by a ringing sound.

Cam frowned. "I'm sorry." She reached for the telephone. "I had turned off my other phones but forgot about this one. I actually don't use it very often."

Tony watched as she inspected the caller ID information on the receiver and grimaced. "It's Vincent." She glanced at Tony. "Why doesn't he just leave me the hell alone!" She placed the phone back in its cradle.

"You're not going to answer it?"

"Hell no," Cam snapped. She shook her head. "Biggest mistake I ever made in my life." She pointed at Tony. "You didn't like him the minute you met him, did you?"

Tony smirked and opened his hands in feigned protest. "I never said that."

Cam pointed again. "You and Rose were too classy to do that. Why didn't you tell me he was a no good son of a..." She gritted her teeth.

Tony shrugged. "Would you have listened?"

"No," Cam whispered and lowered her head. "I guess I got what I deserved for being so stupid."

"You weren't stupid," Tony retorted and cupped Cam's chin with his fingers. "You were in love and sometimes that—hey!" He listened to the music for a few seconds. "That's a great piece." He stood and pulled Cam to her feet. "It's a classic. My dad used to play this song on the guitar. This is when they were steppin' on some serious jazz. I haven't heard it in years." He placed his hands around Cam's waist and swayed to the music, basking in the intoxicating fragrance of her lavender perfume. "Your past is the past, dear Cam. Right now you have this moment—and you have me." He kissed her on the forehead.

Cam snuggled close to him and mirrored his movement. "Oh, Tony. Where were you years ago?"

Tony tilted her head with his fingers and kissed her on the lips. "I'm here now."

*

Tony sat up in Cam's king-sized bed, half covered and alone. After a few minutes of kissing and caressing in the living room, Cam had suggested he climb the stairs to her huge second floor bedroom and get into bed while she put away the snack tray, turned off the downstairs lights and set the alarm. "I won't be long," she had assured him. "Better not," he had playfully demanded. Taking advantage of the hopefully short break, Tony had taken the time to freshen up in the bathroom and brush his teeth. Now he waited, naked and filled with anticipation. He ran his fingers over his six pack abs, his thighs, his erection.

One minute later Cam sauntered into the bedroom. She smiled at Tony before approaching a writing table pressed against the wall opposite the foot of her bed. She slowly lit six candles held by a sterling silver candelabra, then returned to the doorway and flipped a switch, turning off the matching lamps sitting on two nightstands near the head of the bed. Finally, she sat on the bed next to Tony, grabbed a remote and pointed at a compact stereo resting in the middle of a bookshelf next to the writing table. Soft jazz music drifted into the room. She kissed Tony briefly and bounced back up. "Be right back."

"Okay," he said, "but don't be long." He glanced at the alarm clock sitting on the night stand, which read seven forty-five.

Within ten minutes Cam emerged. She wore a red, satiny, chemise and had untied her hair so it flowed across her bare shoulders. The center of her breasts was barely covered by a ribbon that untied the front of the chemise like a gift. The candlelight caressing her light brown skin gave her a sexy glow.

"Wow!" Tony exclaimed.

Cam took short steps and approached the bed. "I know. Now you see what I look like without my makeup. Pretty disappointing, huh?"

"You're joking, right?" Tony said. "You have one-of-kind beauty inside and out, Cam." He scooted over a few inches and pulled back the covers, exposing half the bed while still remaining covered. "Come here. Don't make me come after you." Cam giggled and climbed into bed and into Tony's waiting arms. At first they exchanged soft kisses, but as their ardor grew they took turns forcefully pushing their tongues into each other's mouths. "I've been looking forward to this day for some time," Tony admitted.

"So have I," Cam whispered. "You have no idea how much."

Tony kissed Cam passionately. He loved the feel of her lips and tongue. He pulled on the ribbon of her chemise, revealing a pair of beautiful round breasts. He proceeded to caress and kiss them, and playfully bit her nipples, producing soft moans from Cam. "Marvelous," he said. "Perfect. Beautiful."

Cam reached for the flesh between Tony's legs and gasped. "Oh my God!"

Tony arched his eyebrows. "What's wrong?"

"You-you're quite well-endowed."

Tony smiled and shrugged.

"If you ever give up teaching you could always be a porn star."

"God gives us what he gives us," Tony replied. He deftly worked on Cam's chemise with one hand, removing the two skimpy pieces she wore. After dropping them onto the floor, he resumed kissing her. He reached to separate her legs and massaged her soaking wet, shaved area with his fingers while kissing and fondling her breasts. "Do you like this, Beautiful?" he asked. "I'll stop if you want." He already knew what her answer would be.

"Don't stop," Cam demanded. "There. Yes, right there. Please don't stop."

Tony gladly obeyed. After only two minutes he felt Cam clamp her legs tight around his hand and shake her entire body, writhing in obvious orgasmic ecstasy. He kissed her shoulder and waited for her to finish. After she did, he felt her pulling him on top of her.

"That was so wonderful," Cam panted while stroking his manhood. "Now come inside me. I can't wait any longer." Her considerable chest rose and fell due to her heavy breathing.

Tony responded by kissing Cam again and again, forcing his tongue inside her mouth and sucking on hers. He felt her hand around his hardness and lifted himself so the tip of his head grazed the lips of her opening. But instead of complying with her request, he kissed her breasts, then inched down to kiss her navel and slowly slid downward in the bed until he could smell the heavenly nectar of her secret garden.

"You don't have to do that," Cam said. Tony ignored her protest and lingered over the opening to her tunnel of love. Cam attempted to repeat her statement. "You don't have to...to...oh yes...yes..."

Tony focused on the source of her pleasure, licking, kissing and sucking while enjoying her moans that expressed fervent delight and pleasure. Five minutes passed before he heard Cam announce her intentions.

"I'm going to..." she whimpered. "I'm going to..."

Tony grabbed Cam's legs and held on while she arched her back and shook as if having some sort of seizure. He enjoyed waiting for her to settle down, which took some time, pleased he had once again brought her to orgasm. He felt her pulling him by the arms.

"Oh, you wonderful man!" she exclaimed.

Tony grabbed one corner of the bed sheet to quickly wipe his mouth. He lay on top of Cam and kissed her on the forehead. She responded by throwing her arms around his neck and pushing her tongue into his mouth. The two kissed passionately for several seconds.

Cam grabbed Tony's pleasure object and pulled it to the entrance of her sex. "I've never wanted anything so badly in my entire life."

Tony could deny her or himself no longer. He eased inside her, gradually, carefully, concerned about hurting her. "And now the moment I've been waiting for," he whispered. He moved in and out, slowly at first, then increased his speed, all while kissing Cam, who wrapped her legs around his and moaned. Even though she couldn't quite take all of him, Tony reveled in their immense mutual pleasure, as if their bodies had been made for each other. After a few minutes of valiant resistance he realized he had reached the point of no return. "You want it, baby?" he asked.

"Yes, oh yes, please," Cam pleaded and placed her hands on Tony's butt cheeks.

Tony breathed in short spurts, grunted and felt his burning hot semen gush out like hot lava formerly contained inside a volcano. "Take it. All of it," he said. He could feel Cam's body shaking under him and knew she had joined him in erupting.

After another minute, Cam stopped shaking. She covered her face with her hands and wept. "Oh God, Tony, what are you doing to me?"

Tony smiled and gave Cam two quick kisses on the mouth. "Giving you what you need and deserve," he replied.

*

Tony awoke. He lay behind Cam in bed but side to side, spoon fashion, so he had to lift his head over hers to check the time. Nearly eleven thirty. He lay back down and heard Cam's voice. She spoke without turning over.

"I have to tell you something. I hope you won't be angry."

"What is it?"

Cam confessed without moving. "I called Rose this afternoon and tried to back out."

Tony was surprised, not at her admission but because it was the first time he had thought about Rose since he had rung Cam's doorbell. He gently ran his index finger up and down Cam's back. "Really? And what did she say?"

"Well, you're here, aren't you?"

Tony snickered. "I guess great minds think alike."

"Mmmm..." Cam purred, responding to his touch. She remained on her side but moved as if slow dancing in bed. "Mmmm....what do you mean, great minds think alike?"

"I called Rose this morning and tried to back out, too." Tony felt himself growing erect again.

"And?" Cam asked.

Tony caressed her shoulder and kissed her smooth back. "Well, I'm here, aren't I?" He rubbed her arm and nibbled her neck. Cam responded by squeezing his hand. Tony responded by pushing himself inside her. "You're so beautiful and sexy," he whispered as he thrust his hips back and forth.

*

Tony turned his key in the lock and opened the front door to his home. At nearly eight o'clock in the morning the sun shone with brilliance but the air felt cool. He felt slightly apprehensive, like a naughty child who had done something wrong and now awaited punishment by a parent. He heard soft footsteps, then like so many times over the past fourteen years, Rose appeared. She wore oven mitts and was still clad in her pajamas and bedroom slippers. Her appearance immediately broke the spell of the euphoria Tony harbored from the previous night. He felt happy to be home, happy to see his beloved wife, who immediately stepped into his embrace.

"Hello, honey," Rose said, kissing him and grabbing his overnight bag. "So how was your first day at your new job?"

SIX: AFTERWARD

"**S**o Dad, tell us more about this new job you started last night."

Rose sipped her orange juice and watched for Tony's reaction to his daughter's inquiry. The father, mother, son and daughter, engulfed by the competing aromas of various hot breakfast foods, sat boy-girl-boy-girl at the family's all-purpose kitchen table.

"Well, sweetheart," Tony replied. He lowered his fork, which held two small slices of dry pancakes. "It's a temporary situation. I, um, provide help to another, in a way."

"But what kind of job has you stay overnight?" Adam asked. Clad in a green and gold Boston International Academy sweatshirt and sweatpants, he struck a handsome athletic figure. Eschewing his father's example, his pancakes swam in a pool of syrup.

"And you're a teacher," Zoë added. "What do you know about national security?" She also wore a sweatshirt and sweatpants identifying the school she and Adam attended. The sunlight flooding through the patio door bathed her with an almost angelic hue.

"I never said anything about national security," Tony countered.

"That's kind of what Mom told us yesterday," Adam volunteered with a head gesture toward Rose, who sat at his left.

Rose stared at the two biscuits and three strips of bacon on her plate. For years Tony had remonstrated against her telling the children white lies, but she didn't see what harm it did to offer innocent little untruths for the children's own good. Although she focused her attention on her meal she could feel the burn of Tony's disapproving gaze, and attempted a rescue. "Now kids, maybe I told you more than I should have. I'm sure your dad's tired from all his..." She paused and arched her eyebrows. "...hard work." She had tried not to let her voice evince jealousy over her knowledge about her husband's new part-time job. "Why don't we just enjoy our time together, okay?"

"Okay," Zoë and Adam said simultaneously.

Rose rolled her eyes as the pre-teens repeatedly poked each other while exclaiming "Jinx!" for having spoken the same word at the same time. With the brother and sister occupied, she stole a glance at Tony, who smiled at the twins and at her.

"Come on, now, that's enough. Finish your breakfast," Tony commanded with a laugh.

Rose resumed eating but continued to peek at Tony. He didn't look any different to her. He looked like the same person who had kissed her yesterday morning before going to work. He was still her man. Her husband. The father of her beautiful children. The man with whom she had pledged to spend the rest of her life. The man who had fervently pledged to love only her forever.

Zoë eventually settled down and returned to peeling her orange. "Dad," she said, "don't you think it's time I had my own flute instead of renting one from school?"

Rose watched Tony more intently. This would be the first test of whether he accepted their newfound financial largess.

Tony scratched his head. "Maybe we should talk about it right before school lets out for the summer, when you'll have more time to practice."

Rose frowned. He was also the man who had pledged to give her a good life after he finished law school. The man she had chosen over Phil Masters.

"I've got to admit it," Adam jumped in. "My older sister—by five minutes—really is quite good on that flute."

Zoë spoke quickly. "Mrs. Lewandowsky said she knows a place where we could get a good second hand flute for under a thousand dollars that—"

"You tell Mrs. Lewandowsky," Rose interrupted, "if we decide to buy a flute for our talented daughter we don't need any advice from her."

Silence followed. Tony broke the tense atmosphere with a casual tone. "I'm sure Mrs. Lewandowsky was just trying to help, honey."

"She's just trying to show the local Negroes how superior she is," Rose snapped. "I bet she doesn't tell the white kids at that school they can't afford to buy their children what they need."

Zoë reached across the table and squeezed her mother's hand. "Mrs. L's not like that, Mom. She's very nice and she's a good teacher."

Rose stared at her daughter's big, beautiful brown eyes and regretted having hurt her and spoiled their family gathering. She squeezed the child's hand in return. "Your brother's right, you *are* quite good." She smiled. "I'm sure Mrs. L is a great teacher, dear." She slapped her hands together. "After we finish eating, before you run off to hang out with your friends on this gorgeous Saturday, would you play that song I like? You know, the one you've been practicing for the Christmas concert?"

Zoë beamed. "Of course. Would you like to hear it too, Dad?"

Tony put his hand on Zoë's shoulder. "I'd be delighted."

Rose glanced at Tony again. He seemed to have already forgotten the momentary unpleasantness. In fact, he seemed to be in quite a pleasant mood this morning. Perhaps, she assumed, he was in such good spirits from being on top of Cam all night and possessed that smug feeling men get when they've been satisfied sexually. Rose had to admit she had fallen short in that department lately, but who could blame her when the man she loved had fallen short in his obligations for years?

"So you'll think about the flute, then?" Zoë asked, rocking her head left and right to glean a hint of affirmation from her mother or father.

"Your mom and I will talk about it later," Tony answered.

"Yes," Rose agreed. We'll talk about a whole lot of things later, she thought.

*

Rose's heart swelled with exhilaration as she approached the end of her task. She carefully placed another bill on top of the tenth row of bills lined up next to her prostrate figure on the bed. "...Nine thousand, nine hundred..." she said and held up the last one. "Ten thousand." She rubbed her palms together as if she had just dug a trench with her bare hands and twisted her torso to check the wall clock behind her—the one which Tony had put up such a fuss because of the cost.

Ten thirty. The twins had spent the morning playing basketball. During the afternoon and evening they had attended a church youth group outing. They had gone to bed a half-hour earlier, thoroughly exhausted. Tony had spent the morning holed up in his home office grading papers, then had joined the children as one of the adult chaperones at the church event. Rose had spent the day shopping—groceries for the family and a few personal items for herself. While her activities had kept her busy, to her disappointment they had failed to drown out her invasive thoughts about Tony and Cam.

After waiting all day, she and Tony could finally talk about what to do with the ten grand he had earned the easy way, as far as she was concerned. She turned to address Tony, standing at the foot of the bed, having just showered and now stepping into his pajama pants. "Of course we're going to get caught up with the kids' school tuition," she opened.

"Of course," Tony agreed. "And I think we should pay a little on everything we've fallen behind on—the credit cards, the car notes, the mortgage. And we should put something toward the kids' college fund."

Rose nodded. "How much should we each get personally?"

Tony shrugged. "I hadn't really thought of that. Um, how much would be okay? Maybe a couple of hundred?"

Rose started counting the money again. "I was thinking more like five hundred each."

"Five hundred?" Tony asked. "We should get as much as the church?"

Rose put her hand over the stack of bills as if to protect it. "Who said the church is getting five hundred?"

Tony sat at the foot of the bed, careful not to disturb Rose's pile of cash. "Honey, we agreed to give the church five percent of everything we earn. It really should be ten percent but we've been in such dire straits these days. Let's say five hundred for the church and two-fifty for each of us."

"Four hundred for each of us, three for the church," Rose insisted.

"Three hundred for us, four for the church," Tony countered.

"Three fifty each."

"Okay, three fifty each."

"Done and done," Rose declared. She rolled over onto her back and held up a hundred dollar bill to examine it in the light. "It's just not fair."

"Now baby, we said we wouldn't forsake our obligations to the church."

Rose sighed. "I'm not talking about that. I'm talking about Cam."

Tony ran his index finger across Rose's bare foot. "What about Cam?"

Rose wiggled her foot and let out an exasperated sigh. "Why does she have all the luck? She just ups and pulls together ten grand just like that."

Tony stood and unfolded the shirt to his pajamas. "I'm sure it wasn't just like that, honey. I'm sure she works for what she has, just like we do."

Rose sat up straighter. "Oh, so one night of passion and now you're on her side all of a sudden?"

"I'm on *our* side," Tony said. "That's what this whole thing is all about, remember? Both of us making sacrifices so we can dig ourselves out of this deep hole."

"Both of us?" Rose replied. She rolled out of bed and began scooping the money back into the paper bag. "I'm the one letting my husband play 'hide the salami' with another woman, with some wet dream he's probably been secretly lusting after for years."

Tony put his hands on his hips. "Don't, Rose. We agreed we weren't going to let this hurt us."

Rose cranked her neck and scowled. "I don't see how this hurts *you*." She wanted to stop talking but couldn't help herself. A day's worth of pent up jealousy and loneliness had overwhelmed her. She stared at her husband, who still hadn't put on his shirt. He was so handsome, with his muscular arms and six pack abs. She noticed how other women drooled over him. She had always felt such pride in having something so many other women wanted but belonged exclusively to her, and now she couldn't enjoy that feeling anymore. "You got to spend all night doing the horizontal dance with a bikini model while I looked after our children and lied to them about what their father was doing."

Tony shook his finger but spoke softly. "I never told you to lie to them. In fact, I've told you a hundred times to stop lying to them."

"And what should I have said?" Rose asked, raising her voice slightly. "Mr. I-Don't-Want-to-Talk-About-It, huh? What should I have said when they asked me where their father was? Daddy's out rolling around in bed with your Aunt Cam?"

"You agreed to Cam's proposal," Tony retorted. "You talked me into it. I even wanted to back out at the last minute. Hell, Cam wanted to back out." He closed his eyes, obviously regretting the last statement.

Rose placed her hands on her hips. "My, you two are getting to be quite chummy, aren't you? Nothing like a little roll in the sack to loosen the tongue—in more ways than one, I'm sure."

"Baby, please," Tony begged. "You know tomorrow morning you're going to regret every word, so do us both a favor and stop right now."

Rose threw the full paper bag onto the bed and stomped toward the bathroom. She reached the threshold, stopped, turned around, raced into Tony's arms and sobbed.

Tony, still bare-chested, hugged her and whispered. "Don't do this to yourself."

"Did you tell her you love her?"

Tony held Rose tightly. "Please, baby, we said we wouldn't talk about—"

"While you were making love to her," Rose whined, "did you tell her you love her like you do when you're with me?"

Tony kissed Rose repeatedly on each cheek. "No, honey. How could I say something that's not true? There's only one woman I love, and that's you, my wife."

Rose held onto Tony for a few seconds longer before wiping her eyes with the sleeves of her pajamas. "I'm sorry," she whimpered. "I won't carry on like this again. I promise."

Tony stared deeply into Rose's eyes. "Look, if this thing is going to cause problems we can just tell Cam we're—"

"No!" Rose grunted. "We're going to finish what we started." She pulled away and marched into the bathroom with her head up.

"You're sure?"

"Of course," Rose answered with a hint of annoyance in her voice. "Let's get to bed. It's getting late. We've got to get up for church." She stared at herself in the mirror, eyes swollen from crying. She scowled at the person looking back at her and vowed never to display such vulnerability again.

*

Rose pushed open the door to her car and stepped into the not yet crowded parking lot. A few isolated snowflakes floated down from the overcast sky but she didn't expect any accumulation. In fifteen minutes she would start a long nine a.m. to nine p.m. shift. With four weeks to go before Christmas a store like Emerald's would be extremely busy all day. Rose reveled at the memory of the past week's events since Tony had arrived home bearing ten grand. She especially enjoyed recalling the look of surprise when she had counted Zoë and Adam's overdue—and current—tuition in cash to that supercilious bursar bitch at Boston International Academy. Rose had even deliberately dropped one of the hundred dollar bills on the floor just so the bitch would have to bend her fat ass over and pick it up.

She had also put some money toward a few of the bills on which she and Tony had agreed, not all, but certainly enough to temporarily satisfy anyone who might be a pest. She had, of course, kept a little more than the three hundred fifty she and Tony had agreed to keep for themselves. After all, she had several bills that had to be paid from her secret box hidden in her dresser drawer, and if a woman didn't look out for herself, who would? She rationalized she had kept no more than she deserved. Both Tony and Cam were getting something out of this arrangement while she was the one sacrificing the most, allowing another woman to partake of her husband's generous gifts.

Speaking of which, she had vowed to refuse Tony's sexual overtures more often than usual so he would be on fire the next time he rendezvoused with Cam—she had to make sure they would go the entire year—but she was only human. With Cam and Tony not scheduled for three solid weeks, last night she just had to let Tony have her. She thought for sure they were going to wake up the children or even the neighbors. God, can that man make the whole earth move or what! "I love you" he had told her over and over. Cam would just get his body, and just temporarily. Only his wife would have—

"Mrs. Monroe?"

Rose inspected a man, in his early forties, slowly approaching her. His open, long wool coat revealed a dark business suit. A thief doesn't dress so well or announce his victim's name. Just the same, she reached into her purse and retrieved a can of pepper spray.

The man held up his hands and remained about six feet from her. "I don't mean to startle you, Mrs. Monroe. You are Mrs. Rose Monroe, yes?"

"Who wants to know?"

The man slowly placed his right hand into his jacket pocket. "I'm just getting my card." He handed it to Rose.

Rose read the card. James Rivers. Rivers Investigations and Collections. She inspected the man again; ruggedly handsome with a brown complexion. More likely Jaime Rivera before he changed it. She thought it best not to show any emotion. "Okay, what do you want?"

"Can we walk into the mall, Mrs. Monroe?" Rivers asked. "I don't want you to have to stand out here in the cold."

Rose checked her watch, noted the eight forty-five time and nodded. The two strolled toward one of the mall's main entrances.

"The stores will be crowded now until Christmas," River noted.

Rose said nothing.

"I do all my Christmas shopping online," Rivers said. He allowed Rose to enter the revolving door first, then followed her. They were greeted by an instrumental version of "Santa Claus is Coming to Town" pumping through the airways. In spite of dozens of people milling about—the stores would not open until nine—they walked to a spot near a wall, which afforded them some privacy. "I've been retained by Lieberman's Jewelers, Mrs. Monroe," Rivers announced. "I've left you numerous messages. You owe them..." He reached into his jacket pocket again and produced a small black book. "...three thousand, seven hundred and forty-two dollars."

"I know," Rose replied without any emotion. "And they hired you to do what? Come here to threaten to break my legs?"

Rivers laughed. "Nothing like that. Lieberman's just want their money. They sent you letters and called but got nowhere, so they handed over your file to me. I sent you letters and called but got nowhere."

Rose looked around, afraid someone from Emerald's might see them. "I'll get you the money."

"When?"

Rose had engaged in these types of discussions on numerous occasions before but the man's surprise attack in person had rattled her. She needed to stall for time. "How about five hundred a month starting next month until it's all paid off?"

Rivers shook his head. "No, that won't do. I'm afraid they want it all now."

"A thousand then. A thousand a month."

Rivers ran his fingers through his salt and pepper hair. "Okay. I'll need the first payment right now."

Rose scoffed. "You think I've got a thousand dollars on me, mister?"

Rivers frowned. "No, I suppose not. Tell you what. Have it tomorrow. I'll give you a receipt when you do." He dug into another pocket and brandished a red rectangular book.

"I'm not working tomorrow," she lied. "I have a doctor's appointment."

"That's not my problem."

"I can have it for you for sure in three weeks."

"Mrs. Monroe," Rivers said, "I'll need one thousand dollars in cash by—"

"In cash?"

"In cash by tomorrow noon or I call your job and talk to your supervisor. A lady named..." He produced yet another small book, a blue one, and flipped through it. "...Devorah Silverman. Or maybe I call your parents or visit your husband at Alexander Hamilton High School and ask him to—"

"Okay, Okay!" Rose said, her voice quiet but sharp enough to cut a diamond. "I'll switch my schedule or something. Meet me here with a receipt for one thousand dollars at six-fifteen in the evening."

"At noon, Mrs. Monroe."

"At noon then," Rose growled and walked away. "Asshole," she muttered under her breath while grinding her teeth with indignation. She checked her watch and quickened her pace. Too bad, she thought; she had been having such a good morning. Ironically, she could pawn some jewelry and come up with the money. Also, she thought, she'd have to keep her legs closed and make sure Tony stayed healthy and horny so that he—*they* kept getting paid for the next eleven months.

SEVEN: CLOSE AND FAR

Cam enjoyed the view from her position on top. She slowed her rocking motion and lowered her face to kiss Tony again. He lay in the middle of the bed on his back palming her naked hips, eagerly accepting her kisses. After a few seconds of tongue wrestling Cam straightened up and resumed her movement, but slowly. She had to be careful. If she got carried away and leaned too far back she feared Tony would split her in half.

They had been in bed for over thirty minutes. They were accompanied by soft, instrumental jazz Christmas music playing on the stereo; December 25 was only a few days away. Similarly to their first encounter in November, they had spent over an hour just relaxing in Cam's living room talking, sipping wine and enjoying each other's company. Unlike the previous month, however, this time they had scrambled up the stairs in a sudden passionate frenzy and dove into bed, leaving a trail of clothes along the way. Last month they had moved with tentativeness and uncertainty. This time they spewed fire, grabbing, grunting and moaning. Their spontaneous combustion had left no time for such amenities as candlelight; the candles stuffed into the candelabra on the writing table stood untouched, like silent sentries. The dimmed recessed lights overhead allowed them access to the stimulating sight of each other's nude, well-toned body.

Cam lowered her head and kissed Tony, then shook her long, curly locks to shroud both their faces. She suddenly flung her head backward, causing her hair to flip over to the middle of her back. She knew men found such an ostentatious display sexy. "Oh dear Tony," Cam cried—literally—as she shifted her body in rhythm with his graceful moves.

"You're so beautiful, Cam," Tony replied while caressing her breasts.

She loved his touch but resisted the onset of her eruption because she didn't want to be selfish. Her next orgasmic explosion would be her third, but Tony had not even experienced his first. "Baby," she moaned, "you're amazing," and wiped the tears from her eyes with her hands. She meant every word. He was such a magnificent, totally selfless lover. Cam had never experienced such a man. Although hung like a stallion, he used so many other parts of his body to offer her indescribable pleasure.

Cam rode Tony forward and backward, up and down. She felt her torch about to be ignited and increased her speed. She couldn't help herself. It was too wonderful, too powerful. "Please, Tony," she begged through breathless pants, "do what you need to do."

Tony smiled. "Seeing you in all your dazzling beauty?" he replied. "I *am* doing what I need to do. I'm in heaven."

Cam closed her eyes. Oh how the man could sweet talk. Overcome by the flames of ecstasy, she grabbed a pillow, dropped it on his chest, buried her face in it and screamed.

*

Cam lay with Tony, resting her head on his nearly hairless chest and caressing his washboard abs. A few minutes had passed since her muffled release. She squeezed Tony's hand. "Are you ready to take your turn?"

"Not yet," Tony replied. "Let's just stay like this for a while. I like it."

Cam snuggled closer. Was she dreaming? Did such a man truly exists among mere mortals?

Eventually the two resumed the conversation interrupted by their desire. They talked about the twins, their work, their favorite movies, her travels and their friends but avoided one subject: Rose. Cam enjoyed their exchange. She had never spent time with a man who listened to her so intently when she talked. She wondered if Tony always displayed such behavior or acted this way because, as he sometimes declared, "This time is for you"; just like her female therapist would frequently say. Cam respected his consideration but wanted to understand him; wanted to do something for him besides share a bed. Yes, she was giving him a considerable amount of cash but understood he was accepting it for Rose and the children. It certainly had not been his idea.

"Can I ask you a question?" she asked.

"Yes," Tony replied.

Cam spoke slowly. "Why teaching? I mean, I think it's great, but after finishing law school, what made you decide you wanted to teach rather than practice law?"

"Well," Tony opened, "in the second place, I didn't like the adversarial nature of practicing law; the gamesmanship, bending the truth, win for your client even if they're secretly dumping tons of toxic waste into some poor community's water supply or if they fired some poor schmuck because he was getting close to retirement age. Corporate law wasn't for me."

"Okay," Cam said, "but that's not the only type of law. There are others: criminal, immigration, entertainment. Why not try one of them? I'm not questioning your decision. I just want to understand it."

"You're not the first person to ask," Tony assured her. "Corporate law was where I had started. By the time I admitted I didn't want to do it I was eighty-five percent done with law school. So I decided to, well, dance with the girl I brought to the party, then go home."

"You said that was in the second place," Cam reminded him. "What was in the first place with you and teaching?"

Tony shrugged and laughed. "I just love it," he declared, his voice rising with obvious excitement. "I get a bunch of teenagers on the first day of school. I can see 'history is boring' stamped on their foreheads, but in about a month I'm watching a spirited discussion between them about why the Supreme Court would rule that African Americans weren't citizens in the *Dredd Scott* decision. At the end of the school year kids come to me and say, 'You know, Mr. Monroe, I used to hate history, but you made it interesting, even fun.' "

Cam hugged Tony and nuzzled his chest. "That must be a great feeling."

"It is," Tony agreed. "I mean, which of us can't name a teacher who's made a difference in our lives? Well, in some cases, I'm that teacher."

Tony's words struck a chord with Cam. She remembered Mr. Yamamoto, her high school Advanced Placement calculus teacher in Los Angeles. She had always been good in math but had initially struggled in calc, sitting in a room full of mostly Asian and white kids whose parents earned high six- and seven-figure salaries. Mr. Yamamoto had been patient and kind. Eventually, Cam recalled, she earned a B in the class but felt more pride in that B than in all the A's she had earned in school before and since. Tony's words had resurrected the pride she had felt in herself and, although she had no right to feel this way about another woman's husband, inspired pride in him. "Those kids are so lucky to have you," she gushed.

"Thank you, doll," Tony responded. "I'm glad *you* feel that way."

Cam chuckled, recognizing he had used the term of endearment because he had heard her use it so often when talking to Rose or the twins. She also recognized the way Tony had emphasized the word "you" but she offered no opinion on the subject. She knew better than to stick her nose into someone else's marriage. Privately though, she felt indignation. God had created a very special man when He created Anthony Monroe, and if Rose couldn't see that, it was her loss.

Tony broke the silence. "But you know what?"

"What?"

"I've never told anyone this," Tony volunteered, "but lately I've been interested in taking the bar exam, not because I want to be a lawyer, but because I just want the license, the piece of paper, you know what I mean?"

"I think so," Cam answered. "If you want to, I think you should do it."

"You do?"

"Yes," Cam said. "I could help." She lifted her head and rested it on her hand, supported by her bent elbow on the mattress. "There are courses to help you study for the bar. Why don't you let me pay for you to take one? Or I could hire you a private tutor who could meet you at work." She waited for a reply but heard none. "What? What did I say?"

Tony kissed her. "Cam, is this what you do with the men in your life? See an opportunity and jump in with your credit card or checkbook?"

Cam frowned. "What's wrong with wanting to help someone I care about achieve his goal? Men buy gifts and homes and cars for women all the time? Is that wrong?"

"Not in itself," Tony replied, "but would those women be with those men even if they couldn't buy them the gifts and homes and cars?"

Cam put her hand over her mouth and giggled. "Some. Many, I guess maybe not." She scrunched up her face. "But why is it so different for a woman as opposed to a man?"

Tony touched Cam's cheek with his finger. "How can I explain this? A man needs a woman who's supportive and who inspires him to bring out the best in himself."

Cam shrugged. "Okay..."

"But," Tony continued, "she must understand he needs to climb the mountain himself." His voice became softer. "And when he reaches the summit he wants the people who love him to be proud of him."

Cam snuggled back into Tony's arms. "I know your family is very proud of you."

Tony smiled and kissed Cam on the top of her head. "And as for you, you incredible, sweet lady, you deserve happiness and love from someone who appreciates you for the beautiful queen you are." He kissed Cam again at the same spot. "You know that, don't you: that you're a beautiful queen?"

Cam kissed Tony on the lips. "If you say so, I'll believe it, dearest Tony." She kissed him again and again, each time lingering longer to savor his taste. His breath smelled of wine and her juices, and she found the cocktail piquantly intoxicating. She shifted her attention to the sheet and blanket covering the area between Tony's legs and noticed the spot rising like a tent. She reached for the source of the phenomenon and wrapped her hand around it and began stroking.

Tony inhaled and exhaled deeply, then forcefully pushed Cam by the shoulder until she rolled over onto her stomach.

Cam desperately wanted to please him. She got on all fours. "Is this what you want?"

"Yes," Tony replied as he positioned himself behind her.

Cam felt euphoric, so vulnerable, so totally into the moment. She also felt Tony's hand massaging the back of her head, followed by a slight tug as he pulled her by the hair and guided himself into her. Cam liked sex a little rough sometimes and was glad Tony had picked up on that. "Yes, lover. Give it to me," she moaned. "I'm yours. I belong to you." She surprised herself by making such a pronouncement aloud, revealing her private, willing submission but recognized she couldn't take it back. She couldn't stop the words from escaping if she wanted to—and at that moment she didn't want to.

*

Cam made up part of the circle gathered in the brightly lit narthex of Community African Methodist Episcopal Church, a large, inner city church in Boston that boasted over two thousand members. The 3200 square feet area outside of the sanctuary had been lavishly adorned for the holidays. Dozens of poinsettia plants rested on tables and mantels. Thousands of multicolored lights hung from the walls. A ten feet tall, garishly decorated Christmas tree stood proud within a seven feet wide wall niche specifically constructed to host seasonal decor.

Cam stood next to Rose, who stood next to Tony, who stood next to his parents, who stood next to Rose's parents. They took turns showering Zoë and Adam with praises for their performances in the church's youth Christmas Eve service. Hundreds of parishioners and visitors stepped around them, many rushing into the sanctuary for the next scheduled service. Men of all ages slowed down to catch an eyeful of Cam before moving on. She wore a form-fitting red dress with a green belt and a pair of sexy black boots with four inch tapered heels, bringing her towering height to six feet and two inches.

"I've never heard anyone sing 'Go Tell It on the Mountain' so beautifully," Tony's father, Paul Monroe, told Adam. "Has someone already offered to be your manager? I'll do it." In his youth the tall, bald man had been a jazz guitarist before settling into making a living as a sound technician for a local television station. "I get twenty percent."

"Fifteen," Adam rejoined, to a tide of guffaws. He wore a white shirt with black pants; one among over a hundred children and teens similarly dressed who had participated in the service.

Rose's mother, Ethel Griffith, stepped closer to Zoë and pinched the girl's cheeks. "Your mother told me you were getting good on that flute but I had no idea you were practically a professional!" She had unblemished dark skin that contrasted with her perfect, white teeth.

Zoë, who also wore a white blouse but with a black skirt, grinned. "Thank you, Grandmother." The twins called Rose's parents Grandmother and Grandfather; Tony's parents were addressed as Grandmom and Granddad. The girl seized the opportunity to make a pitch for her own instrument. "Mom and Dad told me they might buy me my own flute."

"Of course they will," Rose's mother insisted. She playfully pulled her son-in-law by the ear. "Won't you, son?"

Tony twisted his mouth from one side to the next and laughed. "I suppose we're going to have to give it some serious consideration." He checked his watch. "It's after six thirty. We better get going." Their circle gradually morphed into a V formation as the group moseyed toward the eight feet tall pair of mahogany front doors.

Rose spoke over the torrent of voices surrounding her. "We'll see you all tomorrow." She took Cam by the hand. "Are you sure we can't persuade you to drop by tomorrow?"

Cam smiled at her friend. She had discerned no trace of discomfort or resentment in Rose's eyes or body language all evening. It was as if their monthly arrangement didn't exists. The subject never surfaced when they talked. "I'd love to, doll," she replied, "but I'll spend tomorrow at my parents' house helping my mother in the kitchen while my dad sits in his easy chair watching one sporting event after another. But thanks."

Cam wrapped herself with a long, black cloak she had personally designed and sewn; presenting such a unique, stylish look that dozens of people stopped and stared. She pretended not to notice and walked with the two families, joining the adults in offering additional effusive remarks to Zoë and Adam. She exited the door being held for everyone by Tony and thanked him for his courtesy without making eye contact.

Tony nodded.

Cam stepped outside, took in a deep breath and sighed with relief. The darkness, quieter environment, and cold, fresh air were a welcome respite from the noisy, warm church interior with its aroma of coffee, hot desserts and perspiration.

"Brrrr, it's cold," Tony's mother, Gladys Monroe, remarked, tightening the collar on her coat. She turned to Cam. "Where are you parked, dear?" She was a handsome, tall, thin woman with short, salt and pepper hair.

Cam pointed. "I parked just down the street. The lot was full."

"Tony, I'll start your car myself and get it warmed up," Rose suggested. "Why don't you walk Cam to her car?"

Cam held up her hands. "Oh, he doesn't have to do that. I'm fine."

Rose's mother nudged Rose's father. "Carlton, let Tony go with Rose and you walk Cam to her car. You could use the exercise after all that pie you ate."

Cam smiled, recognizing Carlton Griffith would take the joke at his expense in stride. She also smiled because she remembered over the years Rose had disclosed how her mother had repeatedly admonished Rose to never leave an attractive woman alone with Tony. "Don't trust no woman with your man. I don't care who she is," the mother had insisted. Apparently, Cam assumed, she judged her husband to be past the age of temptation.

Tony broke from the herd and joined Cam before his rotund father-in-law could respond. "No need, Father Griffith. It'll be my pleasure. I was just about to suggest the same thing myself. You can't be too careful these days."

Cam surrendered to the idea and bid everyone a good night and Merry Christmas. She caught Rose's mother staring daggers at her before the woman raced over to Rose, presumably to repeat her lifelong advice. Cam snickered out loud.

"What's so funny?" Tony asked with a puzzled look on his face.

"Nothing," Cam replied. "I was just regaled by the memory of the kids' performance and the wonderful service. Thank you for inviting me."

"Thank you for coming. The kids really enjoyed seeing you."

"It was my pleasure," Cam said. The two chatted about the chances of snow overnight and agreed there would be no white Christmas in Boston this year. In a few seconds they reached Cam's BMW coupe. She pressed a few buttons on the remote; the car started and the door unlocked itself. "Thanks for walking me to my car," she said softly and forced herself to look at Tony. Unlike Rose, his eyes indicated a hint of conflict, a touch of longing, a pinch of affection. She wanted to reach for his face but didn't. He held the door for her. Cam wished him a Merry Christmas. Tony expressed the same sentiment to her and after closing the door, turned and headed back into the church parking lot to join his waiting family.

Cam enjoyed watching his confident stride. She knew he would not turn around even to admire her car, a vehicle for which he had expressed great awe in the past. She smiled; aware she was one of the fortunate few who knew intimately what lay under that long topcoat. A half-hour ago he had dropped to his knees in church to pray, but just a few days ago he had been on his knees pulling her hair and smacking her ass before roaring like a lion and spraying a river of semen into her body. Cam stared at the cross perched on the church steeple. "I know we'll be forgiven for this," she said, hoping...praying.

Suddenly her heart filled with loneliness and yearning, yearning for Tony. She blinked her eyes twice, turned on the headlights and let out another sigh. How could she and Rose have imagined this arrangement would leave them all unchanged? Perhaps, she thought, she should end the arrangement. "Who are you kidding, Cam?" she growled aloud. "Wild horses couldn't drag you out of this now." She drove to the end of the block, pausing due to the stop sign and remembered checking her calendar this morning: One more day until Christmas; twenty-seven more days until she and Tony met again. She could hardly wait.

*

Cam watched her rearview mirror for the closing of the automatic garage door before getting out of her car. She strutted past her coupe and SUV while humming "Go Tell It on the Mountain." She disarmed the home security system and unlocked the back door leading into the kitchen, both via her telephone, then entered the house and stopped to bend down and pet Elvira, who greeted her. "Hi sweetie!" she exclaimed in a high pitched voice. "You miss Mommy? I don't think they would've let me bring you to church." Cam kicked off her boots and walked barefoot into the living room with Elvira alongside her.

She hung up her coat, put on a pair of slippers and approached the first stair leading to the second floor but stopped. Something wasn't quite right. She hadn't yet plugged in the lights to the eight feet tall artificial Christmas tree Zoë, Adam and her housekeeper, Isabella, had helped her decorate, but that wasn't it. Nothing looked disturbed. No, the house appeared to be the same. It was something she had noticed before easing into the garage, something on the front door.

She turned on the porch light and opened the front door. There it was. Taped to the doorknob. A small envelope.

Cam grabbed the envelope, closed and locked the door and flipped the envelope over to see if any writing appeared. It did: CAM SPENCER in block letters.

"One of the neighbors wishing me happy holidays," she mused aloud. She grabbed her letter opener from the table next to the front door, opened the envelope, read the card and closed her eyes in agony. "Damn that man to hell!" she yelled before reading the card again.

Merry Christmas, darling!
I know what you've been doing.
Love, Vincent

EIGHT: LACK OF PRIVACY

On the third Tuesday in January Tony sat behind his desk in the back corner of his classroom at Alexander Hamilton High School. Wearing a tie, dress shirt and dress pants, he stared at the screen of his five-year-old desktop computer, pondering how to tweak the questions for the upcoming first semester final exam. He checked his watch, the one the twins had given him for Christmas; the 11:42 a.m. time matched the information provided at the bottom right part of the computer screen.

He read the question about the sinking of the *RMS Lusitania* in 1915 for the third time, then directed his attention to a family photograph taken over the summer. He picked up the framed photograph and ran his fingers over the beaming faces of Rose, the twins and him.

He had lost his concentration. His thoughts kept returning to his unconventional personal life. How had things gotten so complicated? Before agreeing to "the arrangement," as he and Rose had come to call it, he had suggested if they weren't careful, her agreeing to Cam's drastic solution to their financial mess could conceivably affect their marriage. He returned the photo to its spot and vowed to prevent anything from upsetting his family life.

He read the *Lusitania* question yet again and decided to rephrase it; last year a significant percentage of students had answered it incorrectly. He typed a few words and wondered what Cam was doing right now. In three days they would meet again. He looked forward to seeing her.

He ground his teeth with frustration when comparing Cam's overt affection to the interaction he and Rose had shared the previous night. If he didn't know better he'd swear Rose deliberately refused his sexual overtures just to hurt him. Perhaps, Tony assumed, she became more resentful or jealous as his date with Cam approached. But didn't she realize avoiding making love to him increased his desire for Cam and inflamed the passion between them?

Speaking of which, he had no complaints about his time with Cam. She possessed fewer inhibitions than Rose, far fewer. Cam was more attuned to her body, more open to sexual enjoyment for its own sake as well as for emotional connection. Cam took care to make him feel like he was sexually desirable. He couldn't remember the last time Rose had made him feel that way. Yes, his wife loves him but she seemed distant and distracted when they made love lately, infrequent as the event had become. Tony suspected she was keeping something from him but couldn't fathom what it was.

He switched his thoughts to the memory of his evening with Cam a few days before Christmas and sighed with self-satisfaction. He could tell she was pleased with their encounter—and the feeling was reciprocated. If he were single, Tony recognized, he could see them falling in love. However, he was a married man who loved his wife and children. He would keep his emotions in check and after nine more months return to his normal life with the family finances greatly improved.

Tony shook his head. "Back to work, Mr. Monroe," he whispered. He heard a knocking sound and turned his attention to the opposite corner of the room; someone opening the only door leading into his classroom. "Hello, Monique," he said. "What's up?"

Monique Carter strutted past the empty, herringbone-arranged student desks and sat down on top of the one nearest Tony. She was a very attractive woman in her late twenties with dark skin and a thick mop of hair that extended in every direction like a dandelion seed head. The pinstripe vest she wore over a white blouse and dark slacks accentuated her hourglass figure. "Hey there, mentor," she said, flashing a dazzling smile. "How about that snow on Friday and Saturday? Did you get shoveled out?"

"Yeah," Tony replied. "How about you? I missed you at the Dr. King celebration yesterday downtown."

"My dad and brother came by to help me dig out," Monique reported. "And as far as the Dr. King celebration, no offense but fuck those bourgeois Negroes and their speeches," she growled, waving her hand. "Self-important folks go to those things so they can brag about themselves or tell everyone they met the governor or sat next to the mayor. I don't have time for such bullshit." She leaned back on the desk. "I'm not talking about you, of course."

Tony ignored the appealing sight of the woman's curvaceous body basking under rows of fluorescent lights and shook his finger in mock anger. "Monique, how many times am I going to talk to you about your mouth?"

Monique leaned forward. "Hey, ain't no man ever voiced any complaints about my mouth." She winked. "If you know what I mean."

Tony laughed. It had taken him a couple of months to become accustomed to Monique's shameless flirting. He had grown to respect the second year teacher who possessed a love for history. She had refused to meet with the mentor the principal had assigned her, selecting him instead. "Okay, no further judgment about your mouth," he conceded, "but seriously, this is our prep period. Shouldn't you be in your room correcting papers or something?"

Monique nodded. "Yeah, I guess so, but I came in here to tell you something juicy I found out that's gonna knock your socks off."

Tony went back to his computer and typed a few strokes. "And I've told you to avoid all that teacher gossip and drama around here."

"It's about you."

Tony stopped typing and made eye contact with his younger colleague. "Me?"

"Um-hum," Monique said. "Remember you told me Dr. Martinez had asked you to sit on some education commission a while back?"

Tony rubbed his hand over his smooth chin. "Yeah, I remember. Must have been when school first started, um, let's see, a good five months ago. Nothing ever came of it. I forgot all about it."

"Well," Monique said, "you better unforget it because you're on the short list to sit on this fancy commission that's going to report to..." She paused, clearly attempting to prolong the suspense.

Tony frowned. "Come on, Monique. I've got work to do and so do you. Just tell me—"

"The fucking president of the United States!"

Tony arched his eyebrows and widened his eyes. "Monique, your antennae is way off. At best, the members of the commission will report to some bureaucrat in the Department of Education."

Monique leaned back again on the desk and clicked the heels of her boots with obvious amusement. "Nope. What I just told you is true."

"How do you know it's true?" Tony asked.

Monique jumped off the desk. "A friend of a friend at the superintendent's office told me. I guess our superintendent and the secretary of education went to college together, so they wanted a teacher from Boston on the commission—and you're being considered. When the members finish they're gonna meet with the secretary and the president."

Tony shrugged. "I never did understand why Dr. Martinez asked me."

Monique straightened up and opened her arms. "What are you talking about? You've been Teacher of the Year."

"That was years ago."

"You coached two high school varsity basketball teams—the boys and the girls—to national championships."

"And what thanks did I get?"

Monique sighed, exasperated. "What the fuck, Tony. Why are you—"

"There goes that mouth again."

Monique put her hand over her full lips. "Oops, sorry. And let's not forget the most important thing..." She paused again, waiting for Tony to prod further. Hearing no such request, she continued. "You look good on television, with your fine self."

Tony laughed again. "Thanks, but if that were the reason, I'm sure there'd be a hundred other teachers chosen instead."

Monique threw her arms up again. "Tony, don't tell me you don't see all these girls here giggling and pointing when you're nearby?"

Tony shrugged. "They're just kids. I'm old enough to be their father. And besides, *you* get the same thing from the boys here. We know it doesn't mean anything."

Monique returned to sitting on top of the desk. "And the female teachers give you the once over when you're not looking, too."

Tony shrugged. "I wouldn't know, or pay any mind if I did. And again, you get the same attention from the male teachers here."

Now it was Monique's turn to shake her finger, brandishing one of her burgundy, acrylic fingernails. "But I don't have your exemplary record and I'm not the poster child for self-sacrifice."

"What do you mean?"

"You know," Monique replied and exaggerated playing the violin. "The golden boy law school graduate who turned down jobs from top law firms so he could teach public high school and make a difference." She stopped playing. "The media eats that shit up."

Tony took a deep breath and scratched his head. "That's not exactly accurate, but—" His sentence was interrupted by the ringing telephone. He read "Principal" on the caller ID screen and picked up the receiver. "Mr. Monroe here."

"Tony," the voice of a middle-aged man with a slight accent said. "How are you?"

"I'm fine, sir," Tony replied. "What can I do for you?"

"Remember that education commission I asked you to be on months ago?"

"Vaguely."

"Are you still interested?

Tony nodded. "As long as it doesn't take me away from the classroom or my family too often." He watched Monique put her index finger into her mouth and stick out her tongue as though gagging. He made a face at her.

"Well," the principal continued, "there is some travel involved but you'd really be doing me a favor."

Tony turned his chair to lessen the distraction of Monique's silent histrionics. "Of course I'd be honored to serve."

"Good," Dr. Martinez said. "Stop by my office later so we can discuss the details."

After exchanging a few pleasantries and saying good-bye to the principal, Tony hung up and faced Monique. "I guess you were telling me something approximating the truth." He shook his head. "Dr. Martinez is a good administrator but he still doesn't understand how hard it is to keep a secret at this place." He checked his watch. "The bell's going to ring in fifteen minutes. I better—we better—get some work done."

Monique ignored the hint. "Tony, you've never really told me what happened with you and the basketball team, well, *teams*."

Tony winced. "Truth be told, I've been trying to forget the whole thing. That was before you and Dr. Martinez came here, when we had that other idiot as principal. There's no point in rehashing ancient history."

Monique plopped back on the desk. "You told me if I ever had a question I could ask. I'm asking."

"Not now. Some other time, I promise."

Monique bowed and spoke slowly with a fake Chinese accent. "Please, oh great Zen master, honor this unworthy servant with your story, so she may know the capricious ways of Alexander Hamilton High School."

Tony smiled. He would have to finish his work after school. "Okay, the short version: A few years ago the basketball coach got fired—"

"For putting his nasty hands where they didn't belong on some cheerleaders, right?" Monique declared, scowling. "The pervert."

"You want me to tell this or not?"

"Sorry."

"But you were right," Tony admitted. "That's why he got the boot. No one wanted to coach a perpetually losing team but someone remembered I had played basketball in college, so I was all but ordered to take over the boys' basketball team in the middle of the season. They were good kids but they lacked discipline. Well, we won more games than we lost in the second half of the season, giving us the first .500 season in..." He paused and shrugged. "...I don't know, something like five years. So I kept coaching and we kept winning more games every year until we won the state championship my fourth year, my third as the head coach for a full season."

Monique applauded. "You da man, Tony!"

Tony frowned. "Maybe to some, but the next year there were a couple of star players who slacked off on their schoolwork, and I had a strict rule: No grades, no basketball."

"Good for you," Monique cheered. "Those white folks ain't gonna slave our black and brown children on their hardwood plantation if Tony Monroe has anything to say about it."

"Well, I did,' Tony replied. "At least I thought I did. I suspended them from the team but when I checked, their grades had been changed. To make a long story short, the principal told me to just go along. I didn't and resigned as coach."

"And the team fell back into the toilet," Monique declared. "Serves 'em right. What about the girls?"

Tony scratched his head. "The principal pressured me to take over the girls' basketball team because he said I had already been paid extra to coach basketball, but he just wanted to embarrass me." He laughed. "The girls program was a complete mess. Undisciplined. Out of shape. Constantly fighting among themselves. Poor grades. Nobody cared. I focused on the fundamentals: skill building, working as a team, conditioning, getting to practice on time, keeping up with their school work, shutting their mouths and listening when the coach talked." He pointed at himself when making the last remark. He was about to say more but checked his watch again. "Well, you know the rest."

Monique nodded. "Um-hmmm. In three years *they* won the state championship. You showed those butt faces a thing or two."

"Maybe," Tony said with a frown. "Then there was that big brouhaha about changing students' grades and cheating on the state proficiency tests. The principal tried to blame me on the grade thing but I had documented my complaints, so..."

"They didn't know who they were messing with."

"...he and his whole corrupt team lost their jobs or were reassigned and Dr. Martinez was brought in."

Monique shrugged. "Okay, you won. So why don't you coach anymore? You're obviously good at it."

Tony shrugged again. "I just soured on the whole thing, you know?" He turned back toward the computer. "Now get out of here. The bell's going to ring in a few minutes."

Monique bounced off the desk. "Okay, I didn't mean to take up so much of your time."

Tony heard the three-inch heels of her dress boots click against the tiled floor and wanted to make sure she knew he was joking. "It's okay. I can always make time for you."

Monique took three steps toward the door, then turned around. "You know, there's something different about you lately. I don't know what it is, but you seem more relaxed. Happier even." She stepped closer. "It's very sexy."

Tony looked up. Before he could respond to Monique's assessment she pulled him by his tie and kissed him on the lips. He felt her tongue enter his mouth and responded by rolling backward in his chair, away from her. "Monique, what are you doing?"

Monique turned and pranced toward the door. "Something I've been dying to do for over a year," she purred. She covered the doorknob with her hand but turned to address Tony. "I really appreciate how much you've helped me, especially last year when I didn't know what the hell was going on." She opened the door and cranked her neck to introduce yet one more issue. "Hey! I wonder how long it'll take the FBI or Secret Service or whoever to vet your ass." She shrugged. "Shouldn't take too long. It's not as if you're secretly meeting with terror-ists or something. See you later."

Tony watched helplessly as Monique closed the door behind her. Her kiss had surprised him and produced a mixture of pride and sexual arousal but he dismissed both feelings and chalked the incident up to a young woman's misplaced gratitude. He would deal with it later if he had to. However, her words about being vetted had alarmed him. She was right. He would have to be thor-oughly investigated before being selected to sit on a pres-idential commission: his health, his family life, his finan-cial situation, the works.

Tony covered his mouth with his closed fist as his thoughts raced. What would happen if some kid with a badge and computer discovered his arrangement with Cam?

He picked up the telephone receiver but returned it to its cradle. He had already told Dr. Martinez he would serve on the commission. Too late to back out now. "Dumb move, Tony," he whispered. However, he surmised, the process wouldn't start immediately. He would still have an opportunity to enjoy Cam. Much to his dismay, this Friday could be the last time they shared a bed—and the last time he collected ten grand afterward. "Damn," he thought as he heard the bell ring. Rose would not take this news well. No, not well at all.

NINE: FOR THE FAMILY

R ose pushed open the door to the master bedroom and flipped the wall switch. The light from a pair of lamps, one sitting on each nightstand, bathe the room in a soft glow. It contrasted sharply with her mood of irritation and cheerlessness, brought on by one upsetting incident after another.

First, she had been summoned to work the late shift at Emerald's on her scheduled day off. Next, while driving to work, that cockroach James Rivers had called again to pester her for not adding to the one thousand dollar payment she had delivered in November. After that, at Emerald's she had been publicly scolded by the store manager because someone had anonymously reported that two young women under her supervision—one African American and one Latina—had been texting on their mobile phones when they should have been working, something almost every white person under the age of twenty-five routinely did. To make matters worse, much worse, her improvident husband had jeopardized their financial recovery.

Rose had held off dealing with the latest bit of bad news until after bidding the children goodnight. However, when Tony, who trailed behind her, closed the bedroom door she started right in on him. "I can't believe this," she declared. "What the hell were you thinking?" In one hand she clutched the matching gray jacket to the pants suit she wore, and in the other, a pair of black shoes. She dropped the latter onto the carpeted floor near the foot of the bed, which landed with a dull, subdivided thud.

Tony, already in his pajamas and robe, frowned. "Well, when Dr. Martinez called me this afternoon I was rewriting a test and there was somebody in my classroom and—"

"Who?"

"Just another teacher."

Rose didn't like the sound of this. With a witness present it would be harder for Tony to back out. "Who?" she inquired again. "What other teacher?"

Tony spread his arms wide, then lowered them. "What difference does it make?"

"Can't you just tell Dr. Martinez you won't be able to do it after all?"

"Sure," Tony replied. "I'll just march into his office tomorrow and tell him never mind what I said yesterday. My wife won't let me go."

Rose shuffled to a corner and sat on the loveseat next to the nightstand. "I don't know what's going on with you these days," she said. "We finally get a chance to crawl out of our financial hole and you go and pull something like this."

Tony joined Rose in the corner and stood in front of her. "It's not as bad as all that, honey." He knelt and took her hand. "The commission might not even happen. You know Washington these days. It takes forever for those clowns to decide who sits where at a committee meeting."

Rose ran her fingers through her hair. "You know better, Tony. If they weren't putting the commission together for sure your principal wouldn't have called."

"Maybe," Tony replied, "and then again, maybe not. Besides, no one says I'm even going to be selected. Dr. Martinez called it a definite maybe. His exact words."

"It doesn't make any difference whether you're selected or not," Rose insisted, raising her voice slightly. "Either way you're still going to be investigated." She couldn't believe how calmly he was taking this. "Aren't you even a little bit concerned?"

Tony shrugged. "What good does it do to get all bent out of shape for something that hasn't happened?" He pointed at the heavens. "Remember what the Lord said in the Sermon on the Mount: 'Can any of you by worrying add a single hour to your span of life?' "

Rose stood and spoke more softly but her voice was drenched with sarcasm. "Well, the Lord didn't have two mortgages, two car payments, and two private school tuitions to pay, not to mention five figures worth of credit card debt." She walked to the other side of the bed and began grabbing pillows and tossing them in Tony's direction. He caught the pillows and placed them on the loveseat six feet from the bed. His calm demeanor annoyed Rose so much she voiced further objections. "I just don't see how you can let your ego get in the way of helping your family." She knew she had just entered the zone: the-take-her-frustrations-out-on-Tony zone. She always felt profound remorse afterward but she could never stop herself. Her mood hadn't been helped by viewing a new Phil Masters commercial on television that morning. Tony's former law school classmate had flashed that smug smile of his and encouraged the viewer to surprise a sweetheart with a new car for Valentine's Day. Rose could almost swear he was deliberately taunting her.

"I would never let anything interfere with helping our family," Tony said.

Rose would hear none of it. "You know what? Anticipating getting into Cam's vagina in three days must be making you lose all sense of what's important."

Tony grabbed the pillows on his side of the bed and dropped them on top of the ones already on the loveseat. "Like I said, there's no need for anyone to lose their head about something that might not even happen."

Rose pulled the comforter back. She wanted Tony to object to her cruel remark but he knew better than to take the bait. Fourteen years of teaching high school had done little for his bank account, but the experience had increased his ability to tolerate irascible agitators. She tried again. "That's right. It's not as if your family matters to you."

Tony walked around the bed and took Rose's hands in his. "It's going to be alright. You'll see." He squeezed and kissed her hands one at a time.

Rose immediately felt shame and self-contempt. She wanted to throw her arms around Tony's neck, smother him with kisses and tell him how proud she felt. How many women could say their husband had served on a presidential commission or even better, met the president of the United States? She wanted to pull him into bed and make love to him all night, but she couldn't. She was in the other zone: the one dictating she punish him for not becoming a lawyer, for making her work at a place where a stupid white woman could humiliate her in public, and for his modest income that allowed their household to become so deep in debt she had to let him gratify another woman sexually for an entire year. "Sure," was the only response she could muster.

Tony kissed Rose on the cheek. "I love you, baby," he whispered.

Rose could feel her resistance to his patience breaking down. In another minute, she would beg his forgiveness. "I love you, too," she muttered. She suddenly remembered something Tony had revealed earlier and decided to pursue it further. "So who was the teacher in the room when Dr. Martinez called?" She retrieved her jacket and shoes, and stepped into the walk-in closet. She disrobed and passed through the bedroom and into the bathroom clad in her robe. "Well?" she called out. "Who was it?"

"Just Monique," Tony replied, his voice flat and void of emotion. "You met her a couple of times at school." He stood at the threshold between the bedroom and bathroom.

Rose, suddenly engulfed by rage, bared her teeth like a snarling wolf. "That hussy who flirted with you at the Open House with me standing right next you?" She glared at his reflection in the mirror and banged on a few cosmetic bottles resting between the double sinks. "So you told Dr. Martinez yes just so you could impress your new girlfriend? Isn't one woman on the side enough for you?"

Tony entered the bathroom and leaned against the wall. "Honey, you know Monique is just putting on airs because she's insecure. You told me that yourself." He opened the medicine cabinet near the door and grabbed his toothbrush. "You were never bothered before about women making eyes at me. You even found it amusing. Why the fuss over some kid at work? Besides, I'm her mentor."

"She's no kid, Tony," Rose retorted. She knew the answer to his question: Before, Tony had never found enjoyment in the arms of another woman, but that had changed last November. Now, Rose feared, once he had tasted the forbidden fruit with a younger, shapelier woman he might want to keep sampling such treats for free after his current contract expires in October. Rose dipped her fingers in cold cream and accidently slapped a glob of it on her face. "Damn it!"

"Lower your voice," Tony whispered. "We don't want to upset the kids."

"Yeah," Rose said, complying. "God forbid they find out their father isn't who he pretends to be." She had crossed a line and immediately regretted her remark. Tony prided himself on being a good father, and over the years Rose had repeatedly expressed her pride at having a faithful, loving husband who routinely set a good example for his children, especially his son.

Tony turned and marched into the bedroom. "I'm calling Cam right now and putting an end to this. I'm not going to be your bitch for the next nine months, that's for sure." He picked up the phone sitting on the nightstand.

Rose ran into the bedroom and snatched the phone from his hand. "No, Tony, don't," she pleaded, hugging him and smearing cold cream on his robe. "I'm so sorry. Please forgive me. Don't hurt the kids because I'm stupid. I'll do better. I swear. Please, Tony, please." She had played her trump card: the children. She hugged him tighter and waited for the inevitable. Tony would relent, of course.

He hugged her and sighed. "You can't do this every month, sweetheart."

"I know," Rose conceded. "I'll do better."

Tony kissed her and stepped back to look her over, the lower half of her face covered in white goo. He snickered. "Just as beautiful and sexy as the day I married her."

Rose laughed as well. She handed Tony the phone and dashed into the bathroom. "Babe," she called. "I don't remember if I put the chicken in the frig. Would you check for me?"

"Sure," Tony said. He opened a top nightstand drawer, lifted a remote and walked out the door, closing it behind him.

Rose heard a faint beep, indicating Tony had disarmed the alarm. She listened to the sound of descending footsteps and quickly re-entered the bedroom. She grabbed her mobile telephone lying on the nightstand and punched a text message to Cam: "Important we get together B4 Friday."

*

Rose lay in bed with her back to Tony, who held her tightly but not uncomfortably so. They had just said their goodnights and exchanged a couple of quick kisses, minimizing the affect of their unpleasant discussion fifteen minutes earlier about Tony's possible participation on a presidential commission. With the door closed and the lights off Rose could see virtually nothing. Just as well. She wanted to close her eyes and sleep away the ill effects of a bad day.

She felt Tony repeatedly kissing the back of her neck and responded by making almost inaudibly soft, short, high pitched, throaty sounds that conveyed pleasure at his show of affection. Tony followed up by nibbling her shoulder. Rose followed up with quiet moans and deeper inhales and exhales. She enjoyed the feel of his massive hardness rubbing through his pajama pants against her pajama-covered buttocks and released a louder moan when he reached inside her top and traced her nipple with his fingertip.

She smiled, pleased he wanted her. With stress from a bad day nearly overwhelming her, she wanted him as well. Given her troubled spirit, Tony would be more than willing to do all the work. She wouldn't have to ask. A few minutes of kissing followed by a few minutes of his face buried between her legs followed by a few more minutes of him on top of her and she would sleep like a baby all night. She felt his large but gentle hands caressing one breast, then the other and felt the urge to roll over, face him and stick her tongue as far into his mouth as it would go.

However, she thought better of giving in to her desires. If she satisfied herself Tony might be less impressive when he met Cam three days from now. She couldn't take the risk. Her only chance of keeping the extra ten thousand every month existed if Cam became addicted to Tony's sexual prowess. Besides, she still harbored some resentment toward him for allowing himself to be considered for that stupid commission.

"I'm very tired, Tony," she whispered. She said nothing further as he slowly removed his hand and rolled over onto his back. The ensuing silence between them was deafening but she knew it would eventually pass. Damn, Rose thought. The sacrifices a woman made for her family.

*

The thick, twenty-five feet high glass walls ushered in the bright daylight, which gently stroked Rose's and Cam's faces. Both wore casual clothes. "Look," Rose said, "I know we said we wouldn't talk about this among ourselves but I need your help here." She hadn't expected Cam to go all noble on her and resists discussing the "arrangement." Rose glanced around to ensure that none of the other two hundred customers enjoying lunch at the crowded restaurant in downtown Boston had overheard.

Cam made a face and stared at her garden salad, displaying obvious discomfort. "But we gave our word," she remonstrated before sipping her hot tea. However, Rose's sour-face response induced her to add, "But you're my best friend so of course I want to help any way I can."

"Well, you might be helping yourself, too," Rose declared. "I shouldn't tell you this but last night Tony was going to call you and tell you to forget this whole thing." She watched Cam closely in order to gage her reaction. Rose liked to believe she harbored no discomfort or hostility toward Cam for their arrangement. Instead, she heaped her resentment toward Cam onto that which she already held against Tony.

Cam widened her eyes and covered her mouth with her hand. "He was? Why? Is it something I did?"

Rose picked up Cam's alarm and felt relieved. The rest would be almost easy. She took her time, savoring the sweet smell of impending success and her fried shrimp. "I don't want to hurt you, hon, but let's just say everybody wins if we keep this thing going for the full year. Don't you think so?" She placed a fork full of rice into her mouth.

"Yes, of course," Cam immediately agreed.

Rose leaned closer. "I did my part—and it wasn't easy—but I got Tony to consent to...you know, keep going, but you've got to do your part as well."

"What should I do?" Cam asked, her voice almost quivering.

"You've got to remind Tony that what we're doing is helping his family," Rose announced. "I don't like keeping secrets from my husband but I can tell you I've got this collection agency asshole hounding me over some chump change we owe him." She reached for Cam's hand and spied the four corners of the room, actually concerned Rivers might show up. "The mortgages, the car notes, the credit cards, the kids' tuition." She paused for dramatic effect and whispered. "You're keeping our family afloat right now, Cam, but that ship's going to sink if we can't keep Tony on board. You understand what I'm saying?"

Cam nodded. "I do. I do. I'll surreptitiously convey that message to him." She sipped her tea again. "Please, let's talk about something else."

The uncomfortable topic settled, the mood immediately lightened and the two best friends chatted incessantly about other matters. When they finished their meal Cam reached into her purse and insisted on paying the bill over Rose's perfunctory protests. Cam dropped a few paper bills on the table, and as they stood and negotiated the corner of the table they heard a man's voice behind them.

"Sister Rose?"

Rose turned and greeted a man nearly as tall as Tony, in his mid-thirties and ruggedly handsome. "Why, Brother Sam. How are you?"

The man approached Rose. "I'm good." He turned to Cam. "Good afternoon. I remember you. You've visited our church in the past, right?" He smiled.

"Cam, this is Sam Parker," Rose said, "Detective Sam Parker, with the Boston Police Department. She watched the two new acquaintances shake hands. "I'm sorry you didn't arrive earlier," she lied. "You could have joined us for lunch."

"I've eaten here before," Sam explained. "The food is good but I'm here to follow up with problems a few businesses in the area have had with some stolen credit cards."

The three exchanged a few pleasantries as they eased toward the front door. Cam excused herself to visit the ladies room, leaving Rose alone in the foyer with Sam.

"Um, Sister Rose," Sam said, "your friend, Cam. She's so beautiful. Is she seeing anyone?" He stroked the goatee that decorated part of his copper skin and waited.

Rose smiled. Sam was tall enough and good-looking enough to dance with Cam, but she didn't see a police detective as a suitable mate for her affluent friend. Besides, the last thing she wanted was Cam to become romantically interested in another man and risk losing Tony's extra tax-free income. "Sorry, Brother Sam," she said. "She's got somebody. She's not available."

*

Rose knocked gently on the door to Zoë's room and unlike Tony, entered without waiting for an answer. She backed into the door to close it while keeping her hands behind her. She could hear "Gavotte" by Francois-Joseph Gossec playing in the background on the stereo. Zoë, holding a book, sat under a six feet tall floor lamp in a loveseat near the window. She wiggled her foot, as if directing the flute lead in the flute-piano duet. Rose smiled, pleased her children were home on a Friday night for a change rather than off on some school or church event. "What are you reading, sweetheart?"

Zoë raised her book. "This? It's just a story about a pair of star-crossed lovers. Kinda like a modern *Romeo and Juliet*." She shrugged, apparently embarrassed not to be caught reading something more substantive. "What's up?"

Rose remained near the door and inspected her daughter's room. It was a neat, simple space with brighter colors than her brothers'. The room had been totally remodeled two years earlier. A black and mostly off-white music motif, reflecting Zoë's passion for the past four years, had replaced the previous girlie-girl pink and red colors. Rose took a step closer. "I have something for you," she whispered, and glanced at the walls surrounding them, adorned with posters of various contemporary and past great flutists.

Zoë placed a marker in her book and set it on the desk next to the loveseat while getting on her feet, covered with thick wool socks. "Really?" What is it?"

Rose extended her hands, showing Zoë a black instrument case. "Take a look."

Zoë rushed to her mother and carefully placed the case on her bed. She opened it, widened her eyes and jumped up and down while clapping her hands. "Oh my God! Oh my God! Oh my God! Oh my God!" she exclaimed in rapid succession.

Rose put her fingers to her lips. "Shhh," she said. "Keep it down."

Zoë lifted the largest part of the obviously brand new flute, the part with the most keys called the body joint, and ran her fingers over it. She returned it to its hollowed spot in the case and hugged Rose tightly. "Thank you, Mom," she gushed. "I love you, you and Dad. I know Dad's at his other job but when he comes home tomorrow morning I'm going to tell him how much I appreciate it." She closed the case and started for the door. "I'm going to go get Adam."

Rose grabbed the girl by the wrist, stopping her forward progress. "No, you can't tell your brother about this."

"Mom, you're hurting me," Zoë whined. She faced her mother, who released her. "Why can't I show this to Adam? It's beautiful. It's—" She paused and stared at the foreign item on her bed, then stepped around Rose to inspect it closer. She opened the case and after a few seconds closed it again. "But Mom, this is the one the man at the music store showed us that costs way too much money."

Rose frowned as she recalled the smug white man with the British accent, pathetic comb over, and condescending attitude they had met a month before. He had certainly straightened up when she had returned yesterday and demanded to speak directly to the store owner. Rose's reply came with a slightly sharp tone. "Who says my talented, budding music star can't have a nice instrument just like the white kids?"

"But why can't I tell Adam?"

"Because he would tell your father."

Zoë sighed. "But what's the problem with that? Dad knows, doesn't he?"

Rose sighed and stared at the poster of flute legend Sir James Galway. After a few seconds she returned her attention to Zoë. "No, honey, he doesn't know—and we're going to keep it that way."

TEN: HOME SWEET HOME

Cam fluttered about in her home like a bee sampling nectar, She fluffed pillows, straightened chairs—and chastised herself for getting such a late start preparing for Tony's visit. She had spent most of the third Friday in January working on a lucrative project: designing a wedding dress for the daughter of a billionaire oil tycoon. Although no longer the proprietress of a prominent fashion design company, eleven years in the business had provided her with contacts from all over the globe. Subsequently, she continued to generate substantial income—often in cash—from individual contracts. Hence, in a few days she would be flown by private jet to Brazil and treated like royalty.

Cam raced into the kitchen and checked the contents of the seven feet tall, built-in refrigerator; no change since she had last checked ten minutes earlier. She closed the door and pranced into the living room with feet covered by thick bedroom slipper-socks, producing almost silent footsteps against the hardwood floor. She spent a full minute rearranging two pillows on her sofa.

Finally satisfied, she stared at the cable box clock and noted the time: 5:44. She would hear Tony's Cadillac SUV roll into her driveway in about fifteen minutes. Burning anticipation engulfed her like a gasoline fire.

Cam raced past the kitchen into the powder room and inspected herself in the oval-shaped mirror, which reflected her image from head to knee. Suddenly, she disapproved of her clothing. She wore a long-sleeved cotton blouse with a plunging neckline and no bra. A belt snugly tied around her waist accentuated her hourglass figure. She also sported a pair of hip-hugging but relatively comfortable blue jeans.

While Cam pondered what to do about her attire, a sultry, smooth, jazzy piano solo playing on the stereo in the living room attracted her attention. She sighed and slowly swiveled her hips from side to side in rhythm with the music. The image of her lover holding her in a pre-coitus mating dance ignited a rush of sexual excitement. "Tony," she whispered. "Sweet Tony." How funny life could be, she mused. A few months ago any man who dared touch her would have gotten his hand bitten off. Now, the thought of making love to Tony invaded her thoughts several times a day.

The music faded and the song ended, inducing her to check her watch; too late to dash upstairs and change. A re-examination of her appearance caused her to disapprove of her hairstyle as well. She had combed her long hair to the right side of her head and tied it into one long curly tail. "What are you, twelve years old?" she asked her reflection.

The chime of the doorbell surprised her. Tony sometimes arrived a little early but never this early. Perhaps he felt as eager to see her as she felt to see him. She trotted to the front door and opened it without checking the peephole, simmering desire prompting such an impetuous action. That desire quickly turned to disappointment. She pushed the storm door open and addressed her unexpected caller. "Yes, Officer, can I help you?"

The porch light shone on the baby face of a nearly six feet tall male police officer who stood at the door holding the arm of a slightly taller man; the latter with his hands behind his back. "Sorry to bother you, ma'am," the officer said, touching the brim of his cap, which covered a thick mop of dirty blond hair. He stared at Cam for a couple of seconds in obvious admiration; the burst of cold air had caused her nipples to protrude quite visibly through her blouse. The officer continued. "This man says he's your husband, but I caught him prowling around on your property trying to peek into one of your side windows."

"I wasn't prowling anywhere," the man snapped, his voice laced with indignation. Dressed in a long, black overcoat, he turned to reveal the handcuffs that bound his hands. "Cam, tell this kid that you know me and to take these damn things off." The cold air converted his heated words into white smoke.

Cam put her hands on her hips. "Vincent, what are you doing here?" She had not seen him in a year. He was still handsome, but had grown a thin goatee and obviously hadn't lost his taste for expensive suits and shoes. His debonair appearance notwithstanding, the sight of him repulsed her, like a huge cockroach crawling across a just-scrubbed kitchen floor.

The officer reached into the upper pocket of his bulky jacket and produced a handcuff key. "I'm sorry, ma'am. So he *is* your husband?"

"God no!" Cam barked. "He's my ex-husband, and I've told him a hundred times to leave me alone. He just doesn't seem to get the message."

"Oh," the officer said. "Well, in that case I could book him for trespassing, but you'd have to come to the station to prefer charges."

Cam considered the suggestion but shook her head. "No, I suppose not." Tony would arrive shortly. She'd much rather roll around in bed with him than sit at some rinky-dink police station answering questions and signing forms.

Vincent smiled. "Thank you, Cam. No matter what's happened between us, I know we both still have feelings for each other."

"Oh shut up, Vincent," Cam demanded. "The only feeling I have for you is disgust."

"Camellia," Vincent replied with exaggerated pain. "You hurt me deeply when you say such things. "He lifted his hands as best he could and addressed the police officer. His tone switched to disdain. "Unlock your little toy and go drink your cocoa, Junior. I think I hear your mommy calling."

Cam couldn't believe Vincent's stupidity. Any African American male with even a modicum of intelligence could appreciate the precarious position in which he stood. She decided to play the higher card she had been dealt. "Shame on you for talking that way. The man's just doing his job."

The officer nodded at Cam, then grabbed Vincent by the arm and shook him. "This nice lady gave you a break, but nothing says *I* have to. Your driver's license has expired. So has your insurance coverage on that fancy car you've got illegally parked about half a block up the street." He descended down the porch steps pulling Vincent with him. "So Junior here is taking you to the station and having your car towed."

Cam was regaled by the shocked expression on Vincent's face as the officer led him down her driveway.

"Bye, Vincent," she called in a mocking tone, waving. "You always did talk too much."

"You bitch!" Vincent yelled. "This isn't over, not by a long shot!"

The officer produced a small canister from a holster on his belt. "If you say one more insulting thing to that classy lady you're going to be screaming in pain when I spray this all over your face." He tugged on his prisoner. "Come on, smartie pants."

Mortified by the entire scene, Cam closed the door and, taking comfort in the refuge of her home, rubbed her arms to warm them. Hopefully, the officer and Vincent would be gone before Tony arrived. Perhaps a night in jail would prevent Vincent from bothering her again. The exhilaration she had felt a few minutes earlier had been replaced by rage and embarrassment. She covered her face with her hands and took deep breaths. She needed Tony right now. Nothing like hot, steamy sex to chase away agitation.

She ran to the powder room to examine herself again but just stood before the mirror in an absent-minded trance replaying the events of the past couple of minutes. After a few seconds she started to giggle. "Smartie pants," the officer had said. She hadn't heard anything like that since junior high school. "Come on, smartie pants," she said before bursting into laughter and scrambling into the kitchen to survey the refrigerator again. "Nothing new in there, smartie pants," she declared and let out another hearty laugh.

She moseyed to the stereo and pressed a few buttons. The soft music abruptly stopped. Cam leaned closer. "Shoot, not what I wanted." She hadn't adjusted the CD player without the remote control since she bought the device two years before. Resolving not to be defeated by a machine, she pressed more buttons, resulting in the CD door opening and closing; then she heard a voice on the radio:

"This is Phil Masters at Masters Motors. We've gotten a new shipment of..."

"What did I do?" Cam asked, clearly annoyed. She dropped to one knee and pressed additional buttons. Phil Masters stopped talking, only to be replaced by static. The doorbell chimed. "He's here!" Cam whispered. She shook her finger at the stereo. "You win this time," she conceded and ran to the table adjoining the sofa to grab the remote. The return of the music, even if the selection started over from the first song, brought her some relief, and she rushed to the door. This time she utilized the peephole. The sight of Tony brought her unbridled joy. She swung the door open. "Hello there, handsome."

Tony stepped inside. "How's the lovely Cam this evening?" He handed her a perfect red rose.

Cam accepted the flower, offered profuse thanks and grabbed the lapel of Tony's jacket with her free hand to pull him close to her for a kiss. She paused to enjoy the scent of his aftershave but felt an immediate spark of passion when their lips touched. God, he tasted so sweet! "I'm fine, baby" she whispered, "now that you're here."

Tony removed his coat and hung it in the closet. After closing the door he turned and rubbed his hands together. "I want to hear everything about your upcoming trip," he commanded, his voice high with keen interest and excitement.

Cam pressed her body, aching with longing, against his. She threw her arm around his neck before answering his request with one word. "Later."

*

Cam opened her eyes and yawned. She had dosed off, drifting into the realm of contentment and bliss. Six lit candles on the candelabra atop the writing table several feet from her bed provided enough light to see all she needed. The wall clock directly above the candles indicated the time as quarter past seven; she had been asleep for twenty minutes.

She turned her head and stared at Tony, who lay on his back next to her, his eyes closed. The two lay side by side, linked arm in arm. Cam took his large hand in hers and savored the thought of their time together. They had started making love downstairs on the sofa a few minutes after he had shed his coat but they had finished in bed. Cam felt simultaneously euphoric and relaxed; the stress from the ugly scene with Vincent had disappeared, if not the memory. She repositioned herself in bed to avoid lying in the wet spot, then inhaled, relishing the pungent smell of their lovemaking.

Tony opened his eyes and smiled. "Sorry, didn't mean to fall asleep."

"I like it," Cam gushed. "I just woke up myself." She pinched Tony. "Dang, we knocked each other out." She enjoyed this part of the evening. Now the two lovers would talk for a while. Almost as much fun as the lovemaking. Almost. Tony would let her start.

"I have something to tell you," Cam opened.

"What is it?"

"Well, that fool of an ex-husband has been bothering me."

Tony made a quarter turn to face Cam and rested his jaw on his hand. "What do you mean, bothering you?"

"On Christmas Eve he left me a snide card. And he's been calling me and leaving messages I never return. Finally, tonight he paid me a visit."

Tony sat up. "You mean here, at the house?"

"Yes, but don't worry," Cam assured him. "The police picked him up and hauled his ass off to the police station for driving with an expired license and some other stuff." She caressed Tony's muscular arm. "It's nothing. Really."

"If it's nothing," Tony replied, "why didn't you tell me?"

"I'm telling you now."

Tony slid back under the covers. "I don't like it." He took Cam into his arms and kissed her on the forehead.

"Why don't you like it?" Cam asked. Whether Tony was more concerned about her or himself mattered to her—even if he was only a rental.

Tony smiled. "Because you're very important to me and I want you to be safe."

Cam cuddled closer. What a wonderful man. No hesitation, no games. Just unabashedly gives her what she needs. She felt so warm and comfortable in his arms. If he were her man for real she'd never share him with another. She'd make him so happy he wouldn't even think of being with someone else.

"Cam," Tony said, "can I ask you something I've wanted to ask for a while?"

"Yes, darling, these breasts are mine."

Tony laughed. "I know that, honey. What I wanted to ask is: What's with you and my brothers? You know, Rose said—um, I mean, I understand most of your romances have been with black men. Given your heritage..." He paused to squeeze Cam gently as he brought the fingers of both hands together and counted. "Okay, now let me get them all right: Dad is one half African American and one half Philippine. Mom is one quarter Mexican, one quarter Irish, one quarter Paiute, and one quarter Shoshone."

Cam applauded. "I'm impressed. Even I have trouble keeping them all straight." She and Tony laughed. "To be honest, I've dated men of all races, but I've just been the most comfortable among black men. Maybe because of my dad, who insisted that I, his only child, be raised black. He said I would never be accepted by other groups anyway."

"Was he right?"

Cam shrugged. "Yes and no. Times are different now. No more one drop rule. Identifying oneself as being bi-racial or multi-racial is accepted and embraced."

Tony nodded. "That's true."

Cam continued. "I've got friends and acquaintances of all races, but truth be told, the people who've accepted me the most are blacks—even though it means I've kissed a couple of frogs thinking they were princes."

"A couple?"

"Okay, more than a couple," Cam admitted. She snuggled close to him again. "But now that I know what a good man is, I'm sure I won't ever make the mistake of choosing another bum like Vincent again."

"I hope not," Tony said. "You're too wonderful, beautiful and special for that."

Cam beamed with affection and self-satisfaction. She cuddled more, enjoying the soft beat of Tony's heart: slow, steady, soothing. They conversed for another forty minutes—about her upcoming trip to Brazil, their work, the Boston Celtics, Zoë and Adam, everything but Rose—intermittently kissing and caressing with increased aggressiveness. Eventually Cam rested her head on Tony's shoulder and ran her index fingertip close to the inside of his thigh, knowing the effect her gesture would have on him. She heard his breathing become heavier. "Baby..." she whispered.

"Yes?"

"What's going to happen after October?"

Tony sighed. After a long pause, he answered. "We both know what has to happen, Cam."

"But," Cam interjected, "will we be able to just shut off our feelings after what we've been sharing?"

"No," Tony answered. "They'll become treasured memories...treasured forever."

Cam nodded in agreement. She wanted Tony in more ways than one but would never venture to take another woman's husband. Still, his reply made her heart feel like a stone falling into a bottomless hole. She tried to overcome the feeling by kissing his chest. Enough talk. Time for Round Two. She continued kissing him and worked her way to his lips. "I'm sorry. I shouldn't have asked such a stupid question." She writhed about, settled on top of him and sat up so he could admire the view. She took pride in her own washboard abs, thanks to a ninety-minute workout five days a week that included ten minutes on an ab crunch exercise machine.

Tony traced around one of her nipples with his finger. "You are one incredibly beautiful and sexy woman."

Cam grabbed his hand and kissed it. "Speaking of treasured memories..."

"Yes, dear Cam?"

She reached under the sheet. "Are you ready to add some more?" The stiff organ she held in her hand provided all the answer she required. She lifted herself and asked one more question while their bodies joined. "By the way, did you start that thing we talked about?"

"As a matter of fact, I did."

"And no one knows?"

Tony palmed Cam's hips as she slowly moved up and down. "No one."

*

Home alone on a Saturday morning, Cam sat at her desk in her spacious office, her attention focused on a website detailing how to file a harassment prevention order in the Commonwealth of Massachusetts. The sun covered the twin, east-facing windows to her left, belying the cold temperature outside. The west wall displayed dozens of laminated magazine covers and photographs featuring Cam's designs worn by beautiful models of all nationalities. A half-dozen papers containing sketches lay scattered across a drafting table behind her near the north wall.

Cam cursed Vincent for making her waste time when she had a million things to do before leaving for Brazil the following week, in addition to numerous other business projects that required her attention. Because it was Saturday she couldn't simply drop the ex-husband-is-stalking-me matter into the hands of one of her attorneys, so she sought some basic information via the Internet. According to the website, harassment prevention orders weren't difficult to obtain. Cam hadn't decided to definitely procure one against Vincent but resolved to do so if he continued to pester her.

The clock in the bottom right corner of her monitor read three minutes after eleven. She sighed. Tony had been gone for only four hours and already she missed him. They had slept in each other's arms all night. She had awakened wanting him again, but Tony had reluctantly declined, reminding her of the "no sex after sunrise" clause on which Rose had insisted.

The telephone rang, jolting her back to the present. Out of habit she grabbed her mobile telephone and scoffed, and instead checked the caller ID information on her home telephone, which read "Unavailable." Against her better judgment, she picked up the receiver. "Hello?"

"Cam Spencer?" the female voice on the other end asked.

"Yes," Cam answered, relieved the call had nothing to do with Vincent.

"You don't know me," the caller said, "but I want you to leave Vincent Moreau alone."

Cam shook her head. So much for assumptions. "Leave *him* alone? Who is this?"

"Never mind who this is," the woman replied. "You got your white policeman boyfriend to throw Vincent in jail over some bullshit charges after luring him to your place. That's why a black man should stick with a real black queen, not some wannabe with a trust fund."

"You got your information all wrong, dear," Cam said. "Vincent got himself thrown in jail by running his big mouth. Don't call me again." She ended the call.

Cam took deep breaths, causing her ample bosom to heave with rage and resentment. Vincent was a crafty and cowardly one, getting someone else to do his dirty work. What had he said yesterday: This isn't over, not by a long shot? Cam turned her attention back to the computer screen, feeling more justified in her research. Her anger mixed with apprehension. She suspected that Vincent was running out of money, and for a man accustomed to living large, no telling what he might do.

ELEVEN: LIFE IS A BOXING MATCH

Rose pushed the glass door open and escaped the twenty-five degree temperature and gusty winds, not uncommon in Massachusetts during the first week of February. She entered the mall with an expression on her face conveying irritation due to her mission. She found the bright overhead lights to be welcome relief from the darkness outside.

Oblivious to the scores of people meandering in every direction at six thirty in the evening, it took her less than a minute to board the escalator. Once she reached the second floor she walked the two hundred feet to the food court where fast food restaurants, squeezed together like children's blocks, formed an arc around an area two-thirds full that could seat one hundred people.

Rose visually searched for James Rivers, who had been a nuisance to her for the past month. Although she had not yet eaten dinner, the competing aromas from the cheap eateries actually suppressed her appetite. A teen-age boy holding a half-full tray of toothpick-impaled meatballs approached her and asked if she cared to try one. Rose politely declined his offer. Finally, she spotted Rivers sitting about forty yards away. He stood and gestured for her to join him. She forced herself to walk in his direction. The sight of him reminded her of her father's assertion that life is similar to a boxing match: one must strive to win rounds but avoid being knocked out. Unfortunately, she had lost this round.

She hated the thought of giving him any money but the threat of legal action had convinced her to acquiesce, at least somewhat. The money had come from Tony's "other job," as the children called it and of course, he knew nothing about the impending transaction. Rose shivered, partly still recovering from the outside weather but mostly from reluctance to handing money over to Rivers, a man who made his living bothering people like her: upstanding, middle class people experiencing temporary financial difficulty.

Rose approached the durable, round table with an acrylic glass top where Rivers had been sitting, accompanied by two empty chairs. "Okay, I'm here," she muttered. She could think of nothing else to say. The two potential antagonists wore long, dress coats over business suits, indicating the end of the workday for both.

"Good evening, Mrs. Monroe," Rivers said, still standing. "Please, sit down. Can I get you a beverage or something?"

Rose resisted the urge to shout, "This isn't a social call, you asshole!" Instead, she dragged a chair to the opposite part of the table and sat. "No thank you. I have to get home in time for dinner."

"I understand," Rivers said. "Me too." He casually inspected the people roaming in front of the tiny restaurants. "I don't understand why we had to meet at this mall rather than the one where you work."

"My prerogative," Rose replied. She didn't care to explain herself. As far as she was concerned, the sooner they completed their business the better. She reached into her purse, produced a letter-size envelope and slid it across the table. Rivers checked their surroundings again before accepting the envelope, like a scene from an old black and white mystery movie. Rose rolled her eyes when he placed the object in his lap and began counting. "There's a thousand dollars in there," she said, now clearly impatient.

Rivers lifted his head and leaned forward but showed no signs of emotion. "Now Mrs. Monroe, we agreed you would bring two thousand."

"I know," Rose conceded, "but I just couldn't. You know how it is. It's February but we're still paying Christmas bills. I'll give you another five hundred next month."

"You told me that before."

Rose lowered her head, feigning humility. "I know, but it's not like I'm not making the effort. You do have a thousand dollars in your hand. That leaves, um..."

"One thousand, seven hundred and forty-two dollars."

Rose shrugged. "Okay, so three, four more months and you'll be done with me."

This time Rivers lowered his head as he scribbled in his receipt book. He finished writing but paused before speaking. "That's too bad," he lamented. "I don't get a chance to see a woman who's as attractive as you."

Rose arched her carefully pruned eyebrows, glanced at the wedding band on the man's left hand and felt offended. However, after additional consideration she also felt surprisingly pleased. Other than her husband, it had been some time since a man had complimented her on her appearance. She smiled. "Mr. Rivers, you shouldn't talk that way."

Rivers nodded. "You're right. I apologize. You see, um, my wife has MS and well, me and the kids, we have to look after her, so sometimes I feel..." He exhaled. "It's just that you're a classy lady but you're still so down to earth. Not like those spoiled kids fresh out of college who go on spending sprees after getting their first real job."

Rose considered her options. She didn't trust Rivers. He had that Latin lothario look. Probably tossed out that sick wife shtick to anything with a vagina. Nevertheless, her mother had taught her never to let an advantage go to waste, especially when dealing with men. Not that he was bad looking, with his piercing brown eyes. Two years and twenty pounds earlier she would have had him eating out of her hand within five minutes. Today she would have to marshal other resources. What she had lost in beauty she had gained in technique. For now, the wise move would be to step into the ring and jab.

Rivers tore the receipt from his book and handed it to her. "I'm just doing my job, Mrs. Monroe, you understand. I really don't mean to cause you any problems."

Rose brushed her index finger against his while lifting the piece of paper from his hand. "Rose," she said. "Call me Rose."

*

Three days before Valentine's Day, Rose dried her hands in her kitchen and chatted with Cam, who had recently returned from Brazil. Hand-sized, red paper hearts adorned each cabinet door; Rose had chosen a Valentine's Day theme for Zoë and Adam's early Saturday afternoon party celebrating their thirteenth birthday. Cam held her mobile telephone and displayed a photo of the dress she had designed for her client. Rose opened her mouth wide with excitement and envy. "You said billionaire with a B?" she asked, speaking over the gaggle of middle school students laughing, talking, eating and drinking in the great room.

"Yes," Cam replied. "The wedding was like some kind of fairy tale. All this for his daughter, who married the son of the country's president, the bum."

"Who's a bum? The president or the son?"

"The son," Cam replied. "When we were alone the day before the wedding, the groom-to-be tried to grope and kiss me."

Rose gave a tisk, tisk. "Men can be such dogs. Speaking of which, I better get back out there and keep my eye on Tony and that wench Monique."

"She teaches with him at the school, right?" Cam asked.

"Yeah," Rose answered. "Wouldn't you know, her niece and Zoë are good friends. The niece goes to our church."

"So who invited the aunt?"

"Guess who," Rose replied. "The hussy gave the girl a ride to the party and made like she was going to leave, but you know Tony." She imitated his voice. "Please stay. We've got more than enough food." She resumed speaking in her own voice. "Now she's been following him around like a bitch in heat for the past fifteen minutes."

"Then we better get out there," Cam declared.

"Damn right," Rose asserted. She noted Cam's use of the word "we" and smirked as they each grabbed a large pizza box. After all these years, Rose thought, she could still get the best of Cam. The mother of the hosts couldn't keep an eye on Miss Teacher-In-Tight-Jeans and organize the party at the same time. Cam would protect her own interest and thereby protect Rose's as well. "If there's one thing I can't stand," Rose said while taking a couple of steps, "is some woman trying to get a piece of my man." She stopped and twisted her torso, making eye contact with Cam before finishing her thought. "I mean, for free." Her friend's face turned beet red with embarrassment. Rose giggled and continued on her journey. She couldn't help rubbing Cam's nose in their arrangement from time to time.

Rose entered the great room and placed the pizza on a dining table loaded with various foods, including a large pot of her mother's chicken gumbo, with its smell trumping the other competitors. "More pizza!" she announced. "There's pepperoni and other meats on this one and veggie or cheese on the one Aunt Cam, um, Ms. Spencer is holding." She and Cam stepped back. Several teens and almost teens swooped down and circled the table like hungry vultures—loud, squawking hungry vultures.

Rose inspected the noisy room, decorated with red paper hearts and red paper roses. Half the forty-two adolescents in attendance brandished mobile telephones. They were a mixture of African American friends from Community African Methodist Episcopal Church, and mostly white friends from Boston International Academy—with a sprinkling of Asians, African Americans or Latinos/Latinas. Keeping with the Valentine theme, everyone wore a red shirt or blouse—or a red shoulder sash sewn by Tony's mother.

Rose spotted Adam posing near the baby grand piano conversing with two lovely girls obviously vying for his attention, one black and one white. Although not totally comfortable with middle schoolers engaged in such mild coquettishness, privately she hoped the girl from church would prevail; she didn't want a blond daughter-in-law named Heather.

Rose furtively checked on her husband, who stood on the other side of the piano conversing with Monique, and now Cam. Rose alternated between observing the older then the younger handsome Monroe male, flanked by adoring females. Like father, like son, she admitted privately. A jocular thought made her snicker: At least Cam was paying for her share. If Monique wanted a turn she'd have to cough up ten grand and get in line.

Next, Rose turned her attention to Zoë, batting her eyes and chatting with a handsome boy who flashed a mouthful of braces. Zoë had informed her that the eighth-grader, originally from Mexico, was some kind of soccer phenom. From the way he continued to smile at her daughter, Rose assessed, soccer was probably the farthest thing from his mind.

She conceded she couldn't stop her children from growing up but she trusted them because they were both terrific kids with sound judgment. Unlike so many teen siblings, they never argued and because each had discovered his or her own strength they didn't compete with each other. Zoë excelled at music while Adam loved science and had earned nothing less than straight A's since kindergarten. A Grammy-winning concert flutist and Nobel prize-winner doctor; sounded good to her.

Rose continued to inspect the attendees but not too conspicuously, remembering her agreement with the birthday honorees: She and Tony would generally stay out of the way and primarily act as caterers and cleanup personnel. Her stealthy intelligence gathering indicated not everyone elected to participate in the adolescent flirting rituals. Jia-Li, the shy classmate and gifted pianist whose mother drove Adam and Zoë to school every morning, had all but run out of the room after a boy who attended Rose's church had attempted to woo her.

"Better go over there and claim what's yours."

Rose turned and tittered. "I'm not worried, Mom."

Rose's mother put her hands on her hips. "I know I done taught you better than that. Those two, they're pretty enough to rustle up their own husbands instead of throwing themselves at yours." She squinted. "Look how they keep touching his arm."

Rose sighed. "They're just being friendly."

The woman whom the twins addressed as "Grandmother" scoffed. "And somebody should tell Cam the next time she buys herself a husband, buy one who's not into men."

Rose gave her mother a playful scowl. "Now you stop that."

"I don't know why you trust her," the mother whispered. "Can't you see she's in love with your husband?"

Rose sighed again. How could she explain? The truth wouldn't do: *Mom, Cam's just captivated because I bet Tony's giving her the best sex she's ever had—for which we're being well compensated.* All she could say was, "Mom, Cam's my best friend."

Her mother shrugged. "So? Wouldn't be the first time a woman run off with her best friend's man."

Rose felt herself becoming angry and defensive. "No one can take Tony from me," she whispered through grinding teeth. "That's in the first place, and in the second..." She took a deep breath and decided to try another approach. "Mom, will you please go back with the other adults in the TV room and let me handle this? Please?" She felt relieved when her mother strutted down the hall. However, the woman's words had hit their mark. Rose pretended to inspect the table filled with food and began inching toward Tony but stopped when she overheard the conversation of two male teens standing at the other end of the table.

"Them two are like, too fine. I'm talking serious cutie pies."

"Why you preach to the choir, bro? You hear what I'm saying?"

Rose listened further to the boys who attended Community AME, one short, one tall; curious about which pair of girls had caught their attention.

"Just like at church," the tall boy said. "They be flocking to Mr. Monroe like sheep. Look at them two."

"Shoot," retorted the short boy. "Give me a couple more years and I'll take one of 'em off his hands, maybe both. You hear what I'm saying?"

The boys burst into raucous, energetic laughter, being careful not to spill the contents of their paper cups, half filled with soda. Rose shook her head. Just puppies barking. Still, if a couple of runts have formed the same opinion as her mother, no need taking any chances. She glided over to the adult threesome and abruptly brought Tony and Monique's animated discussion on the significance of the 1944 G.I. Bill to a close. "Tony, would you get a couple more bags of ice from the cooler outside?"

Tony nodded. "Sure, hon." With that, he vacated the room.

"Anything I can do to help out?" Monique asked.

"Why yes," Rose answered. She resisted disclosing her real sentiment: Get the hell out of here, bitch! She smiled. "Why don't you help me in the kitchen?" The two walked into the empty kitchen with Rose in the lead. Rose turned and faced Monique but her attention was diverted to Tony, outside on the other side of the patio door surrounded by snow, shoveled and piled knee high, from a storm four days before.

"You have a lovely home," Monique said. "And your children are adorable."

"Thank you," Rose replied. "You seem to admire a lot of things that belong to me."

Monique widened her eyes. "I beg your pardon?"

Rose had not intended to talk this way but seeing Monique up close had stoked her ire. She envied the teacher's figure and beauty and thought it best to ensure history was the only passion between this woman and her husband. She picked up a large knife on the counter and washed it in the sink while still half-facing Monique. Might as well have a little fun. "Tony and I don't keep secrets from each other. He told me you kissed him."

"Oh, well, I-I'm sorry about that," Monique said, staring at the knife. "I didn't mean anything. I was just, um, you know..."

"You were just risking your damn life," Rose asserted while pat drying the knife with a paper towel. "I wouldn't suggest you do it too often, and I assure you once more would be too often. Am I making myself clear?"

Monique shook her head vigorously.

Tony slid the patio door open and entered the kitchen carrying two ten-pound bags of ice. He closed the door and shivered. "Cold out there," he said and kept walking.

"Um, excuse me," Monique said. "I have to be going. Felicia can call me when she wants to be picked up." She scampered out of the kitchen, nearly bumping into Zoë.

Zoë approached Rose, clearly excited. "Mom, they want me and Jia-Li to play something."

Rose scrunched up her face with obvious disapproval. "You mean 'they want Jia-Li and me.' And didn't we talk about this earlier? I told you to say no if anyone asks." The last thing she needed was Zoë calling attention to her flute.

"If anyone asks what?"

The two females directed their attention to Tony, standing a few feet away.

"They want *Jia-Li and me* to play something, Dad," Zoë reported. "Jia-Li and me," she said again, poking mild fun at her mother for once again correcting her grammar.

Tony took a step closer. "Honey, it's their party. I don't see what harm it would do."

Rose knew she couldn't protest too much for fear of arousing Tony's suspicion. She felt a vibration in her back pocket and retrieved a thin mobile telephone to read the text message from James Rivers:

wld like to c u.

Cam entered the kitchen and positioned herself behind Tony. "Rose, do you want me to bring the cakes out now?" Her face displayed obvious self-congratulations. She had insisted on bringing the birthday cakes and in fact had bought two huge choices: a German chocolate cake, Adam's favorite, and a yellow cake with caramel frosting, Zoë's favorite.

Rose blinked several times in frustration. Too damn many things happening at once. She shoved the telephone back in her pocket. Her new admirer would have to wait. "Okay, Zoë, but just one, maybe two songs, then we'll serve the cakes and ice cream." Zoë clapped her hands and raced out of the kitchen, followed by Tony, who was followed by Cam. Ungrateful, selfish brat, Rose thought. She'd deal with her later. Right now she had to make sure Tony didn't notice his daughter was playing a new three thousand dollar flute.

TWELVE: COMPLICATIONS

Tony stared at the television while stretched out on a plush reclining chair in the all but dark family TV room. He still wore the red shirt and jeans he had donned during Zoë and Adam's birthday party. Hours had passed since the Monroe family and Cam had cleaned up the house, with Cam being the last guest to leave. Tony had bid Rose, Zoë and Adam goodnight twenty minutes earlier. Now he relaxed and enjoyed some alone time, concentrating on events over two millennia before: the technology developed by ancient engineers during the height of the Roman Empire a hundred years after the birth of Christ.

Tony listened to a University of Oxford professor describe the elaborate and revolutionary indoor plumbing system in the notorious Roman bathhouses. A computer-generated diagram accompanied the academician's explanation. Tony whistled. "Will you look at that!" he exclaimed softly. A pizza commercial interrupted the program, prompting Tony to recall the noisy atmosphere in his home only a few hours earlier, with over forty kids laughing, eating and carrying on. After an afternoon in the company of middle school children he was glad he taught high school.

At ten o'clock the documentary ended. Tony turned off the television and checked to make sure windows and doors were locked. Afterward, he yawned and climbed the stairs. The lingering and clashing smell of pizza, chicken enchilada and gumbo grew fainter with each step. Upon reaching the top of the stairs and arming the alarm system Tony heard sounds coming from Zoë's room, the unmistakable sounds of angry voices. Because of the closed door, he couldn't quite make out the words but could easily identify the combatants: Rose and Zoë. As he drew closer he could decipher more content.

"I told you to say no if anyone asked, didn't I?" Rose said.

"I didn't mean anything, Mom," Zoë asserted, her voice peppered with sarcasm. "I just got a little carried away. I don't know why you're making such a big deal out of it."

"You watch your tone, young lady," Rose replied. "Don't get the idea I'm going to allow you to talk to me the way your white friends at school talk to their parents."

Tony knocked twice and entered rather than wait for a response, as he usually did. A desk lamp offered the only source of light. Rose stood in the middle of the room with her back to the door while Zoë sat at the foot of the bed. They directed their attention to Tony and both immediately became as quiet as an empty room. "What's going on?" he inquired. "I thought you two had gone to bed a while back." He visually inspected Rose and Zoë, clad in their pajamas and bathrobes, both with scrubbed faces but bearing expressions as hard as granite.

"Nothing's going on," Rose answered. "We were just talking."

Tony glanced at both females but directed his remarks to Rose. "Don't do that, honey. Don't treat me like an idiot."

"It wasn't anything important, Dad," Zoë replied in a soft voice. "It's no big deal."

"Really?" Tony said. "Well, if it's no big deal, one of you won't mind telling me what it was all about." He leaned against the open door frame and folded his arms. After a few seconds of silence, he spoke. "I'm waiting."

Rose approached him and put her hand on his forearm. "Sweetheart, it's a mother-daughter thing. Can't you trust me to handle it?"

Tony looked at Rose, then Zoë, then Rose again. He generally deferred to Rose about how to deal with the children, especially Zoë, assuming a mother knew more about bringing up a daughter. "Okay," he said, and turned to leave. He put his hand on the doorknob but before tugging on it added one more pronouncement. "But Zoë, I heard enough to agree with your mother about your tone. I don't want to hear you speak to her in such a way again."

"Yes, Daddy."

Tony continued. "I believe you have something to say to the woman who carried you and your brother safely inside her body for nine months—and at great risk to herself, I might add."

Zoë nodded. "I-I'm sorry, Mom—and you were absolutely right about everything."

Tony beamed at the sight of his wife and daughter hugging and kissing. "Well, my job's done here," he declared in a playfully officious voice, mimicking an old TV western he had seen as a child. Rose and Zoë laughed. "Happy birthday, sweetheart," he added and took a step backward. "Your mother and I are both very proud of you. Nothing's happened to change that."

Zoë ran to Tony and hugged him. "I love you, Daddy."

"I love you too, baby," Tony whispered. "Goodnight." He kissed her and ambled down the hall past Adam's room and heard Rose bid Zoë goodnight as well. He waited for Rose by the door to the master bedroom and closed it after she entered. Tony shook his head and chuckled. "That son of ours could sleep through a hurricane."

Rose laughed. "Just like his father."

Tony took her in his arms. "You want to tell me what that was all about?"

Rose shrugged. "It was nothing really. "I was just scolding Zoë about showing off. I told her she and Jia-Li could play one or two songs but she played three."

"Well," Tony said, "was it that big a deal?"

"How many times have you said if we let the kids disobey us about little things today they'll disobey us about big things tomorrow?"

"You're right. And you're sure that was all?"

"Yes, that was all," Rose said. She threw her arms around Tony's neck and pecked him on the lips. "And thanks for backing me up."

Tony held Rose by the waist and felt himself becoming aroused. He pulled her against him and covered her mouth with soft, lingering kisses. He and Rose had made love three nights before but he had not been completely satisfied because on weeknights they tended to be rushed. The fact that both Monique and Cam had shown him so much attention earlier made him feel virile and energized. Monique and Cam's interests notwithstanding, he held in his arms the woman with whom he will gladly spend the rest of his life. He kissed her again. "Rose," he whispered. "My Rose."

"It's getting late," Rose said. She calmly wiggled out of his grasp and took a leisurely walk into the bathroom. "We've got church in the morning."

Tony sighed, disappointed. He had always possessed a strong libido but for the past year Rose's responses to his advances had been less than enthusiastic. However, he chose to say nothing about his frustration. In his mind asking his wife to react positively to his sexual overtures was tantamount to begging. Instead, he checked the desk calendar on his dresser and counted. Six more days until he sees Cam.

"Tony, are you still there?"

Tony returned his attention to the present. "I'm sorry, honey. What did you say?"

"I said, did you know that the father of the woman in Brazil Cam designed that wedding dress for is a billion-aire?"

"A billionaire, huh?" Tony answered. Six days. He could hardly wait.

*

On the third Saturday in February, Tony, nude and lying on his side, awoke and turned his head to check the time on the wall clock: a little after seven o'clock in the morning. The sun had appeared in Weston, Massachusetts for less than a half-hour. He attempted to ease out of bed without waking Cam, no simple feat given her position behind him clinging tightly like a rescued swimmer to a life preserver. He gently lifted her arm, which was as unclothed as the rest of her.

She responded by opening her eyes, then hugging him and whimpering. "No, baby," she whispered. "Stay."

Tony rolled over to face her and kissed her on the forehead. "I would love too, honey, but...you know, I've got to get home." He could see the expression of hurt on her sleepy face underneath her smile.

However, she refused to release him. "Just a couple more minutes, okay?"

Tony rubbed his nose against hers. "Okay."

Cam slowly caressed his chest, then his stomach, then his inner thigh. "My, my, my," she said in a low, sultry voice. "You were sure on fire last night, lover."

Her comments caused Tony some concern. He realized he had been somewhat aggressive the previous evening but perceived Cam's response at the time as encouragement. In the light of day he feared he had misread her signals. "I hope I didn't hurt you."

"Hah!" Cam snorted. "Hurt so good. Seriously, don't let my name fool you. I'm no flower. I loved every minute of it. In fact, feel free to turn the heat up further."

"Okay, if you insist," Tony replied with an impish grin. He couldn't help but feel elated with what he had come to see as his fantasy life. He was being paid handsomely to make love to a beautiful woman—with his wife's consent. "You were pretty amazing yourself," he declared. They continued to caress each other, but in the ensuing silence Tony's mind drifted to his permanent life, his life with Rose and the children. He loved them but realized he wanted more from his chosen life partner. If only Rose would be as uninhibited as Cam.

He glanced at the clock again and committed himself to rise out of bed, but Cam reached for his penis, creating a different rise from him. However, he remembered the "no sex after sunrise" clause and tapped her on the arm. "I really have to get going."

"Did I do something wrong?" Cam asked. "I've got morning breath, don't I?" She mashed her lips together but continued moving her hand in smooth, leisurely strokes.

"Nothing's wrong," Tony assured her. He responded to the up and down gliding of her hand by kissing her until she parted her lips and returned his kisses. "Last night was wonderful, as it always is, but I have to...yes...yes...I like that." He rolled on top of her.

"You're not bored with me already?" Cam asked. "You don't mind coming here?"

Tony kissed her with increased passion and enjoyed the taste of her tongue in his mouth, morning breath and all. "I love being here." He positioned himself so the tip of his penis touched the wetness of her opening but went no farther. "We shouldn't."

Cam put her hands on his buttocks and pulled. "I know the rules, but I can't get enough of you. I want more."

Tony closed his eyes and relished the initial pleasure of their joining. "Oh God, Cam," he moaned. "What are you doing to me?"

Cam smiled and gave him two quick kisses on the mouth. "Giving you what you need and deserve," she replied.

*

An hour later Tony reached into the closet next to Cam's front door for his jacket. He quietly placed the paper bag that would bring Rose such glee inside his overnight bag. Cam puttered in the kitchen to avoid being a witness to that part of his visit. By habit, she would see him off after he announced his departure. Tony felt guilty about accepting the money. Originally, he viewed it as a necessary evil, now he had grown to resent it. However, he appreciated the importance of the transaction for his family. He also felt reluctance about leaving Cam. He treasured their time together. They talked well. They made love well—and they did indeed make love. They made warm, passionate love.

Tony started for the door. "Cam honey, I'm leaving."

Cam shuffled out of the kitchen and into his arms. She rested her head on his chest and after a few seconds attempted to speak. "Tony..." That's all she could manage to say.

He put his hand under her chin and lifted her face. "Please don't make this any more difficult for me than it already is."

"I'm sorry," Cam said. "But I'm...I mean...you know, it's more than we thought it would be—for me at least."

Tony nodded. "I know. Me too."

Cam suddenly brightened up. "So...see you next time?"

"Looking forward to it," Tony confirmed. He gave her a gentle kiss and walked out the door to his car, parked in the driveway. The below freezing temperature meant he would have to scrape a thin layer of frost from his windshield. He didn't mind and didn't regret declining Cam's offer to move one of her vehicles outside so he could park his car in her garage.

He disarmed the alarm and noticed a small envelope under the windshield wiper on the driver's side. "What's this?" he muttered. Tony tossed the envelope inside the vehicle, started the engine and dropped his overnight bag into the trunk. He scrubbed the windshield and paused for a few seconds to admire the peaceful atmosphere of a suburban landscape, with its acres of white, untouched snow surrounding beautiful, pricey homes. Although a city boy at heart he wondered if Zoë and Adam would benefit from an environment less congested than the city. He tabled that internal discussion and got back into the car. Before shifting the gear into reverse he opened the envelope and took out a piece of paper with large words handwritten in capital letters.

DO YOUR WIFE AND CHILDREN KNOW WHERE YOU ARE, TONY?

Tony grimaced. "Vincent, you really are a no good son of a bitch."

*

The following Tuesday after his visit with Cam, Tony knocked on the door to Monique's classroom and entered. They shared the same prep time so he knew neither of them had class during third period. As far as furnishings, her room appeared almost identical to his. However, Monique's choices in history-oriented displays tended to reflect a more Afrocentric taste. All the posters on the walls featured African American historical figures. "Mind if I come in?" he asked almost sheepishly.

Monique, sitting behind her desk, stood. She wore dark slacks, a white blouse unbuttoned at the top and a thin tie with the knot dangling two inches below her neck. "Actually," she replied, "I was just about to leave and check on my, um, copies."

Tony pointed at the stack of papers on the table next to her desk. "The ones I saw you carry into the room a few minutes ago?"

Monique put her hands on her hips. "So what, you're stalking me now?"

Tony opened his arms and dropped them at his side. "I don't know what's going on, Monique, but I do know you've been avoiding me for over a week. I was concerned, but now I don't give a damn." He turned to leave. "We're high school teachers, not high school students. If something's on your mind and you want to act like an adult and tell me what it is, you know where to find me." He reached for the doorknob.

"Wait! Wait!"

Tony returned and slowly closed to within five feet of Monique's desk. "Are you in some kind of trouble? If you are, you know I'll do anything I can to help."

Monique walked to the front of her desk and leaned against it. "I'm sorry for being such a bitch, but I didn't want to tell you and cause trouble at your house."

"Tell me what?" Tony asked. "At my house? What kind of trouble?"

Monique stepped closer to Tony and after glancing at the door, whispered. "At the party, your wife threatened to kill me if I didn't stay away from you."

Tony shook his head and scowled. "What? That can't be true. Why would Rose possibly do such a thing, huh?"

Monique gave him a forceful shove. "Fuck you, Tony!"

Her action shocked him. Although she had not hurt him physically, he put his hand on his chest. "Have you gone crazy? Why would you say such a thing to me?"

Monique returned to the chair behind her desk but remained standing. "God, Tony. Are you the only one on this planet who doesn't know how I feel about you? But it looks like I'll have to take a number and get in line behind that rich mutt with her fancy BMW. What's her name? Cam?"

Tony considered what would constitute an appropriate reply but the only words that came to mind were the ones his father had repeatedly offered him, credited to Abraham Lincoln: "Better to remain silent and be thought a fool than to speak and remove all doubt."

The ringing bell broke the uncomfortable silence between mentor and mentee. Tony felt relieved he had an excuse to return to his classroom, located around the corner from Monique's: teachers were required to station themselves outside their classrooms during the four-minute passing time. "Monique," he finally said, "we'll straighten this out later." Monique said nothing. "I'm sure you misunderstood but I'll see you after school, okay?" He dashed out of the room feeling bewildered and upset but knew he would have to calm down before the start of his next class. Surely, he thought, Monique had misinterpreted something Rose had said. He would clear up the whole matter after school.

*

At 2:10 p.m. the school day ended for students at Hamilton High School. Twenty minutes later Tony peered through the four inch wide glass window on Monique's classroom door to find the room dark and unoccupied. He slammed the palm of his hand on the door in frustration. "Damn," he said, then peered over his shoulder to make sure no students had overheard him. Highly unlikely. Social studies classes were held on the second floor on the side of the building opposite the front door. The area practically became a ghost town ten minutes after final dismissal. He had intended to see Monique right after the last bell but a group of agitated honors students had paid him an unscheduled visit, fretting about an upcoming quiz.

Tony walked through the empty corridor back to his classroom, replaying in his mind the unspoken retorts he had prepared to rebut Monique's allegation. Halfway into his trek he reached into his back pocket and produced his telephone. He had Monique's number but decided against calling or texting her. Better to wait until tomorrow and talk to her face to face. Perhaps he should speak to Rose first.

He placed a call to Rose but changed his mind about discussing such a sensitive matter over the telephone. Better to wait until he got home and talk to her face to face as well. He listened impatiently for Rose's recorded greeting to end and spoke quickly. "Honey, it's me. Don't forget I have class tonight so I won't be home until around eight. I love you. Bye."

He returned to his classroom and noticed the telephone on his desk with its red light flashing, indicating he had just missed a call. Perhaps Monique, he hoped, but most likely a concerned parent. Tony pushed a few buttons, causing the red light to stop flashing, and listened to an unfamiliar voice with a faint accent:

"Hello, Mr. Monroe. My name is Robert Kwan and I'm with the Department of Homeland Security. We do background checks for several departments including the Department of Education. As you know, you're being considered to sit on a commission sponsored by DOE so I'd like to ask you a few questions. It's purely routine. I'm going to be out for the rest of the day but would you please call me back tomorrow?"

Tony wrote down the caller's telephone number and extension, before saving the message. He spent twenty tortured minutes arranging items on his desk and table with his thoughts bouncing from Rose to Monique to Cam. Finally, he stuffed papers into his tote bag and turned off the lights, all the time frowning as he imagined the emotionally charged discussion he and Rose would have this evening. He closed the door and chuckled when recalling more tidbits of wisdom from his father: "Women are sweet, son, but they're complicated."

THIRTEEN: SACRIFICES AND SECRETS

A few minutes before nine p.m. Rose pursed her lips. Her short evening with Tony had been uneventful; now she anticipated it would end unpleasantly. She shivered due to a sudden chill and tugged on her pajama sleeves so they extended past the sleeves of her bathrobe. The identical table lamps, one on each nightstand in their bedroom, offered soft lighting. "Go ahead," she said in a low, husky tone. "I'm listening."

Tony, freshly showered and now in his pajamas and bathrobe, sat next to Rose on the loveseat. He had been home for less than an hour after attending a class that would enable him to renew his five-year teaching certificate. After partaking of a light dinner, he had asked to speak to her alone behind closed doors. He spoke slowly. "Well, a couple of things happened today at work that I need to tell you about."

Rose felt an immediate twinge of annoyance and almost rolled her eyes. More problems due to Tony's damn job. As far as she was concerned he shouldn't be working at a public high school anyway, trying to help a bunch of lazy, disrespectful, ghetto kids who don't appreciate him. Rose put on a performance, acting as if she cared about Tony's profession. "What happened at work, honey?" she asked, her voice as sweet as raspberry jam.

"Well," Tony replied, taking Rose's hand. "I know she's got it all wrong, but—"

"Who? Who's got it all wrong?"

"Um, Monique."

Rose squinted. "Oh, her. So what did she do this time?"

Tony squirmed. "Well, honey, she said at the party, you know, the kid's birthday party the week before last. She said something pretty incredible."

"Incredible?" Rose asked. "What did she say?"

"Believe it or not," Tony said, "Monique told me you threatened to kill her if she didn't keep away from me."

Rose jumped to her feet. "Why, that lying ass heifer! She's got a lot of nerve flirting with my husband, then coming to our home—uninvited, I might add—eating our food, and now making up some ridiculous nonsense just to stir up trouble." She pointed at Tony. "What did you say?"

Tony stood and put his hands on Rose's shoulders. "I told her she must have misunderstood or misinterpreted something you said or did. I mean, we didn't really get a chance to talk about it because the bell rang and I had to get back to my room."

Rose scowled. "That's all? You didn't back me up?"

"Of course I did."

Rose wiggled her shoulders, shaking off Tony's touch. "And just how is saying I did something that caused the problem backing me up, dear husband, huh? That's what I'd like to know."

"I didn't know what else to say," Tony explained. "I mean, she caught me totally by surprise. It was so...bizarre. I know you didn't cause anything. I'm just saying, Monique's young, and young people often jump to conclusions. In the law it's called assuming facts not in evidence. That's what Monique did."

Rose frowned. The last thing she needed was to be reminded that Tony forsook a career in law—and for what? So a junior teacher could pester him? He should be earning a six-figure salary at a prestigious law firm with his own swanky office and his own secretary— preferably a homely one—and resisting the advances of some middle-aged temptress offering to make him part- ner if he danced the horizontal tango with her. "So are you going to set Miss Thang straight?" she inquired. "Or do I need to pay her a visit?"

Tony shook his head. "I'll take care of it, baby, but I wanted to talk to you first. Tomorrow I bet she'll agree the whole thing was one big misunderstanding. But you know me, I like to get my ducks in a row."

"So," Rose said, "you want to interview your witness before presenting your case."

Tony nodded. "In a manner of speaking, yes." He ges- tured for Rose to return to the loveseat. She did. He re- mained standing.

"Go ahead, counselor," Rose said. "Call your first wit- ness."

Tony grinned. He put his hand behind his back and began to pace. "So, Ms. Monroe, did you and Ms. Carter spend any time alone during the party? I seem to recall seeing you two in the kitchen and she left shortly after- ward."

"Objection!" Rose declared. "Learned counsel is an- swering his own question."

"Um, sustained," Tony replied. He stopped pacing. "So what, if anything, transpired between the two of you on the day in question? Please tell us in your own words."

Rose considered her options. She debated with herself about how much to reveal, then decided to reveal very little. Tony would certainly believe whatever she told him. "Monique and I went into the kitchen," she reported, "to get more food or something. Monique told me she had kissed you. I think she was trying to taunt me, you know? Like you said, she's young and just wanted to play high school girl games."

"And what did you say?"

"I told the bitch you had already informed me about the kiss, such as it was," Rose fired back.

"Go on."

Rose shrugged. "That was about the long and short of it. I didn't want to give her the satisfaction of believing she had hurt me or upset me in any way."

"Did you say anything else? Anything at all?"

"No."

Tony kneeled. He took Rose's hand and spoke in a soothing voice. "I'm sorry if what she said did hurt you, baby, but you know I'm not interested in her." He kissed her hand.

Rose smiled and placed her hand on Tony's face. "I know that." She inhaled and took pleasure in the faint scent of his aftershave, just a finger's dab on each cheek.

Tony scratched his head. "But honey, I have to confess, lately I've been under the impression you're keeping things from me." He held up his hands. "I'm not saying you have, but it's just a feeling I've had. You know I don't believe in husbands and wives keeping secrets from each other or lying to each other—unless it's some kind of pleasant surprise like a Christmas present or something. You know how strongly I feel about that." He resumed sitting next to her on the loveseat.

Rose made a face to suggest the infliction of an emotional wound. "I swear, as God is my witness, Tony, I'm not keeping anything from you. I never have and I never will."

"But you didn't tell me about the conversation between you and Monique."

Rose raised her hand and brought it down sharply, dismissing Tony's remark. "Believe me, I forgot all about it because it was as important as a piece of dirt on the bottom of my shoe. From what you've told me about how much work teachers have these days, you'd think she has more important things to do than start some mess."

"Don't be too hard on her," Tony requested. "She's a good teacher. She's just full of drama, the way young sisters can be sometimes. Try to forgive her, okay?"

Rose smiled. "Okay, for your sake. So what are you going to say when you see her?"

Tony stood. "I don't know. I'll probably tell her what I've been saying all along: that she misunderstood and you wouldn't hurt a fly."

"You don't have to go that far," Rose rejoined. "Don't make me have to come to that school to claim what's mine." She cranked her neck and continued. "Because I'll show up and pulled her head off her shoulders if she ever touches my man again."

Tony laughed. "I don't think that'll be necessary."

"I strongly recommend you see that it doesn't," Rose said, grinding her teeth. She recognized her indignation had seeped out and shifted her tone to a more casual one. "But you said there were a *couple* of things that happened at work."

Tony scratched his head again. "Yeah, well, a man from the Department of Homeland Security called—actually, left a message, about that commission I might be on with the Department of Education."

"And?"

"And I guess he's doing a background check. I have to call him back tomorrow."

Rose clasped her hands together. "My, my. You've sure got a busy day tomorrow. And what are you going to tell *him*?"

Tony sat at the foot of the bed and sighed. "I don't know. I thought I'd just answer his questions as best I can."

"Damn it, Tony," Rose said. "I don't understand how you can jeopardize what we've got going. You told me Cam's ex has inserted his sorry ass into our business. Isn't that enough? We're making headway on clearing up our debts but we're not even halfway through and already you want to throw it all away—and for what?" She pounded the arm of the loveseat with her fist. "To sit on a commission that's not going to change anything." She stood and stormed into the walk-in closet. "Am I the only person who understands how important this is, who's willing to make a sacrifice for this family?"

Tony followed her and stood at the entrance to the closet. "Oh, so you're the only one sacrificing here? Just you?"

"Yes, just me," Rose asserted. "Jesus Christ! You're getting your dick wet and getting paid for it. Cam's getting her empty cock pocket filled."

"Please lower your voice," Tony requested. "The kids haven't turned in yet, and you know I don't like it when you use that kind of language. You're getting all worked up."

"Who's worked up?" Rose asked. "I've got eyes. When Cam visited our church for the kids' Christmas concert, you practically pushed my dad out the way so you could walk her to her car."

"Now that's just not true."

"Yes it is," Rose retorted, "and don't think I haven't noticed how you've changed your eating habits, and how fit and trim you've gotten over the past few months...well, extra fit and trim. You look like you did in your pictures when you played basketball in college. And please don't insult my intelligence and say you've done all that for me."

"Well, it sure hasn't earned me any points in our own bed, that's for sure." Tony barked. He winced and reached for Rose. "I'm sorry, sweetheart. I didn't mean that."

"Of course you did," Rose insisted, backing away from Tony's hands. "You're a man. Everything's still about sex to you."

Tony shook his head. "No it's not. You're the woman I love. The woman I want to grow old with. I-I know couples slow down a bit after they've been married for a while, but admit it, we've slowed down a lot."

Rose turned to inspect the parallel racks loaded with a vast selection of clothes. She sighed: so many beautiful outfits into which she could no longer fit. She spoke while facing the garments. "Well, forgive me if I'm pre-occupied with how we're going to keep a roof over our heads and keep sending our precious children to a good school."

"I want that too, honey," Tony said. "I just don't obsess over it the way you do."

Rose faced Tony. "And forgive me if can't keep up with Monique and Cam, neither who've had children. I'm just your wife, just the woman who had to lie in bed for three solid months sicker than a beaten dog so I could give birth to your children." She turned and resumed thumbing through her clothes so Tony couldn't see the shame she felt.

Once again she had crossed the line, especially given that Tony had hired a full-time nurse to take care of her during the last three difficult months of her pregnancy, and when not at work, had personally waited on her like a faithful servant. Not being able to stand the silence between them. She grabbed a skirted suit and blouse at random and hung them on a hook behind the closet door.

Tony lowered his head and broke the silence. "Okay, okay. I'll tell the Homeland Security guy tomorrow I don't want to be on the commission."

"Whatever," Rose replied and walked past him. "I'm going to say goodnight to the children."

*

The following morning Rose heard the sound of a female voice for less than three seconds before Tony turned off the clock radio. The room was dark. She felt very cozy under the warm, thick comforter and wanted to stay there. Tony was an early bird. He arose at four thirty in the morning, frequently to go jogging outside, especially if he hadn't made it to the gym straight from work the previous evening. During inclement weather he'd utilize the five thousand dollar treadmill located in the fourth bedroom: the one Rose had insisted on buying and had used for one month. She, on the other hand, got up at five thirty with Zoë and Adam, and sometimes not then if she had worked late at Emerald's the evening before.

She felt Tony's lips on her cheek. He always kissed her before rolling out of bed virtually wide awake. His kiss caused Rose to be filled with shame, self-loathing and regret for her behavior the previous evening. She pulled on his arm, keeping him with her. "I don't know why you put up with me," she whined. "I don't give you nothing but grief."

"I put up with you because I love you," Tony whispered and kissed her again.

"I hate myself when I hurt you," Rose moaned. "I just can't seem to stop myself."

"I know you don't mean it, baby," Tony replied. "It's already forgotten."

Rose pushed Tony onto his back and dived under the covers. She kissed his chest, then his navel, then worked her way lower. She didn't need any light. After fourteen years of marriage, she knew every inch of him, and where to find the special part of his body with selected generous inches. Her target located, she began stroking, licking and kissing.

"Sweetheart, you don't have to do that for me," Tony protested.

Rose stopped just long enough to offer a reply. "It's not for you. It's for me."

*

Rose sat at the kitchen table sipping orange juice, having finished her simple breakfast of cereal and milk. The house was empty save her; Tony had gone to work and the twins to school. She watched the large screen television in the great room, only partly observing a nine o'clock news report about a historical observation in Virginia for George Washington's birthday. She didn't understand all the fuss over February 22. After all, hadn't the country's first president been a slave owner virtually his entire life?

She yawned and changed the channel to a shopping network and recalled her highly unusual early morning behavior with Tony. Rather than feel pleased by the memory, she felt regret. Perhaps, she thought, she shouldn't have shown such weakness. Her mother had often told her a woman should hold back a little of herself in order to keep her man under control; make him want more. Rose shrugged. "Well, no use crying over spilled...semen," she declared aloud.

She turned her attention to yet another text message from James Rivers, whom she hadn't seen since their clandestine money exchange at the mall three weeks before. She read the message on her mobile telephone for the third time.

pls can i c you PLS?

It marked the sixth message he had sent in three weeks. Rose shook her head. The man was obviously not very smart about these things. A text message could be saved or printed. If need be, she would be able to use the messages to her advantage. Rose put her dishes in the dishwasher and walked up the stairs to shower and change for work; another late shift. As was her ritual before getting into the shower, she examined her naked body in the bathroom mirror. True, she didn't have the figure of a swimsuit model but Tony had never conveyed any disapproval about her appearance, and now another man had expressed open attraction to her. She liked the feeling.

She threw her bathrobe back on and returned to the bedroom to call Rivers using her mobile telephone. She could feel her heartbeat accelerate while listening to the rings.

"Hello?" Rivers said.

Shoot, Rose thought. She had hoped to just hang up when his voicemail message played, so he would know she had called. She didn't really want to talk to him. However, she had prepared for the possibility of an answer. "Hello, James," she said. "It's Rose Monroe. I wanted to call you but I had some problems with my phone and just got it fixed."

"That's okay," Rivers said in an eager voice. "Can we meet today?"

"I'd like that very much," Rose replied, "but I can't. We have to be careful, you know."

"I understand," Rivers agreed. "How about tomorrow?"

"I can't tomorrow."

"Then when?"

"Soon," Rose answered. "I have to go but I'll call you again."

"When?"

"I'm not sure," Rose said. "Oh, I'm going to be just a little late with the next payment."

"Don't worry about that," Rivers said.

Rose smiled. Bingo! "I'll talk to you soon, James. Please be patient. This is all so new to me. Bye." She ended the call and sashayed back into the bathroom. She turned on the shower and took one final look at her body in the mirror. She knew she was playing with fire but was confident she could handle it without getting burned.

FOURTEEN: IN LOVE

Cam sat behind the desk in her home office perusing yet another printed spreadsheet. She rubbed her eyes and continued reviewing one of nearly one hundred pages gathered for the preparation of filing her income tax return, due in about a month. She had stayed home all day, clad in sweatpants and a sweatshirt, all but confined to her office. Hours of mind-numbing tedium had begun to take their toll; even the lively Haydn symphony playing in the background couldn't induce her to remain focused on her task. A glance at the calendar reminded her of the soothsayer's warning to "beware the Ides of March" in the Shakespearean play *Julius Caesar*. "Beware indeed," she mumbled.

Similar to most Americans whatever their income, Cam disliked the annual chore, but she respected its necessity. Her finances stood in very good shape but over the years the process required to document them had grown increasingly complicated and time-consuming. Fortunately, most of the heavy lifting had already been done by two experienced accountants from a reputable accounting firm, and Lakshmi, her full-time personal assistant, who had left for the day.

Cam stretched out her arms and yawned. Due to daylight saving time, the sun would set ten minutes before seven o'clock, so in less than an hour she would bounce from room to room in the house, drawing shades and curtains. She had other matters on her mind: one being it was nearly time for dinner. She sniffed the air and savored the smell of the haddock, brown rice and asparagus awaiting her downstairs in the kitchen, prepared by her housekeeper, Isabella, who had likewise left for the day.

Cam yawned again and tried to refocus on a huge list of charitable tax deductions. The Lutheran church in Boston she had joined when she was a teenager—and still often attended with her parents—had been a significant recipient of her largess. However, she seemed to be a soft touch for education-related projects, especially those serving Native American children, African American children and children living in impoverished villages in the Philippines; such beneficiaries had received donations totaling six-figures the previous year.

"Hmmm," Cam said, "that reminds me." She typed an electronic sticky note onto her computer desktop, reminding her to check an airline's baggage rules before she embarked on her business trip to Europe at the end of the month. She enjoyed traveling and learning new languages, an interest that resulted in being reasonably fluent speaking Spanish, French and Italian. She also spoke passable Tagalog, Mandarin Chinese and, after six weeks of intense studying and a week in Brazil, Portuguese.

Cam flipped another spreadsheet page and smiled, but not due to anything on the paper. Tomorrow would be what she had come to call Tony Day. It would be their fifth meeting. So far the deal had far surpassed her expectations. Tony had become more than a wonderful part-time lover. He had become a valued friend—within the confines of the agreement.

A pop-up notice appeared on her computer screen reminding her of a late morning appointment with her therapist the following day. Speaking of whom, Cam felt guilty for not informing her therapist about her arrangement with the Monroes; but the fewer people who know the secret the less likely the secret would be compromised.

She deleted the notice and recalled her last rendezvous with Tony. They had broken "the no sex after sunrise" rule and it had been, as one of her British acquaintances would say, bloody marvelous! She reveled in the memory of that morning, especially the ecstasy she had felt as he thrust in and out of her. The memory caused her breathing to become more labored. She closed her eyes and inched her fingers over the top inseam of her pants. "Don't stop, Tony," she whispered.

The ringing home telephone snapped her out of her trance. She grabbed the receiver and checked the caller ID information. It read "Rose Monroe" but the number didn't match any she knew to be Rose's. Could it be Tony? She swallowed and answered. "Hello?"

"Hello, Aunt Cam."

Cam blinked twice. It took her a couple of seconds for the familiarity of the voice to register. "Zoë? Why hello there. How are you?"

"I'm fine," Zoë replied. "How are you?"

"I'm fine, sweetie."

"Are you busy?"

Cam examined the stacks of papers scattered across her desk as well as those forming a semi-circle at her feet. "No, I'm not busy. Is everything alright?"

"Yes, ma'am. Everything's fine," Zoë assured her. "I just want to talk to you about something. Something personal. Is that okay?"

Cam leaned back in her chair. "Of course, but shouldn't you be talking to your mom or dad?"

"Well," Zoë replied. "I can't really talk to mom."

"You can't?"

"No, not about personal stuff."

"Why would you say that?"

"Well," Zoë said, "Mom just doesn't listen."

Cam felt uncomfortable about the girl's assessment and changed the subject. "Okay, I'll listen. Maybe that's all I can do, but what about Tony—um, your dad?"

"Dad's great. He listens," Zoë declared, "but he works all the time and he's taking this class. Did you know he has another job and has to stay overnight once a month?"

"Is that so?"

"Um-hmmm," Zoë said. "In fact, he's gonna be gone tomorrow and won't be back until Saturday morning. Mom says he doing it for our family and...I probably shouldn't tell you this, but it has something to do with national security."

Cam slapped her hand over her mouth to suppress a giggle.

"Aunt Cam? Are you there?"

"Of course, doll," Cam said. "So go ahead, what's going on?" She heard no response and waited. Her mind flooded with disturbing thoughts of the possibilities. Rose had told her horror stories about problems plaguing families of children who attended Boston International Academy: drugs, riches to rags humiliation, alcohol abuse, sexual molestation, parental infidelity...Oh God! Did Zoë believe her father was having an affair?

"Well, there's this boy I like who goes to my school..."

147

Cam exhaled. So it's thirteen-year-old Zoë's first adolescent crush. "Oh, I see."

"His name's Pedro. He's really cute."

"He is, huh?" Cam asked. "Was he at your birthday party?"

"Yes."

Cam didn't hear anything further. The silence made her uncomfortable. "Um, is he that boy your mom said was some kind of soccer star?"

"Yes, that's him."

Cam remembered her therapist would frequently allow silence to permeate the room, which always resulted in Cam breaking the silence. She decided to be quiet and wait for Zoë to talk.

She did. "Well, two of my friends told me he liked me, but I didn't know if that was true so I told them to ask him if he liked me."

Isn't puppy love just adorable? Cam thought.

Zoë continued. "He told my friends that he did, you know, like me, so I told them to tell him that I liked him too. So we started hanging out together at school."

"Well, that sounds nice," Cam said.

"It was," Zoë said. "But yesterday he asked me to be his girlfriend."

Cam smiled. Middle school romances seemed so important at the time. Unfortunately, she didn't know how to answer Zoë's indirect question. "Well..." she replied. What would her therapist say? "Um, what do you think you should do?" While waiting for an answer she grabbed a pen, and scribbled LISTEN on a small piece of paper over and over.

"I don't know," Zoë said.

Cam frowned. The child's probably thinking: Some help you are, Aunt Cam.

"I want to tell him yes," Zoë said. "I'm going to tell him yes."

Cam nodded. "Okay dear, if that's what you want. When are you going to do this?" Her therapist also frequently suggested it was best to state not just what would be done, but when.

"I'll talk to him tomorrow."

"When tomorrow?"

"At lunch," Zoë said. "We have the same lunch."

"But won't there be people around?"

"We usually finish lunch early," Zoë reported, "and hang out alone for a few minutes."

"That sounds good."

"Thank you, Aunt Cam," Zoë gushed. "Thank you so much."

"Well," Cam said, "I really didn't do anything."

"Yes you did," Zoë insisted. "Hey, can I ask you something else?"

"Of course, sweetie."

"Do you want to get married again and have children someday?"

Cam was surprised by the question. "Well, doll, it wouldn't be easy to be married to me. I travel so much. In fact, I'm flying to Paris soon. But to answer your question, I might get married again but I've never really seen myself as a mother. I guess as the saying goes, it's a call I just don't hear. Of course if I could be guaranteed children like you and Adam I'd do it in a heartbeat."

The two talked for a few more minutes, mostly Cam listening to Zoë's report on the progress of her music lessons. Eventually, Cam bid her "niece" good-bye. She returned to her tax prep papers but reflected on their conversation and the subject of children. In a few years her window of opportunity would slam shut on giving birth to a child. She and Vincent had generally agreed children wouldn't be a part of their marriage. Now she understood Vincent's reason: He was such a selfish bastard he would have loathed the idea of her spending money on anyone else but him. She shuddered at the thought of being tied to Vincent for nearly twenty years after their divorce, glaring at him when he picked up a child or children for visitation. At least she hadn't been saddled with that ignominious encounter, and fortunately, she hadn't heard from him for a while.

She tried to return her attention to her tax papers but again her thoughts drifted, this time to the issue of Tony and children. She wondered if he had wanted more children after Rose's difficult pregnancy with the twins. Probably not, she thought, or why would he have undergone a vasectomy? Knowing Tony, probably to spare Rose any further health risks.

Cam turned her attention to her desktop computer and typed a couple of words on a search engine, just for fun: vasectomy reversal. She brought up another window and typed three more words: single parent adoption. Then she brought up another screen and started another search, again, just for fun: Step-parenthood. She checked the wall clock and stood. "Time for dinner. I'll come back to this," she said and left the room.

*

The following day Cam opened the door and flashed a huge smile. "Hello, doll."

Tony stepped inside. He wore casual clothes. "Hello," he said, and handed her a red rose. "I hope you don't get weary of this small token of my esteem." He offered a slightly exaggerated bow.

Cam accepted the rose and curtsied. She wore a pair of black jeans and a red, long-sleeved sweater but no bra. "You honor me, my lord," she said in a mock British ac-

150

cent. "Your esteem is always welcomed here at Castle Spencer."

Their snickering ended when they threw themselves into each other's arms for a passionate kiss. Tony quickly hung up his jacket and placed his overnight bag outside the door of the closet. He resumed kissing Cam but abruptly stopped. "Hey, wait a sec," he said before twirling Cam around and inspecting her. "You've changed the color of your hair. It's lighter."

Cam smiled and nodded. Wow, how many straight men would notice the subtle change in her hair color? "Do you like it?" she asked. "If you don't I can—"

"It's nice," Tony replied, examining Cam again. "I like it. I like it very much. And even if I didn't you wouldn't have to do anything."

Cam smiled. What a wonderful man. She grabbed his hand and slowly led him upstairs. "Come with me. I have to have you right now."

*

Cam heard the closet door being closed and felt her heart, filled with longing and despair, breaking. The dreaded moment had arrived.

"Cam, I've got to go," Tony announced.

She forced herself to cease tinkering in the kitchen and see him off, her misery notwithstanding. The time they had spent together had seemed so short. She shuffled into his arms and embraced him; keeping her head down, struggling with her emotions and the words she wanted to say. She knew she had no right to want her best friend's husband for herself, but she did. Still, she wouldn't do anything to make him hers. "So it's okay that I tell my therapist about you?" she asked.

"Yes," Tony answered. "The law protects your privilege."

"Thank you," Cam said, barely above a whisper. "I-I have treasured our time together."

"So have I," Tony replied, "and I look forward to seeing you again." He kissed her gently on the lips and reached for the doorknob to the front door.

Cam covered his hand with her's. "Tony, I have to tell you how I feel or I'm going to go insane."

"Don't, honey," Tony ordered. "What good will it do?"

"Please let me say it."

Tony turned the knob. "I have to go."

Cam threw her arms around his waist. "Forgive me, my love," she pleaded. "Yes, that's what you are: my love. I love you. I do. I love you so much!" She felt his embrace become tighter. Several seconds passed. God, please make time stand still, she begged.

Finally, Tony kissed her and pulled away. "I love you too, dearest Cam."

Cam shook her head. Did she hear what she thought she had heard? She raised her head and peered into Tony's eyes and knew he had spoken from his heart. She put her hand over her mouth. "Oh God, Tony. What are we going to do?"

Tony pulled the front door open before submitting his one word reply. "Nothing." He pushed the storm door open and stepped outside before Cam could say anything else.

She guided the doors closed and staggered into the living room but didn't know why she had gone there. Elvira appeared and meowed before rubbing against her legs. "I'm in love. Isn't it wonderful?" Cam asked Elvira, then threw herself onto the sofa and burst into tears.

FIFTEEN: BONDING

At nearly quarter past eight in the morning, ten minutes after leaving Cam's house, Tony cruised eastward on the Mass Pike facing a bright sun. He wore sunglasses and had lowered the visor inside his vehicle to shield his eyes. Traffic flowed lightly, not that he noticed. The surrounding vehicles moved in a blur to him, like buzzing mosquitoes. The sound of the heater fan, on low, and the soft, slow, guitar-led jazz music on the CD player blended in the background, not that he noticed. Tony, usually a notorious highway speeder and lane-changer, obeyed the sixty-five-miles-per-hour speed limit and maintained his position in the center lane. He mentally replayed the tortured confession he and Cam had spoken before parting.

"I love you. I do. I love you so much!"

"I love you too, dearest Cam."

Tony had resisted uttering his reply but had been unable to help himself. He did indeed love Cam—and was that a crime? Only if they had been sneaking around behind Rose's back, but they had engaged in no such behavior. In fact, the terms of their monthly rendezvous had been negotiated by his wife.

Tony blinked twice to focus on his driving. He shifted into the left lane to pass an old, rickety pickup truck and shook his head. Back in October Rose had insisted their marriage wouldn't be significantly altered if her husband periodically visited another woman's bed, but she was wrong. The visits had revealed the weakness of their own matrimonial bond.

Tony returned to the center lane and smiled while recalling Cam's crescendoing cries and yelps the previous night as he plunged himself in and out of her. However, the foundation supporting the feelings he and Cam shared consisted of much more than sex. The affection that had grown between them over the past five months had been all but pronounced, so why not acknowledge that mutual love, which had become self-evident?

Because you already have a life, dumbass, Tony thought; a life with Rose and their two wonderful children. He had promised, before God, he and his bride would share that life "until parted by death." As far as Tony was concerned, he belonged with Rose, Zoë and Adam. Yes, he loved Cam, but he had loved Rose longer and loved her more. His feelings for Cam didn't change that.

Still, his love for Cam increased with every meeting. The hours they shared filled him with excitement and joy. The more time he spent with her, the more time he wanted to spend with her. Cam was attentive, beautiful, sexy and intelligent. He thought little of her wealth but it certainly didn't make her less attractive.

He loved Rose, he did, but instead of behaving as husband and wife they were gradually becoming roommates. They made love less frequently and when they did they lacked the ardor and passion he now expressed so abundantly with Cam. While he and Rose fretted about debts and the twins, he and Cam explored their dreams, hopes, ambitions, and how wonderful each found the other. He regretted leaving her on Saturday morning and noticed he departed later each month.

Tony turned at a corner and couldn't believe he had already reached his destination. He couldn't recall a minute of the journey. He parked on the street in front of his home and regretted he had insisted on buying a less expensive home without an attached two-car garage. He shut off the engine and sighed, apprehensive about entering his own home. Rose would be somewhat emotionally aloof and distant all day, as she always acted when he returned from his "other job." However, late in the evening she would lie on their bed with a gleam in her eye and count the money slowly as if caressing a lover.

Tony sighed again and decided perhaps it would be best to find an excuse to be away from home, maybe take the twins to the movies. "No, damn it. No!" he exclaimed aloud. He'd fight for his family. He pushed open the door to his vehicle. The trees lining the street bore thumb-size buds that would grow into hand-size leaves, but for now they offered little protection against the glare of the sun. As he emerged from his SUV the chilly, thirty-degree air helped to snap him out of his funk. He slammed the door and resolved to take action that would reinforce the bonds of his marriage, something drastic.

*

Tony plopped down onto the loveseat next to the bed. "Honey, I've been thinking..."

"Wait a sec," Rose commanded. "I'm still counting." She wore thick socks, jeans and a sweatshirt and lay on the right side of the bed—the side on which she normally slept—facing stacks of cash, which lay on the left.

Tony, similarly dressed, rolled his eyes and glanced at the wall clock. He took a deep breath and waited, noting the nearly ten p.m. time. After an uneventful day for the family filled with chores and errands, Rose entertained herself by arranging and rearranging "their" bounty for nearly twenty minutes. After thirty seconds had passed without any sign Rose intended to turn her attention to him, Tony ran out of patience "It's all there," he assured her. "How many times are you going to count it?"

Rose spoke with an edge to her voice. "I'm almost finished. Okay?"

"Finish later, please," Tony insisted.

Rose dropped a handful of bills onto the bed and gently rolled over to face Tony. "Okay, so what's on your mind?"

Tony took a deep breath before making the announcement. "This is it. The last payment. I'm putting an end to this whole thing."

Rose twisted to straighten a stack of bills, then returned her attention to Tony. "You can't be serious."

"I am."

"But why?" Rose whined. "When things are going so well?"

Too damn well, Tony thought. He leaned forward. "I-I'm just not comfortable with this arrangement. I'm a married man. A father. A respected member of our church."

"Yeah," Rose said. "You're still all those things. You're also a man helping his family get out of debt."

Tony opened his hands. "Baby, I just can't explain it. I just don't want this to go any further. It interferes with who I am, with what I am."

Rose eased off the bed and sat next to Tony. After a long pause, she spoke. "What's the matter? Is Cam making you do something you don't want to do? Is she hurting you?" She avoided making eye contact.

Actually, I enjoy everything Cam does, Tony thought, but nothing positive would result from such a disclosure. "No, it's not that," he replied. "It's just—"

"Over the years she's told me she likes it a little kinky, a little wild," Rose said. "But if you're uncomfortable with some of her demands you can always—"

"I don't want to get into any details," Tony insisted. "You know how I feel about that," he added while standing. "If you recall, we all agreed to something in the beginning..." He rubbed his hands together for a few seconds. "We agreed that any one of us could end this thing at any time."

Rose squinted her eyes, looking perturbed. "I know."

Tony shrugged. "Well, I'm invoking my prerogative under that clause. I want out."

Rose abruptly returned to her position on the bed and resumed counting the money with her back to Tony.

Tony sat behind her and stretched to glean her facial expression. Rose could pout and sulk better than anyone, and right now she showcased a medley of her greatest hits. He put his hand on her shoulder. "Honey, this is for the best. We've made headway."

"Not enough," Rose retorted.

"We're not drowning."

"But we're still in deep water."

Tony ran his fingers over Rose's shoulder. She shook off his touch. Her response hurt him. For a few seconds neither said a word.

"Please," Rose said, "do this for me—and our children."

"It's not right," Tony whispered. "It's not good for us, for me and you." More silence.

Rose finally spoke, her voice saturated with quiet rage. "If you end this now I'll never forgive you."

"Don't say that, honey," Tony entreated, and reached for her again.

Rose shook off his touch again. "I mean it, Tony. If you quit we'll never be the same ever, you and me."

Tony closed his eyes. Her words caused him deep pain. His wife suspected he was possibly being subjected to sexual demands that made him uncomfortable or worse, hurt him, yet she wanted him to continue. The truth about her finally dawned on him: She cared more about the money than his feelings. "Okay," he whispered.

Rose stopped counting. "Okay what?"

Tony sighed. "Okay, I'll keep going."

Rose turned and grabbed Tony's hand and kissed it. "You'll thank me for being strong for both of us, baby. You'll see."

Tony nodded. "You're probably right." He stood again. "Are you going to be done there soon? We better get ready for bed."

Rose mouthed numbers to herself. "You're right. Why don't you take your shower first while I finish up here, okay?"

Tony agreed and walked toward the bathroom.

"And Tony?"

"Yes?"

Rose wagged her index finger. "No more talk about quitting, okay? And don't be moping around next month. We don't want our um...benefactor to be disappointed."

Tony nodded. "It's like sports. I'll be ready by game time." He entered the bathroom and grabbed his toothbrush. I'll be ready alright, he thought. Ready, willing and able.

*

The next day, Sunday evening, Tony sat in the family TV room, located at the back of the house, watching a college basketball game. His preferred team was being beaten badly so he grabbed the remote to change the channel and spare himself further disappointment. He heard the telephone ring, muted the sound to the television and picked up the receiver. "Hello?"

"Hello, Tony. How are you?"

"Um, hello Cam," he said as a rush of excitement caused him to curl his toes inside his bedroom slippers. "Rose isn't here. She took the kids for some 'light' clothes shopping. You know, with Easter only three weeks away..." An uncomfortable silence followed. "Well, I'll tell her you called."

"No, Tony," Cam whined. "Please don't go. Please."

Tony felt his heart melt. The sound of Cam's pleading voice brought him joy and pain at the same time. "Well, the agreement says no contact outside of...you know..."

"To hell with the agreement," Cam barked. "I miss you, Tony. Don't you miss me too?"

Tony stuttered his reply. "Y-yes, of course I do, but you-you know how it is."

"I love you, Tony."

"Don't talk that way, Cam," Tony remonstrated.

"I can't help it. I love you. Do you love me?"

Tony peeked around before answering. "You know I do."

"You do what?"

"I love you, dearest Cam," Tony declared. "You've awoken something in me I didn't even know had been sleeping."

"Same here, my love. I get dripping wet every time I think of you."

Tony smiled. "Now, behave yourself." He grabbed the remote and turned off the television. "Okay, we can talk for a couple of minutes, but saying certain things on my home phone is like...well, it's like taking a woman into the marital bed."

"I understand," Cam said. "We'll talk about something else."

"Good."

"You're such a spectacular lover."

Tony laughed. "Baby, that's not exactly what I had in mind."

"What?" Cam asked. "You want to talk about the NCAA games? The state of the economy? The ongoing problems in the Middle East?" She laughed. "Seriously, I've always wanted to know how you came to be so marvelous in bed. Tell me about your first time."

Tony chuckled. "Why would you want to know about that?"

"I'm just curious."

Tony shrugged. "You won't believe this but my first time was with my high school teacher." He could hear Cam gasping on the other end of the line.

"You're not making this up, are you?"

"No," Tony answered. "I was in the eleventh grade and my English teacher was this woman who had just turned thirty."

"Was she pretty?"

"Very," Tony said. "Of course all the boys loved being around her. The girls too, for that matter. More on that later."

"I can't wait."

Tony took a sip from his cranberry juice and continued. "Anyway, one evening the varsity's basketball practice had been cancelled. I didn't tell my parents because I wanted to hang out at school. My teacher—Maritza Colön was her name; she was from Puerto Rico—she asked me to help her load some boxes into the trunk of her car. Then she asked if I would ride with her and help her unload them into her house."

"The sneaky little cradle robber," Cam said. "Keep going."

"Well, we went to her house. I helped her unload the boxes. She invited me into the house for a soda. When we got inside she started complaining about her ex-husband, some bum who repeatedly cheated on her. I said something like, 'he's crazy, as beautiful as you are.' The next thing I know she's got her tongue in my mouth and is unzipping my pants."

Cam let out a single snort. "I assume you didn't put up much of a fight, but what she did was still wrong. How long did it go on?"

Tony scratched his head. "For about six months."

"Really? Six months?"

"For the rest of the school year and half the summer," Tony said. "She sure taught me a few things. That's when I realized that I really liked sex, a lot."

"You and about a billion other males on this planet," Cam added. "So how did it end?"

"Hmmm...let me think," Tony replied. "Her mother got sick and she went back to Puerto Rico to take care of her. But not before surprising me with a going away present."

"Which was?"

"A beautiful Chinese co-ed for a three-way. It turned out Maritza was bi-sexual."

"And you never told anyone about this?"

"Not a soul. Ever."

"Humph," Cam said. "Usually boys can't wait to run their mouths about something like this, but she must have chosen you because somehow she knew she'd be safe. And your parents never suspected anything?"

"Nope."

"And you've never shared this with...um..."

"Rose just knows my first time was with someone in high school," Tony said. "You're the first person I've ever told about the details."

"I'm honored that you trust me," Cam said. "How do you feel about your former English teacher now?"

Tony paused before answering. "Like you said, I know what she did was wrong, and it did have an effect on me."

"In what way?"

"I tended to gravitate toward women who were older than me for a while after that. I even had an affair with the wife of one of my college professors when I was a sophomore at UMass Boston; another sexually adventurous woman eager to teach me."

"And you don't believe you were damaged by any of this?"

"Not long term," Tony said. "Perhaps it's different with males. I think of it as just a part of my past. Now don't get me wrong..." He stood and slowly strolled to the front of the house. "I wouldn't want Adam to go through anything similar—and of course I'd beat a thirty-year-old teacher to death if he ever put his hands on Zoë when she's in the eleventh grade." He laughed. "Hey, what about you? You know, your first time?"

Cam laughed. "Oh, just some classmate I thought I was in love with when I was seventeen years old. A real rabbit jumper. Totally disappointing and totally forgettable."

The two lovers talked and laughed for several more minutes. Tony moved the drapes slightly that covered the large picture window in the great room and spotted the headlights of Rose's SUV piercing the dark as she eased behind his car and stopped. "It's the family. I have to go. Have fun in Paris. I'll see you in three and a half weeks."

"Can I call you on *your* phone, darling?"

Tony grimaced. "Cam, this has been nice, but I don't want us sneaking around seeing each other, calling each other. Please try to understand."

"Okay," Cam said. "You're an honorable man. That's one of the many things I love about you. But just so you know: When I see you next month I'm going to wear you out."

"Back atcha," Tony retorted. He said goodbye and went to open the front door. Rose, Zoë and Adam entered, bouncing, laughing and toting large shopping bags overflowing with clothes. "Good hunting?" Tony asked.

Rose, the last to enter the house, kissed him on the cheek. "Would you get the rest out of the trunk, honey?"

Tony arched his eyebrows. "The rest?" He obediently marched outside into the frosty evening air and walked down the stairs. "Oh," he said as he passed Rose. "Cam called."

Rose stepped into the house, then checked to ensure the children were out of earshot and poked her head past the plane of the door's threshold. "Cam called on the house phone?"

"Yeah."

"That's odd," Rose said. "Maybe she wanted—you didn't try to cancel, did you?"

"No, honey," Tony said. "She called asking for you."

"Good," Rose declared. "Hurry up and get out of the cold."

Tony retrieved the merchandise from Rose's SUV and climbed the stairs while balancing two full shopping bags. When he got inside he sighed. "What's all this?"

Rose shrugged. "Stuff we need. Did you study for your class?"

"Hmm-hmm," Tony reported. "How much did all this cost?"

"Not as much as you think, honey," Rose replied. "We got some things for you too."

"I don't remember asking for anything."

Rose frowned and clapped her hands. "Kids, take your stuff upstairs and put everything away." After watching the twins rumble up the stairs she eased toward Tony and kissed him on the lips. "Well, it's just like you not to ask for anything for yourself, but the kids are growing out of all their clothes and I know what's best for them—and you."

Tony stared at the shopping bags on the floor and resumed his inquiry. "Exactly how much did knowing what's best cost?"

"We'll talk about this later, honey," she whispered.

Tony shrugged in resignation. "I guess we will." He walked up the stairs with the intent of going to his office. He heard Rose's voice.

"Aren't you going to see what we got you?"

"I'll come back for it later," he replied. She's not going to change, he thought, and for the first time in fourteen years he seriously worried about the state of his marriage.

SIXTEEN: CHANCE ENCOUNTER

A week after talking to Tony on the telephone, Cam, clad in black jeans and a gray, body-hugging cowl neck sweater, scrutinized clothes hanging in the back of a boutique. The 1600 square feet boutique was one of three dozen upscale specialty stores in the Milton Mall, located in Milton. The affluent suburb of less than 30,000—three-quarters white and fifteen percent African American—was located just south of Boston.

Cam momentarily glanced at a lavender blouse with a ruffled collar hanging on a brass pole before pushing it from right to left, forcing it to join a score of other rejects. She shook her head, causing the thick, single braid of hair hanging down the middle of her back to swing like the pendulum of a grandfather clock. So far nothing appealed to her. Not that she needed to buy additional items to wear. There were no shortage of clothes at home in her closet, which had formerly been a bedroom adjoining the master suite.

A dozen mostly well off, mostly well-dressed, female patrons primarily in their thirties and forties also occupied the boutique as Cam sorted through clothes on the last Sunday afternoon in March. A few shoppers kept one eye on the various selections in the store and the other on their bored and antsy children. Cam assumed many of the customers, like her, were searching for something eye-catching but appropriately reverent for services on Easter Sunday, exactly two weeks away. Breezy music by a jazz trio—a pianist, bassist and drummer—mixed softly on loudspeakers hoisted along the perimeter of the ceiling. Two attractive, professionally dressed female employees—"fashion consultants" according to their name tags—wandered about, offering assistance.

A variety of internal distractions competed for Cam's attention. First, she missed Tony so much she had been sporadically sighing like a lovesick teenager every day since his last conjugal visit. The fact that she couldn't stop thinking about him became apparent when she tentatively grabbed a purple, one-shouldered blouse and wondered whether he would second her choice. She shook her head again and returned the item to the twelve feet long bar along with the other vetoed items.

A second source of distraction: Along with sorting through clothes, Cam also mentally sorted through the necessary errands and chores that had to be done before embarking on her trip to Paris in four days. She would stay for a week, serving as one member of a seven-member international panel judging a slew of independent French films. Having attended a language immersion school from kindergarten to the eighth grade, and having visited France several days a year for over twenty years, she spoke and wrote fluent French. Cam looked forward to the trip. She had a loyal, almost cult following of Parisian admirers who lauded her contributions to the fashion industry.

Cam wrinkled her face due to another source of distraction. Her past Friday morning therapy session had not gone well. She had finally disclosed the "arrangement," and her feelings for Tony, to her therapist. Although her therapist had articulated no overt disapprobation, Cam could tell the psychologist did not approve. "Another man who cannot commit exclusively to you?" the woman had asked.

Finally, Cam felt a little self-conscious shopping for clothing at Otra Cosa, which at one time she had owned. For some inexplicable reason she had felt slightly embarrassed when the toothy, twenty-something fashion consultant with the Spanish accent had greeted her and asked if she needed any assistance. Cam had sheepishly told the woman she was just browsing.

Cam lifted a hanger containing a silk, long-sleeved, fire engine red blouse. It was cross-draped at the waist and had a plunging neckline. She ran her fingers over the material. "Mmmm, that's more like it," she purred. She had been somewhat disappointed with the quality of more than one selection at the store. About twenty percent of the merchandise she had examined in the ten minutes she had been there would never have made the cut back when she owned the place.

Cam reexamined her current surroundings. Little had changed since she had gotten out of the business without a second thought two and a half years earlier. The Brazilian teak floor she had personally selected still glistened beneath her chic black ankle boots. The shop's dinner plate-size circular lights embedded in the ceiling, along with the strategically placed track lighting, still allowed her to easily examine each piece of merchandise. The mahogany and marble furnishings still evinced elegance. The five feet tall posters of beautiful female models sporting trendy designer clothing still hung from the walls. The locked, brightly lit, glass top cabinet still showcased an assortment of jewelry, accessories and—

"Shit. One hundred ninety-five dollars for a blouse? What the fuck!"

Cam peered from behind her potential purchase to see a scowling woman standing next to her holding a black and white striped blouse she had passed over. The woman wore a double-breasted blouse covered by an unzipped leather jacket that barely reached the belt loops of her tight jeans, an outfit meant to show off her curves, which Cam acknowledged privately, were admirable.

Cam returned her attention to the blouse in her own hand but realized she recognized the foul-mouthed woman four feet from her, or at least had met her. Cam thought for a few seconds...the woman's name was Monique and she taught history at the same high school as her beloved Tony. Cam admired the teacher's smooth, unblemished dark skin and wondered if anyone had ever suggested she consider modeling.

Cam pondered whether it would be advisable to acknowledge the acquaintance. If Monique had likewise recognized her she might think it rude of Cam not to say hello. However, Cam recalled during the twins' birthday party Monique had been somewhat curt when interacting with her. Also, according to Rose, who had heard it from Tony, two days after the party Monique had referred to Cam as a "yellow mongrel."

Cam decided to try on the top. She took a step in the direction away from Monique but out of habit, turned and rearranged the blouses so they hung evenly apart. She and the teacher made eye contact. Cam could see the light of recognition on Monique's face and decided to be cordial. "Why hello there, um...Monique, right? I'm Cam, a friend of Rose and Tony Monroe. We met at the birthday party for Zoë and Adam, remember?"

Monique responded with a tight smile. "Yes, I remember. You drove that fancy BMW and brought the birthday cakes. I'm sorry I couldn't stay to sample them."

From what Rose told me, Cam thought, if you had your way you would love to sample my Tony. "Oh, the cakes were delicious. I had this much of each one." She held her thumb and index finger about two inches apart. "I admit I don't bake much so I bought them at this wonderful bakery in Newton."

"Newton?" Monique glanced around and lowered her voice. "Newton? Whatcha wanna give those rich white folks your money for? They don't need it."

Cam shrugged, feeling defensive. "Well, they're an excellent bakery."

"And they don't have excellent bakeries in the inner city?" Monique said. "Is that what you mean?"

Cam didn't understand the turn of the conversation and regretted initiating one with the disagreeable woman. She had met her type before—beautiful on the outside but always ready to pounce about some real or imagined slight. "I'm sure they do," Cam replied, "but the people who own the bakery are people I know and have done business with before."

"Hmm-hmm," Monique muttered. "I see."

After an awkward silence, Cam spoke. "Well, it was nice seeing and talking to you again." She struggled for a graceful exit and shook the blouse in her hand. "I'm going to try this on." Cam noticed Monique staring at the dangling two hundred seventy-nine dollar price tag.

Monique dropped the blouse she held so it lay on top of the golden brown rack. "I'm afraid I can't afford any of this shit. I'm just a high school teacher, you know."

Cam nodded. "Yes, I know. You mentioned it at the party. I'm sure you're a very good one and I'm sure you and Tony are making a big difference with our kids."

Monique cranked her neck with indignation. "I heard this was supposed to be a place for women of color, but most sisters working as nurses and school teachers can't fork over the kind of bank they're asking for here." She inspected the room. "Shit. Half the women in here are white—and half of them are toting black kids. And look at those two." She gestured with her head toward the middle of the store at the two employees: One stood in front of the cash register ringing up a sale while the other held the door for a tall redhead entering a fitting room. "A Latina and a white lady, and the first one looks likes she's barely old enough to legally buy a drink."

"Well..." Cam looked around as well, her discomfort increasing. "Seems to be a variety of people here ...you know, all kinds. I'm sure anybody's money is welcomed." She glanced at her watch and shook the blouse again. "Well, I better get going. So many things to do today. Nice seeing you again." She turned but winced when she heard the voice behind her.

"Hey Cam."

Cam turned back. "Yes?"

"Can I ask you something?"

Cam felt compelled to reply even though the tone of the question indicated trouble. "Of course. Go right ahead."

Monique stepped closer. "You're fucking Tony, aren't you?"

Cam widened her eyes to the size of silver dollars. "Wh-what kind of question is that? Certainly not the kind of question a lady would ask—or answer. Good day." Her face burning red, she turned again to leave.

Monique scampered, cutting off her path. "You don't have to get all high and mighty with me. I'm just trying to do you a favor."

"Do *me* a favor?"

"That's right, smart ass," Monique said. "I just think you ought to know something: Tony's told me that wife of his is one cold but crazy, jealous ass bitch. She already threatened to kill me at the party while holding a knife."

Cam took deep breaths through her nose and bared her teeth like a riled wolf. "I don't believe you. Tony would never talk that way about Rose. He's got too much class for that. And Rose, she's a wonderful woman and mother—and she happens to be my best friend."

Monique cackled. "Ha! Some best friend you are, riding your best friend's husband behind her back." She snorted and smacked her lips. "Not that I blame you. The man is finer than a motherfucker—and I bet he's packing some serious meat inside those pants, but my guess is you already know that."

Cam took another deep breath and surveyed the room. Customers were beginning to whisper and point at them. "If you're finished I would like to leave."

Monique took a step back to examine Cam. "I admit you've got a pretty face and those big ass tits going for you—I saw how you jiggled for those teenage boys at the party—plus I bet you've got enough money to buy this place, but you might want to stick with old, rich, white geezers with shriveled dicks who'll kick off and drop a fortune into your lap, and leave brothers like Tony to real sisters who know how to handle them."

Cam struggled to retain her calm demeanor but she had endured such remarks before and resolved to endure them no longer. She sympathized with dark beauties like Monique because society devalued them, but that didn't mean she had to take anyone's crap. She pointed at Monique. "I suppose you mean real sisters like you?"

"Yeah, like me." Monique declared in a slightly louder voice. She picked up the blouse with the black stripes again and shook it, causing the price tag to dance like a marionette. "You can rent him but you can't land him—and if you do land him you won't be able to keep him."

Cam prepared to leave but found her path blocked by another woman, the younger clerk.

"Is there something I can help you two find?" the svelte, pantsuit-wearing woman whispered with a heavily accented voice. She glanced at Cam, then at Monique and addressed the latter. "Miss, if you would like to try that on..." She returned her attention back to Cam. "Cam Spencer?" She put her hands to her face and gasped. "Dios Mio! You are Cam Spencer, aren't you?"

Monique grimaced. "What the hell? How come this woman knows who you are?"

The woman gushed. "Are you kidding? This is the founder of Otra Cosa. She used to own this place and the big stores in New York and Los Angeles." She pointed at Cam. "She's a goddess. I know because I'm majoring in fashion design at Mount Ida College. Her designs and books on fashion have sold all over the world. If it wasn't for her—" The woman stopped and inspected Monique before lowering her voice and addressing Cam. "Ms. Spencer, is there a problem? Do you want me to call mall security?"

Monique glowered. "Um-hmm. I see. Two women are having a disagreement and it has to be the black woman's fault."

Cam privately admitted Monique had a point, but the advantage hers, she held up the red blouse and resisted the temptation to speak Spanish, knowing it would infuriate Monique. "I was just looking at this. There's no need to call anyone, um..." She glanced at the employee's name tag. "...Dulce. The lady and I were just having an animated discussion. You know how it is."

Dulce nodded. "Yes, of course, Ms. Spencer."

"Call me Cam."

Dulce smiled. "Oh, I couldn't." She clasped her hands together. "Really? Would you like to try on that blouse, Cam?"

Cam nodded and gestured with her head faintly in Monique's direction. "Yes, the lady and I have finished here."

A middle-aged woman wearing a long overcoat and a little too much blush interrupted the conversation. "Miss, I would like to take a closer look at one of the watches, please." She pointed at the large table next to the cash register.

Dulce glanced at Cam, then back at the customer. "Yes, missus."

"It's okay," Cam said. "Go ahead."

The young woman thanked Cam and trotted away.

Cam started to walk in the consultant's direction but felt a tug on her arm.

"This isn't over, Miss Thang, Miss Big Shot," Monique whispered.

Cam jerked her arm away. "Don't you touch me!" she whispered. "Let me tell you something: This place is saturated with state of the art security cameras. I know because I had them installed. You put your hands on me again and I *will* have that lady call mall security and they'll call the police. And whose side do you think the police will take, huh?" She shook her index finger. "What happens to teachers who get arrested for assault? And did I mention that recently I posed for a picture with your superintendent because I gave one elementary school five thousand dollars to buy Christmas presents for every student there and got nineteen acquaintances to do the same?" She squinted and continued. "Now you get out of here and leave me alone." She paused for just three seconds and finished. "As Brick said in *Cat on a*

Hot Tin Roof: 'You're fooled by the fact that I am sayin' this quiet?' " Her eyes glowed with anger.

A few more seconds passed before Monique smirked. "Got a little spunk there, huh, Miss Thang?"

"And I can back it up, too. You want to try me?"

Monique chuckled. "Not today, not here in your home court, but I'll see you again in more neutral territory." She dropped the blouse on the floor and sauntered out of the store.

Cam picked up the blouse, inspected it and satisfied it had sustained no damage, returned it to the rack. She reached into her back pocket and took out her mobile telephone. She needed to speak to a sympathetic friend—but who?

She wanted to call Tony and tell him what had just happened. Monique worked with him five days a week and would certainly make a point to see him on Monday in order to twist the incident, casting Cam as the bitch. Cam hated the thought of Tony being fed lies about her, but she had promised she wouldn't call him. If she called Rose her best friend would certainly repeat the story to Tony, putting Monique in the worst possible light—which she deserved—but that might cause trouble for Tony at his school, and Cam didn't want that either.

Cam could feel the stares of the other patrons in the store and wanted to leave as soon as possible. She shoved her telephone back into her pocket and strolled to the cash register, stopping to look at herself in a tall, three-way mirror against the wall. Her face had lost the flush generated by her anger. She handed the blouse to the other fashion consultant, a tall blonde in her late twenties with an athletic build who pushed a mound of thick hair to the right side of her face.

"It's a pleasure to serve you, Ms. Spencer," the woman opened. "Would you like to try that on?"

"Please call me Cam," she replied and immediately took note of the woman's accent and name tag, and added in French: "It won't be necessary to try it on, Cosette. I know how the sizes run for this vendor."

Cosette flashed a wide grin and complimented Cam on her pronunciations. The two exchanged pleasantries while the woman rang up Cam's purchase. After they completed their transaction and Cosette handed Cam her purchase, she leaned closer and whispered to Cam, still in French. "Do you want me to call mall security to walk you to your car?"

"That won't be necessary," Cam replied, still in French, "but thank you."

Cam checked her watch and after noting the five thirty time, decided to get home and eat dinner. Upon entering the mall she had admired the myriad of decorations for Easter, but upon leaving she rushed past the displays looking straight ahead. Eventually she stepped outside into the fifty degree temperature trying to project an air of self-confidence, but in addition to toting her purse and shopping bag she also clutched her car remote with her left hand and a container of pepper spray in her right. Due to hills of plowed, melting snow, the asphalt of the parking lot glistened and shimmered with wetness like a freshly waxed floor.

Cam felt relieved when she reached her recently detailed SUV, shining under a sun that would disappear beneath the horizon in ninety minutes. She spotted a piece of paper under her windshield wiper and shuddered with apprehension. She looked around to make sure no one was near, then quickly snatched the paper and climbed into her vehicle. The SUV started and the doors locked, she unfolded the paper and read the note. It contained a message composed from cut out newspaper.

SEE YOU WHEN YOU GET BACK FROM PARIS.

Cam blinked. Clearly, Monique wouldn't have had time to construct such a document—but her ex-husband, who didn't know the meaning of full-time work, had all the time in the world. Cam balled up her fists and grinded her teeth. "I never thought I would ever say this, Vincent, but I hope to God you drop dead!"

She swiveled her head in every direction looking out for passing cars and possibly Vincent. Spotting neither, she eased out of her parking space while fighting back feelings of anger peppered with fear. Clearly, Vincent had followed her to the mall. But how had he known about her upcoming trip to Paris? Cam scolded herself for not following through on filing a harassment prevention order against Vincent, but while zigzagging through the parking lot she resolved to rectify that first thing Monday morning.

SEVENTEEN: FEMALE ATTRACTOR

On the third Friday in April Tony's sixth scheduled rendezvous with Cam surpassed his expectations.

At around nine o'clock in the evening he lay on his back in Cam's bed. She, her hair down and completely nude, joined with him at the genitals, rode on top. In spite of the thermostat-controlled seventy degree temperature, the smell of their musk and sweat, born from boiling passion and lust, filled the room. Cam did most of the work while Tony held on to her hips and enjoyed the view. The light from a half-dozen strawberry-scented candles bathed her in a smoldering hot, sensuous glow. Tony admired her bouncing breasts and washboard abs. "Dearest Cam," he said. "You're so beautiful."

"Oh my God, Tony," Cam exclaimed. "I-I-I can't believe I'm going to fire another round!" She increased her rocking motion as she spoke between short gasps. "I know I've been selfish but I can't help it. Our love is so beautiful." She gripped Tony's hands Greco-Roman knuckle style, then closed her eyes, leaned back and melted with ecstasy.

"Go ahead, baby," Tony said. "You know how much I love seeing you like this." He did. After over fifteen years of being with a woman who was guarded and secretive inside and outside of the bedroom, he relished sharing his body with such a multi-orgasmic woman who expressed her feelings so openly.

Cam's spasms eventually subsided. She sighed and leisurely collapsed onto Tony, pressing her ample bare bosom against his. "I swear," she declared, her voice barely above a whisper, "if I have another climax I'm going to pass out." She opened her eyes and kissed him. "Seriously, what are you doing to me?"

Tony smiled, then embraced Cam and deftly rolled them both over so he lay on top while keeping them coupled. He kissed her once, twice, three times, then began moving his hips back and forth in slow, deliberate strokes. He knew he had to be careful or he could injure her. They cooed and mashed their lips together, twirling their tongues in and out of each other's mouth. He gradually increased his speed and laid the palm of his hands flat under Cam's shoulders to support his weight. Their movements conveyed increased familiarity with each other's body and proclivities, like a pair of dancers who, through practice, have become synchronized, their words proclaimed the love they had confessed to each other for the first time a month earlier. "I love you, Cam," Tony whispered.

"I love you, Tony, with all my heart," she replied. "I'll always love you." She caressed his back with her fingers and closed her legs momentarily around his waist, affectionately squeezing him. "Mmmm, I love the feel of you inside me. So hard, so big, so fucking deep. I'm so happy it's almost unbearable. I want more, darling. Give me more. Don't stop."

Tony enjoyed Cam's proclamations. She was so uninhibited, so expressive. She liked to describe what they were doing and sometimes offer suggestions bordering on commands.

"We're making beautiful love together, Tony," Cam declared. "We're loving each other so much. Yes, darling, thrust into me. Pull my hair. Now kiss me."

Tony gladly complied. She had told him talking in such a way in bed increased her pleasure. He loved it. She didn't play games or hold back. She didn't care how vulnerable she appeared. No wonder she had been hurt so many times by bums who used her. Still, in his quest to prolong their lovemaking he had brought himself to the brink several times over the past forty minutes but had slowed down or stopped. Satisfied Cam had been satisfied, it was time to please himself. "Baby, I can't hold it any longer."

"Yes, I want it all. Don't make me beg, Tony," Cam moaned. "I want every drop. Pour it into me."

"Take it," Tony whispered. "Kiss me while I fill you with love." He covered his mouth with hers, sucked on her tongue and shuddered as he felt a flow of warmth pass from him to her, generating sensations of intense pleasure throughout his entire body.

Cam separated her mouth from his. "I can feel it, my love," she moaned. "There's so much. I can feel how much you love me."

For three minutes they lay together, arms tightly wrapped around each other, neither saying a word. Finally, their breathing and heart rate nearing normal again, Cam covered her face with her hands, which puzzled Tony. He brushed her hair from the side of her face. "You okay, dearest?"

She burst into tears. "I'm sorry. I've tried not to cry but it's too beautiful, too wonderful. I can't help myself. Please don't be annoyed with me."

Tony smiled. He twisted like a contortionist to grab the sheet and blanket and tugged on them so he and Cam were covered again. "It's okay. I don't mind."

Cam smiled back. "Will you stay inside me for a while?"

Tony kissed her on the forehead. "Of course." He lay with his cheek against Cam's and his face lightly pressed against the mattress. They would doze for a few minutes, still as one. He closed his eyes. If only it could be like this between him and Rose but for the past month she had declined his overtures to make love.

*

Thirty minutes later Cam lay in Tony's arms with her head on his chest. "...I'm sorry to put you in a position where you have to believe either Monique or me," she said.

"It's not like that," Tony assured her. "When she told me her version of what had happened it didn't sound like you at all." He shrugged. "Monique has, I don't know, issues. She's had a few problems at work too. Dr. Martinez—he's our principal—has spoken to her for getting into pointless fights with coworkers and students. She's opinionated and takes offense easily. Sees racism everywhere. I've tried to get her to count to twenty before she speaks but, well, let's say it's a work in progress."

Cam nodded. "If she listens to you I'm sure she'll be alright."

Tony smiled. "She really is a good teacher. I'm sorry she upset you."

"She wants you in her bed," Cam said. "You know that, don't you?"

Tony shrugged. "She thinks that's what she wants."

"Is that what you want?"

Tony chuckled. "I've got all I can handle with you." He snickered. "Enough about that. What are you going to do about Vincent?"

"I filed that harassment prevention order," Cam announced. "I had to hire a private investigator to get his current address. He's living with some woman in Boston. She's probably the one who called me, demanding I leave *him* alone. Can you imagine that?"

"Lousy cockroach," Tony said. "You let me catch him sneaking around here."

Cam laughed. "By the way, happy belated birthday. Not a bad performance for forty."

"Thanks. I try."

"You wouldn't let me give you a small birthday present, would you?"

"I would be delighted, honey," Tony said, "but, well...you know."

Cam hugged him. "Yeah, I know."

Tony broke the ensuing few seconds of uncomfortable silence by playfully pinching Cam's nose. "So tell me more about France. Some serious history there. Have you ever been to any of the ancient Roman amphitheatres like the Arena in Nimes?"

The pleasant atmosphere restored, the two lovers talked nonstop for nearly an hour. Eventually Cam yawned and rolled over on her right side so she faced away from Tony. She pulled his arm. "Hold me."

Tony did and kissed Cam at the back of the neck. "Good night, baby."

"Good night, my love."

Tony closed his eyes and considered his position in more ways than one. They had reached the halfway point in their arrangement. He had fallen completely and hopelessly in love with Cam and hated the thought one day this aspect of their relationship would end. A month earlier he would have unequivocally asserted he loved both Rose and Cam but he had loved Rose longer and loved her more. Now he could only say he had loved Rose longer. He loved them both, but differently. Nevertheless, when the time came to end his sexual relationship with Cam he would do it for the sake of his family.

He opened his eyes and declined to ruminate on the matter any further. Just enjoy this time together, he thought. Lying next to Cam felt so good. She was so warm, so beautiful, so damn sexy. He reached and cupped her breast with his left hand. Yes, so very sexy. He kissed her neck and back, then lightly bit her back.

Cam squirmed with obvious delight. "Tony, do you need something?"

"Yes," he admitted. He could feel his hardness pressing against Cam's butt cheek. He lifted her leg and touched her sex, which aroused him even more. "You're soaking wet."

"For you," Cam said. She raised her leg farther and leaned forward while still lying on her side. "Go ahead, my love. Don't deny yourself. Take what's yours—and don't forget to smack that ass."

Tony closed his eyes and grunted as he slid inside Cam again. What a woman. How could he ever go back to a life without her as his lover?

*

The following Monday afternoon Tony sat at his desk in his classroom reviewing his lesson plans for the remainder of April and the month of May. Twenty minutes had passed since the last class of the day had ended. Foot traffic outside his closed door had all but disappeared. There had been no school the previous week, part of Boston Public Schools' odd vacation schedule: a week and a half during Christmas and New Year's, another week during the third week in February, and another week during the third week in April.

Tony didn't know why the district had such a unique schedule rather than take one week off for Spring Break like most other schools. Depending on the number of snow days to be made up, the BPS school year could run very late; sometimes into the fourth week in June. Tony shrugged. The school calendar is what it is. He resumed reading the words on the computer screen and wondered if he could cut a day from the lessons on the Great Depression if he combined—

A group of giggling female students burst into the classroom. Tony stood and straightened his tie. "Can I help you ladies?" He counted four girls, all wearing jeans and collared shirts; two African Americans, one white, one Latina. They appeared to be seniors.

The shortest girl, one of the African Americans, took a step closer. She bore long hair elaborately French-braided. "Mr. Monroe, is this where the Tigerettes are meeting?"

Tony wondered if a better name could have been chosen for the student group committed to improving the academic achievement of girls at Hamilton High, but that wasn't his call. He answered her question by shaking his head. "No, doll. I believe that's in Ms. Harper's room." He pointed at the floor. "It's the room literally underneath us." The girls nodded and exited en masse. He could still hear their voices because they neglected to close the door.

"Goddamn, he's so fine!"

"Umm-hmm. If I was older I'd be on his ass like fucking rain."

"Y'all bitches ain't got no chance. Didn't you hear him call me doll?"

"Niggah, please. He meant a mahfuckin' rag doll."

Their badinage prompted Tony to wince and shake his head again. The compliment notwithstanding, God help Zoë if he ever got a report about her using that kind of language, especially in public. Thankfully, both Zoë and Adam were excellent, well-behaved students for whom he would never be summoned to school for a disciplinary reason. He prepared to take his seat when he heard the sound of footsteps near the door. Another lost student?

"Hey there, Tony."

No. Monique.

Tony smiled and returned to his seat. "Hey there yourself." In spite of her account weeks earlier about an unpleasant encounter with Cam at the mall, the two colleagues had continued their friendship. Tony had told Monique an argument between her and his wife's best friend had nothing to do with them as coworkers. He pointed at the wall clock behind him. "I'm leaving in a minute. I've got to get to class. What's going on?"

Monique strolled closer. She wore a simple off white blouse with dark brown slacks. "Nothing really, I just wanted to see if you've got a yardstick I can borrow. I think one of our colleagues stole mine."

Tony chose to ignore the accusation but made a mental note to pick up a yardstick at the hardware store before the end of the work week and anonymously leave it on Monique's desk, just to keep peace in the family. "Sure," he said. "It's in the closet." He pointed to the side of the room opposite the door.

Monique stared at the closet and scrunched up her face. "Would you mind getting it? I'm not in the mood to deal with those mice that are always hiding in our closets."

Tony snickered. "Monique, you're afraid of mice?"

She frowned, clearly embarrassed. "Can you just go get the damn yardstick?"

Tony chuckled and went to the closet. He returned and handed the yardstick to Monique.

"Thanks," she said.

"Don't mention it," Tony replied in a playfully officious tone. He checked his wristwatch and returned to his desk. The two teachers chatted while he turned off the computer, donned a jacket and placed a Hamilton Tigers baseball cap on his head. He scooped up his briefcase from underneath his desk and grabbed a large tote bag stuffed with papers and notebooks propped against the back legs. "Turn off the lights for me, would you?"

Monique flipped the switch next to the door leading into the hallway, darkening the room somewhat.

Tony approached the door but Monique blocked his path. He arched his eyebrows. "Something else?"

Monique covered the hand in which Tony clutched his briefcase with her own. "Yeah, how about a kiss?"

Tony sighed and set his things down. "Monique, I'd be lying if I told you I'm not fond of you, but I'm a happily married man."

"You're married alright, but I can tell you're not that happy."

"You don't know that."

"Yes I do."

"Well, that's in the first place," Tony said. "In the second place, even if I weren't happy in my marriage—and I am—I wouldn't get involved with you because we work together and," he paused, "in the third place we wouldn't be right for each other. You know that."

"I'm not looking for a long-term commitment, Tony," Monique retorted. She puckered her full lips. "Right now, all I want is a kiss."

"I don't think so."

Monique grinned. "Just one kiss and I'll never bring up the subject of 'us' again."

Tony sighed. He couldn't believe he was considering granting Monique's request. Of course, six months earlier he wouldn't have believed he'd agree to be pimped out by his wife either. He shook his finger. "You promise, one kiss and starting tomorrow we go back to being platonic colleagues?"

Monique raised her right hand. "I swear to God."

Tony backed up two paces and stepped a few feet to his right. "Come here, away from the door." He could see Monique saunter closer like a panther nearing its prey. Without saying a word he took her in his arms. Monique threw her arms around his neck. The two stood in silence, their lips locked tightly together, their tongues dueling. After a few seconds it was over. Tony moseyed to the door and picked up his briefcase and tote bag. "I have to go." Monique had not moved and still had her back to him. "Monique?"

She slowly turned around and sighed. "Oh my God. Wow. I mean like, fuckin' wow, Tony," she whispered, gasping as if she had just run up a flight of stairs.

Tony could see the outline of her nipples pushing through the fabric of her bra and blouse, but he ignored the sight and opened the door. "A deal's a deal." He heard his mobile telephone buzzing and dropped everything to retrieve it from his jacket pocket. He checked the number, which read: Bost Int Acad. "Hello?"

"Is this Mr. Monroe?" the female voice on the other end of the line asked. "Zoë and Adam Monroe's father?" The voice conveyed a privileged background.

"Yes," Tony answered, "and I'm speaking to whom?"

"This is Mrs. Fox. I'm the assistant headmaster at Boston International Academy. There's been some trouble here at school today involving both your son and daughter and some other children. A physical altercation, actually."

"Are Zoë and Adam okay?"

"Yes," Fox said. "It appears they got the better of the situation, but one of the parents involved is talking about filing charges and, well, I must insist that you or Mrs. Monroe come to BIA right away. We've called your wife but we haven't been able to reach her."

That's odd, Tony thought. Rose was off today. Come to think of it he had called her a few minutes earlier and had gotten her voice mail himself. "Okay," he said. "I'll be right there." He ended the call and returned his attention to Monique, who had eased past him and held the door open. "The kids got into some sort of fight at school. They're alright but I have to get down there." He dashed out the door. "Lock up for me, would you please—and remember our deal."

"I won't forget," Monique said. "But if I knew what I know now I never would have agreed to it."

Tony trotted down the hall oblivious to Monique's quip. He had more pressing matters on his mind.

EIGHTEEN: CAT'S OUT OF THE BAG

Rose drove slowly past Tony's driverless Cadillac. "Damn," she muttered. Tony had gotten there first. Scores of creeping and parked automobiles owned by parents awaiting the end of the school day at Boston International Academy surrounded her in the half-full lot. Rose flung her own SUV into a space thirty yards farther away, then shifted into park and checked the dashboard clock just in time to see the LED numbers flicker to 3:01. The "Finale" to the William Tell Overture emanating from the mobile telephone mounted next to the clock redirected her attention.

She read the caller ID information. Tony again, his third call this afternoon, not to mention his two text messages. She waited ten seconds for the music to stop, signaling the call had gone to voice mail. Relieved, she sat in the vehicle with the engine running, twisting her mouth from side to side, pondering what to do next. In nine minutes the bell would ring and four hundred middle schoolers—one third of the student body—would spill out of the building like bees fluttering away from a hive.

Rose turned the telephone off. If Tony asked she would tell him she was having trouble with it. That excuse always worked. No way could she tell him she had spent the past hour fending off the advances of an amorous bill collector. Rose snatched off her sunglasses, flipped down her sun visor to inspect her face in its mirror, and sighed. What a way to spend the afternoon. It was like dating in high school again. She frowned at the unpleasant memory of James Rivers groping, moaning and breathing on her. She hadn't planned on the man turning into a sex-crazed octopus after she relented and gave him a little peck on the lips; she had meant to just keep him on the hook, not have him leap into the damn boat.

"Men," she scoffed aloud. They were such disgusting creatures. Always obsessing about sex. Tony was no better. It had gotten so that almost every night in bed he would squeeze her breast and whisper in her ear, lowing about how beautiful and sexy she was and how he loved her. Well, she was having none of it. If he wasn't going to adequately provide for his family let him settle for soaking his penis once a month for pay.

Her mother had been right all along. Let a man get a woman on her back and he loses all ambition. Rose had to concede, to her regret, she had married a man just like her father. Although she loved Daddy he was small-minded and lacked driving ambition. A gifted carpenter, he had continuously toiled for decades in someone else's firm instead of opening his own business and becoming rich. Rose had vowed not to nag her man, like her mother, but to gently nudge and cajole her husband into being more than what he imagined he could be—but that hadn't worked either.

Rose finally pushed her sunglasses back onto her face and exited her SUV while taking deep breaths, steeling herself for the upcoming event. Her designer jeans, stylish calf-high leather boots, turtleneck sweater and long, all-weather coat more than overcame the crisp, fifty degree air. She pressed her keychain remote to secure her vehicle and wished women could sometimes do the same when dealing with men. The futility of that wish privately acknowledged, she half-trotted toward the Craig Windom Building, named after some old man who had helped raise millions of dollars toward constructing the four-year-old middle school wing of BIA. The building constituted one of the three instructional buildings in the six-unit, forty-five acre private school.

She checked her watch: four minutes to spare before the bell rang. She barely noticed the plethora of flowering magnolia trees, patches of yellow daffodils, or several hundred square yards of green grass that garnished the campus under the soft glow of a generous sun. Nor did she stop to join the gaggle of mothers waiting outside the front door no doubt bemoaning how difficult it could be to hire dependable domestic help these days.

After a hurried exchange with the middle school secretary Rose was ushered through the corridor leading to the windowless inner office of Vera Fox, the assistant headmaster who, like the assistant headmasters at the Lower and Upper Schools, performed administrative tasks but taught one class. Rose knocked on the door and was beckoned to enter. She pushed the door open and counted four persons seated inside. Fox immediately stood. The front corner of her small desk was pressed against the back right corner of the cramped room, allowing her to slide her chair backward and move about.

"Good afternoon, Mrs. Monroe," Fox said. She was a nearly six feet tall, handsome, redhead of almost forty with pale white skin and freckles. She wore a tight-fitting brown pantsuit, but not tight-fitting in a flattering way.

Her formerly athletic body had begun to show signs of expansion due to long work hours and not enough exercise. The assistant headmaster ambled past Tony, who had also stood, and extended her hand. His chair rested against the wall between the desk and the door. The chairs in which Zoë and Adam sat touched the wall opposite the desk next to a file cabinet. "It's a pleasure to see you again," Fox added. "I regret it's under these circumstances." She shook Rose's hand, then looked around and tried to lighten the mood. "I assume you know everyone here?" Just then the bell rang.

Rose politely offered a half smile and a nod.

"Something wrong with your feet, Adam?" Tony asked with a low voice. "Since when do you sit while your mother stands?"

Adam bounced out of his chair. "I'm sorry, Mom," he mumbled, and gestured at his now empty seat, the one closest to his mother. "Sit here."

Rose resisted the urge to defend her son. Tony could sometimes be hard on the boy—harder than on Zoë—but she recognized now was not the time to take up that issue.

"She'll sit in my chair," Tony said. "I'll stand." He and Fox eased past each other. After declining an offer to have another chair brought in, he squeezed Rose's arm and kissed her on the cheek, then leaned against a six feet tall bookshelf stuffed with books and folders near the closed door.

"Thank you, hon," Rose said. She opened her arms. "Come here, sweeties." Zoë and Adam gathered at her bosom like formerly lost calves. She kissed them each twice. "You two okay?"

"Yes, Mom," the twins said in unison.

Rose smiled when she saw Zoë surreptitiously tap Adam on the elbow and mouthed the word "jinx." Yes, they were okay. She sat in Tony's former seat.

The four chairs occupied again, Fox leaned back. "Ms. Monroe, I'm glad both you and Mr. Monroe are here. I already explained to your husband what happened earlier this afternoon, and I'm afraid it's potentially serious. One boy needed medical attention and is on his way home from the doctor as we speak."

Rose felt a twinge of alarm. Obviously this was more than an adolescent spat. "Perhaps you would be good enough to repeat the story for my benefit, Ms. Fox."

Fox shuffled several papers lying between her and a five-by-seven-inch photograph of herself looking slightly younger posing with an attractive female blonde, both sporting tennis gear and rackets. She spoke over muffled sounds of footsteps and voices from students and staff conducting business in the outer office. "Well, I have incident reports here from adult and student witnesses, as well as from Zoë and Adam. It's still preliminary, but from what I can tell, right after her music class, which ended at one fifteen, a couple of boys grabbed Zoë's flute in the hallway and started tossing it back and forth."

Rose felt her heartbeat accelerate. They would have been better off to have snatched the girl's teeth out of her mouth than to have touched that instrument. She glanced at Zoë, who lowered her head. Rose kept a stoic face. With a little luck the truth about the flute's ownership and cost would remain a secret. "Why on earth would they do such a thing?"

"I guess they thought it was funny," Fox answered.

"I assume Zoë didn't agree," Rose asserted.

Fox arched a thick eyebrow. "That's putting it mildly. According to the reports, Zoë ran back and forth, very upset, yelling at the boys to give her back her flute, which was still in its case and was not damaged. Anyway, I guess Zoë and one boy, Kenneth Jerome, wrestled a bit over the flute and he shoved Zoë backward, causing her to fall."

Rose gritted her teeth. "This boy pushed my baby to the ground? What grade is he in?"

"Well," Fox said, staring at her desk, "both boys are in the eighth grade."

Rose raised her voice slightly. "And they've got nothing better to do than take property that doesn't belong to them and push a seventh grade girl to the ground?"

Tony took a couple of steps and kneeled next to Rose. "She's okay, sweetheart." He took her hand and squeezed it.

Rose lightly reciprocated his gesture of affection and took a deep breath. "Well, thank God for that." She returned her attention to Fox. "And no one intervened?"

"Humph," Tony said, and glanced at his son. "As a matter of fact, someone did."

Rose stared at Adam. He returned her gaze. She addressed Tony. "You mean, Adam?"

Tony nodded. "Ms. Fox, I didn't mean to interrupt. Would you please continue?"

Fox cleared her throat. "Yes, well, according to the witnesses, Adam entered the area just in time to see Kenneth push Zoë, so rather than go get an adult as he should have, he called the boy a..." She rolled her eyes and squirmed in her chair. "...well, a bastard and tackled him, sending him backward into a wall. Then the other boy who had been throwing the flute with Kenneth—his name is Bartholomew Ross Atherton—everyone calls him 'BR,' he grabbed Adam—"

"From behind," Adam rejoined.

"Speak when you're spoken to," Tony growled.

Adam lowered his head. "Yes sir."

Fox continued. "BR grabbed Adam—from behind, as Adam said—and pinned his arms back, and called for Kenneth, who had staggered to his feet, to punch him, but he never got the chance because Zoë jumped on BR's back and dug her fingers into the boy's eyes. Finally the head custodian and a teacher broke up the melee. I called BR's mother, who just happened to be next door at the Lower School where he has a sister. She came over and rushed him to a medical facility to have his eyes looked at. I got a call a few minutes ago from her saying he's going to be okay. She's still very upset."

Rose released Tony's hand. "So what happens now?"

Fox shrugged. "I'm not sure, to be honest. Today is Monday. Headmaster Cleveland is away at a fundraiser. I spoke to him on the telephone and he told me to keep all four of them out of school on suspension until he returns on Wednesday."

"If what you told me is true," Rose said, "it's clear that Zoë and Adam didn't start the fight. Adam did just what his father and I have taught him—not to fight unless defending himself or someone else—in this case that someone else happens to be the person who he shared my body with for nine months."

"I appreciate that, Mrs. Monroe," Fox interjected, "I do, but here at BIA, we have a zero tolerance policy about any kind of fighting, no matter who starts it."

"Are these two white kids?" Rose asked.

Fox shrugged. "Um, yes, but I don't see what that has to do with anything."

Zoë spoke up. "When they were separating us, Kenneth called Adam a nigger. I heard him. Everybody heard him."

Fox inhaled and exhaled. "Well, Adam called him a... well, you know."

Rose shook her finger at Fox. "I'm sure you're not equating the two, are you?"

Fox held up her hands. "Of course not. I'm just saying that's what happened."

Rose continued. "So we have two white eighth grade boys—two cowards—picking on a black girl with no provocation, taking her—taking what doesn't belong to them, one about to hit her brother when he was defenseless because he had come to his sister's rescue when no one else would, the same boy who used a racial slur. That about right?"

"Well," Fox said, "that isn't exactly the way I would characterize it."

Tony stood. "Ms. Fox, I'm an educator as well, a high school teacher, and at my school whenever there's an incident or altercation, all things being equal it's the older kids who are held to a higher standard because it's their responsibility to set a good example."

Fox blinked and opened her hands. "I-I-I'm only telling you what I've been told to do." She stood, signaling the end of the meeting. "So please keep Zoë and Adam home tomorrow. I'm sure this will all be straightened out when our headmaster returns."

Rose stood as well. "Okay, but my husband's also a lawyer. If my children get any adverse mark on their record because of this, we're going to contact the media and the local NAACP and give them an earful. There's a news anchor on Channel Eight who attends our church and is a good friend of mine. How would you like a couple of TV vans parked outside your school while a reporter grills you about the racial climate at BIA?"

Fox took a deep breath. "I-I wouldn't like that at all, but I'm sure it won't come to that."

Tony opened the door and held it for Rose and the twins. "I hope not."

"One more thing, Mr. and Mrs. Monroe."

Rose turned. She and her family huddled together on the outer side of the threshold to Fox's office. "Yes?"

Fox approached the clan. "Students are allowed—even encouraged—to purchase their own instruments, but we require that the parents sign a hold harmless form absolving the school from any liability should something happen to the instrument. We also require proof that the instrument is insured."

Oh fuck me, Rose thought. The cat's out of the bag. She glanced at Zoë, who looked absolutely mortified.

Fox continued. "Zoë didn't notify the school that she has her own flute, and a marvelous one it is—I play the flute myself. But before she can bring it back on campus she'll have to bring in those forms."

Tony stepped forward. "What do you, mean, Zoë has her own flute?"

After an awkward silence Fox smirked, clearly relishing her surprise on the unsuspecting father. "I don't know how to make it any clearer, Mr. Monroe." She pointed at the door. "The instrument is out there by the secretary's desk." She turned to Zoë. "It's your *personal* property, isn't that right, Zoë?"

Rose saw the downcast countenance of her daughter and felt a burning rage. How dare this supercilious heifer drag Zoë into her petty bullshit. "We'll take care of it," she said.

*

It took ten minutes for Zoë and Adam to gather their belongings. Afterward, the Monroe family ambled side by side past small groups of congregating students and across the school parking lot, with now only a few scattered cars in the visitors section. Rose and Tony served as bookends; Zoë walked next to Rose, while Adam walked alongside Tony.

"As far as we're concerned," Rose insisted, "you two didn't do anything wrong."

The four gathered next to the empty parking space next to the driver's side of Tony's vehicle.

"You kids ride with me," Rose announced.

Zoë and Adam looked at each other, then at Tony, apparently for rescue.

"Dad?" Zoë asked, almost whining.

Tony checked his watch. "I need to catch the rest of my class." He pointed. "You two go wait by your mother's SUV. I need to talk to her for a second."

The two trotted, then raced to Rose's vehicle.

Rose watched the twins playfully argue over who had reached the SUV first. She forced herself to face Tony, knowing she was in for a rough time. "I'm sure this will all work out."

"Rose," Tony said, "I want to know what the hell is going on. First, I've been calling and texting you all afternoon."

"I'm sorry, I've been having some trouble with my phone," Rose offered sheepishly. "I told you I need a new one."

"You just bought that one a year ago," Tony snarled. "Never mind that. When did you buy Zoë that flute, how much did it cost and why didn't you tell me?"

Rose checked on Zoë and Adam. Adam was chasing Zoë around her vehicle. "We were going to tell you, sweetheart."

"We? Who's we? When did *you* buy it and how much did it cost?"

Rose considered shaving a few dollars off the price but decided against it. She held up her hand and muttered one word. "Three." She saw the whites of Tony's eyes.

"Hundred?"

Rose said nothing.

"Thousand?"

She nodded.

Tony shook his head. "I'm going to class." He gently pulled Rose with him to the driver's door and opened it. "I don't know what to make of this. All the spending and the lying. Can't you see what you're doing to me, to us, to the kids?"

"I haven't hurt anyone, Tony."

"Damn it Rose," Tony said, trying to keep his voice down, "did you see the look on Zoë and Adam's face when that snooty woman asked Zoë about that flute? Are you so self-absorbed you didn't catch the embarrassment on our children's faces—and on mine?"

Rose lowered her head and sighed. "You're overreacting. It wasn't—"

"You told Zoë to lie to me," Tony said, striking himself in the chest with his index finger. "Me, her father. And you told her to lie to Adam. Don't you know how that must have hurt her?"

"I didn't tell her to lie," Rose protested. "I just didn't mention it to you or Adam."

Tony slid into the SUV. "You lie so much you're not even aware you're doing it."

"That's not true."

"Yes it is," Tony shot back. "And what was that a few minutes ago? You know I'm not a lawyer."

Rose rolled her eyes. "Don't remind me."

Tony started the engine, pressed a button to roll down the driver's door window and closed the door. "I'm sick of your lies. It's my fault for allowing it to go on for so long. Take the kids home and don't fill their heads up with bullshit. I mean it. If you do, I'll...I'll—"

"You'll what, Tony, huh?" Rose whispered forcefully, pushing her face halfway into the SUV. "Get a significant job so you can be a real man and support your family properly? And where are you *really* going, huh? Going to see Cam or Monique or some other hussy I don't even know about?" She shook her finger. "Well, don't get sentimental and stick her for free. Get paid in cash up front."

"You're insane," Tony declared through clenched teeth, "but God help us both. Take the kids home but remember what I said." He yanked the gearshift and drove away.

Rose walked toward her SUV and the twins. She reached into her purse for her remote and disarmed the vehicle. "Get in," she commanded. "Now."

Five minutes later she cruised north on Hyde Park Avenue in silence feeling depressed and lonely. Usually the children argued over whose turn it was to sit in the front seat with her. This time they both rode in the back seat with their heads down, their mobile telephones in their hands and their thumbs rapidly moving, firing off text messages. Rose suspected they were actually texting each other.

She wondered how had things deteriorated between her and Tony so quickly. She had never seen him so angry. She couldn't fathom why he didn't recognize their problems stemmed from his career choice and the financial hole it created for their family. She waited for a light to turn green and pondered their situation.

Now that she thought about it, everything started to change after he started sleeping with Cam. Was Cam behind all this, she wondered? Was Cam poisoning Tony's mind against his own wife after the two lovers exhausted each other physically? She resolved to find out. She'd confront Cam very soon and straighten her out about a few things—without jeopardizing the remaining six months of their arrangement, of course.

NINETEEN: TENSION

Cam placed the paper spreadsheet on top of the desk. After a vigorous morning workout in her home gym, followed by a shower and change into a comfortable UCLA sweatshirt and sweatpants, she had been working in her home office for over three hours. With the curtains spread wide open and the blinds up, the generous afternoon sun obviated the need for the use of any electrical lights. Cam picked up the telephone receiver and spoke only one word. "Yes?" She waited for a reply from her full-time administrative assistant and friend, who worked in the adjoining room.

"I know you said you didn't want to be disturbed," said Lakshmi, a middle-aged woman whose faint accent betrayed her East Indian origin, "but it's Zoë."

"Zoë?" Cam asked. "At this time of day?"

"I wouldn't bother you but the poor child sounds so...so...I don't know..."

Cam nodded. "You did the right thing. I'll talk to her." She grabbed a remote to halt the quiet harp serenade coming from the stereo in the corner. It took another few seconds to fit a headset over her thick mound of hair, tied into a ponytail, before pressing the button on the telephone base. "Hello."

"Hi Aunt Cam."

"Hi there, sweetie," Cam said, trying a little too hard to sound cheerful. "I happen to know Boston schools are on vacation this week—but you're not." She checked the clock on the wall. "It's almost twelve noon. Are you at school? Is it lunch?"

"No," Zoë said. "Adam and me, I mean Adam and I, we got sent home yesterday...for fighting."

Cam gasped. "Fighting? Are you two alright?"

"Um-hmm, but Mom and Dad had to come get us and everything."

Cam breathed a sigh of relief and listened while Zoë told her the entire story. She rolled her eyes when the girl recounted the part about the secret of her flute being revealed to Tony. Rose would never learn. "So when are you and Adam going back to school?"

"Tomorrow."

"Really?"

"Yeah," Zoë said. "Dad called some hotshot lawyer friend and she called the school and made some noise. A friend of mine who's a student aide at the office called and whispered to me that the school was contacted by a lawyer for each of the two boys as well."

Cam chuckled. "Whoa. Times have sure changed from when I was your age. It used to be when you got in trouble at school your parents sided with the teachers."

"Not at BIA," Zoë declared. "Ms. Fox called Mom at work about a half-hour ago, and Mom called home and told Adam today's a cooling off period; but tomorrow everybody goes back to school and, you know, stay clear of each other, behave ourselves, blah, blah, blah."

"Is this going to be on your record?"

"Yes and no," Zoë reported. "They're going to hold the whole thing over our heads for one year, and if we don't get into any more trouble it'll be expunged."

Cam sighed. "What did your mom and dad say about all this?" She heard nothing and adjusted the earpiece of her headset. "Zoë, are you there?"

"Something's going on," Zoë said in a hushed voice.

Cam stood and began to pace. "What do you mean, something's going on?"

"Something between mom and dad. Something serious."

"Something like what?"

"I'm not sure," Zoë replied. "They don't argue in front of us but the tension between them, it's bad."

Cam inhaled and exhaled, then returned to her seat. "Well, they'll work it out, sweetheart. Even the best marriages go through a rough patch or two."

"Aunt Cam."

"Yes, doll?"

"This whole thing, it's my fault, isn't it?"

Cam could hear sadness in the girl's voice and wished she could wrap her arms around her and comfort her. "No, of course not."

Zoë spoke a little louder. "Mom said it was. When we were alone she said if I hadn't made such a big fuss over my flute none of this would have happened."

Cam rolled her eyes again and shook her head. "She didn't mean it. She was just upset."

"And there's something else."

"Something else?"

"Pedro was there."

Cam tapped her lips with her index finger, trying to place the name. "That's the boy you're sweet on, right?"

"Yeah, kinda. He didn't do anything to help me," Zoë whined. "When those boys were throwing my flute back and forth, he just stood there and watched like the rest of them. He hasn't even called. I called and texted him but he hasn't answered."

Cam heard the quiver in the child's voice and felt sympathy for her. She didn't know what to say, so she said nothing. After a few seconds Zoë broke the silence.

"And I had even let him kiss me."

Cam felt a rush of sympathy. "Oh, sweetie, I'm so sorry."

"I guess it's best I found out about him before...before we got too serious."

Cam smiled. The girl would recover in a few days or weeks but didn't need to hear that right now. She just needed someone to listen. Speaking of someone, she decided to make one more pitch for Rose. "Zoë, don't you think you should give your mother a chance to help by, you know, sharing your hurt?"

"I told you, Aunt Cam, she doesn't listen."

"Okay," Cam said. A flashing red light on the base of her telephone directed her attention to another line. She read the caller ID information. "Hang on a sec." She pressed a button to mute the sound so Zoë couldn't hear her, then jumped out of her chair, opened the door connecting her large office with the smaller one next door and whispered to Lakshmi. "Tell Rose I'm on the phone and will call her back in a few minutes."

Lakshmi, a short, attractive woman in her thirties, sat at her cluttered desk with her back to the door. She held a remote in her left hand, having just muted the sound of a thirteen-inch television airing the latest entertainment news. She also wore a headset and responded to Cam's request by looking over her shoulder and nodding.

Cam closed the door and returned to Zoë. "Honey, your mother's on the other line. I'm going to call her back later. When I do, is it okay to mention that you called me?"

"No!"

Cam frowned. "I'm happy to be here for you, sweetie, but you might find if you give your mother a chance she'll be able to provide what only a mother can."

"Please, Aunt Cam," Zoë pleaded. "I don't want her to know I called you."

Cam shrugged with resignation. "I don't like keeping this from her but okay." She glanced at the desk calendar. "I'm going to be in New York for a few days but I'll return on Sunday. You know you can call me on my mobile phone if you need to." They talked for a few more minutes, long enough for Cam to assure Zoë she would come to watch her perform at a school event the following month. After saying goodbye Cam pressed the intercom button. "Did Rose leave a message?"

"That's putting it mildly," Lakshmi replied. "She said to call her right away."

*

Six days later on the last afternoon in April, Cam and Rose sat in the family TV room at Rose's home. They both wore jeans and other casual attire. Cam listened patiently while Rose proudly touted the technology behind the Monroe family's latest acquisition: a new fifty-four inch television. Rose jumped into a comfortable, well-worn reclining chair and pointed the remote at the screen, surfing stations to demonstrate the machine's various features. Before that, she had closed the curtains to cover the massive windows that took up significant space among the three outside walls of the former sun room.

Cam dropped onto the sofa next to Rose and smiled with appreciation while privately musing that her best friend put too much stock in material items; of course she declined to express her sentiments. Finally, a few minutes after three o'clock Rose ended her presentation by selecting a jazz music station and lowering the volume, which allowed the two friends to catch up on current events. Cam spoke briefly about her business trip to New York before steering the conversation back to the twins. "So Adam insisted on staying after school with Zoë while she rehearses, huh?"

Rose nodded. "Yeah. He's been real protective of her since that incident with those two punks. Jia-Li's playing piano for the event too, so her mother's going to bring all three home. That won't be until nearly six. Tony won't be home until after four."

Cam smiled, sharing Rose's obvious pride in her son. "That Adam is a real prince, just like his dad." She immediately felt uneasy about her remark. Before their arrangement, her compliment would have been simply acknowledged as a factual statement, but under the circumstances praising Tony took on a different meaning. Cam also felt apprehensive about where the conversation *wasn't* going. Rose had asked to see her, saying it was important but had not yet stated why. After a few more minutes of chatter Cam decided to tacitly admit defeat and broach the subject.

"I'm sorry I couldn't get over here sooner," she moaned for the second time since arriving, "but with my trip and all...you know." She shrugged. "So what was so important you didn't want to discuss it over the phone?"

Rose twisted her mouth from side to side, then shook her head. "I thought I could trust you, Cam. After all, you're supposed to be my best friend."

Cam nodded. "Of course you can trust me. Why would you think otherwise?"

"Well, you might as well know," Rose said. "Tony and I are having some, um, well issues, and I think it's because of you."

Cam felt her breathing become labored. Did Rose know she and Tony had fallen in love? Not knowing what to say, she just pointed at herself and replied in a soft voice, "Me?"

Rose pointed as well. "Yes, you. I'm just going to ask you straight out: Have you been seeing Tony behind my back outside of our agreed upon date?"

Cam shook her head. "No. I've adhered to our agreement." She knew better than to add how difficult it had become to do so.

Rose cranked her neck with obvious indignation. "Have you been speaking against me, poisoning Tony against his wife and the mother of his children, after I made the ultimate sacrifice and let him climb into your bed and bring you comfort and pleasure as only Tony Monroe can?"

Cam shook her head again. "No, of course not. I would never do that. I swear."

Rose leaned forward. "You know, at one time Tony wanted to pull out—in more ways than one, and I talked him into staying because we're in a jam and I put my family's needs first, and I admit I wanted to help you because you're my best friend, but now I'm thinking about pulling the plug on this myself."

Cam covered the bottom half of her face with her hands, then removed them. "What's happened to make you want to hurt me like this, Rose?"

"I want to know," Rose demanded, "what has Tony told you about me?"

"Nothing."

"Nothing?"

Cam gulped. "Nothing, I swear. We never openly said so but we have this unspoken agreement not to talk about you or your marriage at all. You know how Tony is. You know his sense of honor."

"Well," Rose resumed, "what have you told him? Have you revealed things I've shared with you in confidence? You've told Tony about a few measly things I've bought over the years I didn't tell him about?"

Cam wondered if Tony would share the characterization about Rose's massive spending as "a few measly things" but kept the question to herself. She understood the position of power Rose welded. Cam answered Rose's question softly. "I haven't told him anything."

"You're not being honest," Rose insisted, "and after I loaned him to you. How many years have I sat with you and held you while you cried your eyes out over some no-good bum who mistreated you or used you? And did I say 'I told you so' even once after Vincent showed his true colors, which everyone could see but you?"

As a matter of fact you did, Cam thought but again kept quiet.

"And because you're like a sister to me I agreed to let you sleep with the man I love. And why? Because you needed him."

Cam pointed. "But it was your idea."

"Did you tell him about that?" Rose growled, raising her voice.

Cam shook her head vigorously. "No, no, no. I swear. He believes this whole thing was my idea and I've never said anything to contradict his belief. When you called and told me Tony was finally on board I said he doesn't have to know, remember?"

"Then what do you talk about—when you're not doing the horizontal dance, that is?"

Cam shrugged. "We talk about everything, I guess. You know: our work, the twins, history, travelling, our families—but not you, sports, our past, politics, everything."

"Everything but me."

"That's right."

"Because the woman he's been married to for fourteen years doesn't understand him."

"He's never said that."

"Because his wife has gotten fat, and nags him and doesn't provide him with 'fuck me whenever you want to' privileges."

"You're not fat, Rose," Cam retorted. "And Tony's never complained about you. He's too good a man. You know that."

"And you didn't tell him how I had to scare that bitch Monique out of this house by showing her one of our butcher knives?"

"Oh God no," Cam exclaimed. "I was shocked when you told me the truth about that."

"The hell with this," Rose said. She got on her feet. "I'm going to tell Tony to just forget this whole thing."

Cam stood as well and hugged Rose. "There's no need for that." She stepped back but extended her arms, holding Rose by the shoulders and made eye contact with her best friend only briefly. She lowered her head and her voice. "If it's the money, well, maybe I could pay off a bill for you or give you a little extra, um, just between us. Tony never counts the money, you know." She saw the corners of Rose's lips curl upward just slightly.

Rose nodded. "Well, that might help, but I need you to build me up a bit with Tony."

Cam blinked a couple of times. "What do you mean?"

"I want you to remind him how fortunate he is to have two beautiful kids and a wife who's devoted to him—even though he's not providing for us like he should."

"But," Cam replied and released Rose, "isn't it more important he's doing something he loves and he's helping to shape the next generation?"

"Let someone else save the world," Rose snapped. "I've got two kids I'm going to have to put through private college in a few years."

Just for a second Cam considered telling Rose perhaps it would help to stop spending money she doesn't have, but she kept that belief to herself as well. She was in love with Tony and admired him for his choice of profession. She couldn't reveal either sentiment to Rose for fear of losing Tony. Cam understood she would have to give Tony up in six months but wanted to worry about that in six months. Right now, she needed him and although he never overtly verbalized it, she believed he needed her too.

Rose continued. "You above everyone else should know how men are. They have to be handled right or they do stupid things we women have to—" She stopped talking and stared at the doorway.

Cam turned to see what had seized Rose's attention. The sight of the man leaning against the door frame with his arms folded across his chest alarmed and excited her. "Oh, hello there, Tony."

Tony said nothing.

Rose rushed over to him. "What are you doing home so early? I thought you were going to play basketball with your friends? I mean, you're not sick or anything, are you?" She put her hand on his forehead.

"I'm fine."

Rose kissed him on the cheek. "I thought you weren't going to be home until four."

"So I need to punch a clock when I leave and come home?"

Cam could feel the tension between them. Still, the sight of Tony, in his sleeveless sweatshirt that revealed his muscles, made her weak in the knees. It had been ten long days since they had made love. She had stopped trying to satisfy herself with her collection of "personal massagers" because they made her miss him even more. She wanted to rush into his arms, kiss him, and drag him to the nearest bed even if it was the one he shared with Rose. "How are you, Tony?"

Tony answered with one word without looking at her. "Fine."

Rose spoke with an uncharacteristically high-pitched voice. "How long have you been standing there, honey?"

"Long enough."

Cam visually searched the room. "I must have left my handbag near the front door." She passed Tony and they made very brief eye contact. "I guess I better get going." She couldn't tell how much he had heard—and if what he had heard would affect his feelings for her. To answer the first question she'd have to wait a few hours or a day until Rose told her. To answer the second she'd have to wait for nearly three weeks.

TWENTY: MAN TO MAN

A little after nine o'clock that same evening Tony corrected papers in his home office while seated behind his desk; he wore a white cotton T-shirt and a pair of plaid pajama pants. His task consumed more time than it should have because his thoughts repeatedly turned to the troubling aspects of his personal life. After Cam had left, he and Rose had spent the remainder of the afternoon and evening virtually ignoring each other. To his regret, they had become distant roommates rather than husband and wife, their mutual bitterness and disappointment toward each other simmering below the surface like water boiling in a lidded pot.

Tony returned his attention to his task and grimaced at the spelling errors in a one-sentence answer written by an eleventh-grader. Still, he gave the student full credit because the answer was technically correct. His thoughts gravitated toward the conversation he had overheard between Rose and Cam a few hours earlier. So it had been Rose's idea to rent him out to Cam, not Cam's, as both had led him to believe. Also, Rose had indeed threatened Monique with a knife just as Monique had claimed. He owed his impetuous colleague an apology but would be unable to tender one, lest he be accused of being disloyal to his wife. Throw in Rose spending thousands of dollars on that damn flute for Zoë behind his back and it added up to one inescapable conclusion: He was married to a woman he couldn't trust.

Then there was Cam. She had participated in deceiving him but not without prodding from Rose, who had always been the dominant player between the two friends. He loved Rose in spite of herself but he was in love with Cam. Truth be revealed, presently he preferred Cam's company because she expressed her feelings honestly and she loved him unconditionally. Besides, he could sure use some hot, steamy, hair pulling, nail digging, F-word shouting sex right now, and that spelled C-A-M.

The sentiment caused his penis to twitch and struggle against the confines of his briefs. Tony grunted from unfulfilled desire. He had always possessed a strong libido, which his once a month meetings with Cam inadequately satiated. He and Rose still slept in the same bed but they occupied opposite sides like two boxers after hearing the bell announcing the end of a round. Tony sighed with sexual frustration. He would have to wait three more weeks to see Cam but resolved the next time they got together he'd let her have it but good.

He dropped his red pen onto the desk and rubbed his chin between his thumb and index finger, pondering his options. Actually, he didn't have to deny himself. Monique obviously wanted him and could be his for the asking. Tony closed his eyes and recalled their kiss: her arms around his neck, her tongue probing the inside of his mouth, her moans. He shook his head to banish the memory. He wouldn't tempt fate. No telling what would emerge if he opened that Pandora's Box. Wasn't his life complicated enough?

A soft commotion outside the door caused him to blink. He stuffed his bare feet snugly inside his bedroom slippers and rose from his chair. The voices sounded restrained but angry. Tony felt himself becoming slightly annoyed for being interrupted. He walked to the door and slowly opened it. "Somebody want to tell me what's going on?" he asked the pajama-clad combatants.

Adam lowered his head. "Nothing, Dad."

Rose nudged Adam into the room. "Your son needs to talk to you, man to man."

Adam gritted his teeth. "Mom, it's nothing."

Rose rolled her eyes. "Do I need to leave and come back with your laundry?"

"No!" Adam growled. "Dang, Mom, why don't you stay out of my business?"

"Adam!" Tony barked. He took a deep breath to contain his own anger, then spoke slowly while staring at his son. "Okay, something's going on, something obviously upsetting because you've lost your mind, speaking to your mother that way, especially knowing doing so puts you in serious trouble with me."

Adam closed his eyes. "I'm sorry, but why can't everyone just leave me alone?"

Rose approached Adam and gently pulled his ear. "Because we love you." She turned and stepped across the threshold into the hall. "Talk to your father. Here's one subject he knows a lot about." With that, she closed the door behind her.

Tony recognized Rose's remark as sarcasm, not a compliment, but dismissed it. Rather than return to the padded chair behind his desk he sat in one of two chairs in front of his desk and motioned for Adam to take the other. "So what's going on, son?"

Adam sat but kept his face down. "Nothing."

Tony tapped Adam on the knee. "Take as much time as you need but..." He paused. "...you're not leaving this room until you tell me."

After about twenty torturous seconds of silence, Adam spoke, his voice barely above a whisper. "For some reason...out of the blue...I've been..." He glanced at the door.

"It's okay," Tony guaranteed. "It's just you and me."

"I can't say it, Dad," Adam moaned. Tears rolled down his face.

"I'm here, son," Tony said. Another several seconds of silence followed. The sight of Adam in distress caused him great pain. Whatever Adam revealed they would face it together. Maybe he should say that. No, better not to say—

"I-I've been wetting the bed."

Tony felt shock at such a revelation but didn't let it show on his face. "Really?"

"Yes, Dad." Adam whimpered. "Wetting the bed like a toddler...only it's not urine. It's thick and white, and it happens when I have these-these-these dreams."

Tony felt profound relief. "Oh."

Adam finally raised his head. "Oh! Is that all? Oh? It's because you're ashamed of me, aren't you? I-I don't blame you. I'm ashamed of myself. So ashamed I wish I could melt into this chair and disappear." He covered his face with his hands.

Tony shook his head. "I'm not ashamed of you, son, and you've no reason to be."

Adam lowered his hands. "Even though there's obviously something wrong with me?"

Tony shook his head again. "There's nothing wrong with you."

"There isn't?"

"No," Tony assured his only son. "In fact, it's exactly the opposite. "You're experiencing puberty. Your body is changing from a boy to a man. All humans go through puberty. Girls get their periods and boys, well, many boys, go through this." He snickered. "Thank the Lord males go through this phase only for a while when we're teens. Females endure that period thing several days a month for decades."

Adam smiled. "You mean it's normal?"

Tony nodded. "Normal as the sun rising in the morning and setting in the evening."

Adam ran his hands over his head, covered with a one inch thick carpet of hair. "But I wake up with my underwear wet."

Tony nodded. "It's semen. The doctors call it nocturnal emissions, or wet dreams. You're ejaculating because your body is producing sperm."

"And," Adam said, "oh lord, my..." He pointed at his crotch. "My...my..."

"Your penis."

"My penis is getting hard all the time no matter where I am. I can't control it."

"Again, all perfectly natural."

"Do all men go through this, Dad?"

"To one extent or another."

"Did you?"

"Yes," Tony confessed without hesitating. "And I didn't take it any better than you at the time." He laughed. "I secretly tossed my underwear in the garbage and bought new ones with my own money—my precious video game money."

Father and son talked for several minutes about the male human body. Adam asked questions and Tony answered.

Adam closed his eyes. "Dad, the dreams. I mean especially the last one, there was this girl and oh my, she was so beautiful." He opened his eyes. "She crawled into bed with me and she told me she loved me and we..." He clasped his hands together."...we did it over and over. I woke up and felt ashamed for, um, ejaculating but I felt so good at the same time. You know what I mean?"

Tony nodded. "I do."

The two Monroe males talked further about sex and girls—and the misinformation exchanged between ignorant boys at school about both.

Adam leaned forward. "Dad, can I ask you about something else?"

"Of course."

"Have you ever been interested in two girls at the same time?"

Son, Tony thought, you don't know the half of it. He shrugged. "Oh, I suppose. Why?"

"Well," Adam said, "there are these two girls. You met them. They came to our birthday party. Well, I kinda started seeing this girl named Doneesha; she goes to our church. But I don't think she's right for me. I really like her but not like a girlfriend. But the other girl, her name's Lucy and she goes to BIA. I think I'd like to see her."

Tony opened his hands. "And your question is?"

"Is it okay to break up with Doneesha and start seeing Lucy?"

"Is that what you honestly want to do?"

Adam rubbed his lips with his fingers before answering. "Yes, Doneesha's nice, but she's not for me, you know what I'm saying?"

"I think so," Tony said. "You're at an age when you're becoming interested in girls. God has blessed you: You're smart and handsome. Girls are going to flock to you like bees to flowers." He shook his finger. "Just be honest with them and with yourself. Don't be one of those who keep several women at the same time by lying to them. That's no good."

"Did you ever do that?"

Tony nodded and frowned. "Been there, done that, got the T-shirt—and got my face slapped for it. I wished I hadn't."

"Wish you hadn't lied or got your face slapped?"

"Both," Tony said. He rubbed his fingers against his cheek. "But the second certainly contributed to the first."

Adam laughed. "Mom's not going to like me seeing Lucy."

Tony shrugged. "We've only met her once. What's not to like?"

Adam shook his head. "Maybe I shouldn't say this but after the party Mom told me she didn't want me with no white girl—but Lucy's actually Latina."

Puppy love, Tony thought. A few weeks, a few months and it would be over anyway. "Well," he said, "as long as she's got a good heart and respects who you are..." He stopped and glanced at the wall clock. "It's getting late. You better get ready for bed." He stood. Adam stood as well and they both walked to the door. Tony put his hand on Adam's shoulder. Adam responded by gently clutching Tony's wrist. They made eye contact. "I love you, son, and I'm proud of you. I know I can be hard on you sometimes but that's just because I want you to turn out right."

"I know," Adam said and hugged Tony. "I love you, Dad. You're the greatest father in the world. Thank you for being here for me today."

Tony wrapped his arms around Adam. "Today, and tomorrow and all the tomorrows." He kissed Adam on the forehead and watched him open and close the door.

Tony beamed with pride. My boy is going to be a fine young man, he thought. Got a good head on his shoulders. Not shallow like Rose can be, especially about money. He heard a knock and saw the door being opened. Adam stuck his head back into the room.

"Hey, Dad," he whispered, grinning widely. "Did I mention that Lucy's family is filthy stinking rich?"

Tony laughed. "Good night, Adam." After watching the door being closed again he pointed at his reflection in the full-length mirror near the door and muttered, "Dispensing advice about women, huh? Physician, heal thyself!"

*

On the first Thursday afternoon in May Tony pressed buttons on the telephone in his classroom. The school day had ended twenty minutes before. He stood next to the chair behind his desk feeling nervous and apprehensive, as if calling for the results of a tax audit.

Three rings preceded an answer. "Hello, this is Robert Kwan."

Tony swallowed. "Good afternoon Mr. Kwan. This is Tony Monroe. I'm a teacher at Alexander Hamilton High School here in Boston. We spoke back in February when I was being considered for that presidential commission on education."

"Yes. How are you, Mr. Monroe?"

Tony shrugged. "I'm fine, thank you, busy of course. How are you?"

"Same here. Busy."

Satisfied with the disposal of amenities, Tony got down to business. "I'm returning your call, although I confess I was surprised to hear from you. I mean, I mentioned to you a couple of months ago that, for personal reasons, I would like my name removed from the list of potential nominees—although I was of course, honored to be considered."

"I remember," Kwan said, "but someone whose pay grade is higher than mine told me not to remove your name. It appears you've got friends in high places."

Tony recalled being told the superintendent of Boston Public Schools and the secretary of the U.S. Department of Education had been college friends. "I'm flattered."

"Actually," Kwan said, "you're background cleared."

Tony exhaled. Apparently his relationship with Cam had flown below the Department of Homeland Security radar. He wondered if Rose would be pleased or displeased about him possibly serving on the commission. He knew Cam would be thrilled. Still, something in Kwan's voice indicated he was withholding something. "So is that why you called? To tell me I'm in the clear?"

"Yes and no," Kwan replied. "You see, the administration's new transparency policy allows us here at DHS to disclose limited portions of our background checks to those being vetted. And rest assured, we don't disclose what we find to anyone else like the IRS, or Immigration, or your employer, or anything like that."

"I've got nothing to hide," Tony declared.

"I'm sure. How about we meet in person?"

Tony raised one eyebrow, surprised by the suggestion. "Sure, that would be fine."

"Great," Kwan declared. "I'll bring you a copy of my report. Some of it will be redacted, of course, but you might find it interesting."

Tony nodded. Clearly, there was something in the report the man wanted him to see. "If it's okay with you we can meet some evening next week."

"How about a week from today or next Friday?" Kwan asked.

"Next Friday works for me," Tony said. The two men worked out the time and place before ending their call. Tony placed the receiver in its cradle and scratched his head. He squeezed his lips between his thumb and index finger while replaying the conversation in his head. "What the hell was that all about?"

*

Eight days later, a few minutes before six p.m. Tony sat at a small table in a coffee shop located within a medium-size bookstore. He passed the time by pressing one of the five buttons on the wristwatch Rose had given him for his fortieth birthday last month. An attractive but complicated digital wonder, it contained features Tony still hadn't completely divined. Knowing Rose, it had probably cost a fortune, he thought.

He had told Rose he was going to work late and perhaps catch a boys' volleyball game. "Fine" had been her unemotional response. He had indeed watched the first few minutes of the game before dashing off. Now, sitting in a public place surrounded by a dozen people, he felt terribly lonely—and hungry. He had not yet eaten dinner, and the smell and sights of various foods and beverages on display caused him to take more notice of his empty stomach and spirit. God, one more week before he would see Cam.

Tony surreptitiously examined the faces of the patrons, oblivious to his presence; virtually every one tapped on a telephone, tablet or some other electronic device. The bookstore was located in a mall three miles from his school but, he assumed, there was not much chance he would catch one of his students in a bookstore on a Friday evening. Only four of ten tables in the coffee shop were taken, including his. Three customers stood in line a few feet away waiting to order something to eat and/or drink. Soothing classical music flowed from the overhead speakers. Tony couldn't name the composer but suspected Zoë would probably know. He leaned right slightly to admire the parquet floor, which contrasted with the carpeting that covered most of the bookstore's floor. Good quality work.

"Mr. Monroe?"

Tony raised his head to see a handsome man in his late thirties standing before him. The man wore a blue pinstripe suit and a thick mop of black hair conservatively cut. Tony got on his feet, steadied his swinging tie and extended his hand. "Mr. Kwan I presume?"

The man nodded. Standing nearly six feet tall, he switched the briefcase he carried from his right hand to his left and shook Tony's hand. "Yes, and please call me Robert."

"Okay, and it's Tony." He gestured. "Sit down, please."

After an initial few minutes of small talk over coffee Tony discovered the two had a natural chemistry and a great deal in common. They ordered croissant sandwiches and sodas, and chatted like men who had been acquainted for years: about their education, their faith in God, their taste in automobiles, their mutual love of history—Robert had also been a history major in college—and their mutual love of basketball.

Robert checked his watch. "It's after seven. I'm sorry, I didn't mean to keep you." He reached inside the briefcase he had positioned between his black wing-tipped shoes and produced a manila folder. "Here's the redacted report I promised you." He laid it on the table but placed his hand over it to keep Tony from opening it. "Before you look at it, let me tell you a quick story: I used to be married but not anymore."

Tony noted the sadness in the man's brown eyes and shook his head. "I'm sorry to hear that."

Robert took a sip of his coffee. "The most beautiful woman I've ever seen and a hard worker, but she was a big spender. Not only that, she lied to me about it for years."

Tony arched one of his eyebrows and squirmed in his chair. "I see. You've seen my finances. You know I'm a bit overextended myself but I'm taking care of it."

Robert nodded. "I know, but I've been doing this long enough to recognize when one spouse is hiding things from another: an affair, a shady past, whatever."

"And you take it upon yourself to tell the other spouse?"

Robert laughed and stood. "No. I take it upon myself to tell the *husband*, you know, man to man." He checked his watch again. "I didn't mean to keep you so long." He held out his hand to keep Tony from rising. "Don't get up. I'm giving you the information. What you do with it is up to you." He shook Tony's hand. "It was a pleasure to meet you. Good luck on the commission." Those were his last words before he turned and left.

Tony watched the man stride several yards down a long aisle and eventually disappear. An interesting gentleman, he thought. Had they met under different circumstances they probably would have become good friends. They still might.

He picked up the folder and began reading.

TWENTY-ONE: CONFRONTED

Rose lay on top of her bed, which was still made up. The lamp on each nightstand offered enough light for her to examine a home decorating magazine. The closed door prevented the lingering aroma of broiled haddock, which she and the twins had eaten two hours earlier, from entering the bedroom. Rose turned a page before checking the silent clock radio next to the bed: nearly eight o'clock in the evening. Ten minutes earlier Tony had called, saying he would be home soon. He and "Robert, a new friend" had stopped somewhere for a bite to eat. Rose had responded to his report with a one word grunt: "Fine."

She lay on her side in her pajamas glancing at photos of beautifully manicured lawns and flower gardens, but her thoughts focused on how to break the lingering stalemate with Tony. She would definitely have to step up her game, thereby prodding him to make the first move toward reconciliation. Rose flipped her magazine over and considered turning on the forty-inch television located on the other side of the room. Instead, she chose to ponder the time-honored words of her mother.

"Don't go running behind no man crying and begging him to forgive you," Mom had repeatedly admonished both her daughters beginning in their early teens. "We're stronger than they are, not physically, but mentally, so hold out and eventually he'll come to you."

Rose rubbed her sock-covered feet together to warm them. The mid-May evening temperature had dipped into the upper fifties, thus lowering the temperature in the house to the upper sixties. She rolled over onto her back and nodded, silently concurring with the advice from her mother.

For as long as she and Tony had been a couple, after a few days of silence following a quarrel Tony would usually approach her and moan something like, "Baby, we can't go on like this." Rose would relish her victory privately but outwardly offer Tony a hurt, wounded look, which always made him capitulate even more. Sometimes he had been right and she, wrong, but that didn't matter. A woman had to keep her man in line to the extent it served her purpose.

Rose resumed reading her magazine and muttered, "I didn't think you had it in you, Tony dear." That is, he had never endured her silent treatment for this long. Perhaps, as one does with medicine, he had developed a slight tolerance to her tactics. That possibility notwithstanding, a good tactician knew when to make adjustments, and that's just what she intended to do. Women possessed an arsenal of weapons: tears, pouting, silence, nagging, recruiting the children, bending the truth, and the most potent of all—her body.

Rose frowned at the thought of utilizing the last one. She would only reward Tony by spreading her legs after he promised to quit that stupid job and work toward becoming a lawyer—a corporate lawyer. Having confirmed nearly two weeks earlier Cam hadn't been slipping him a little extra nookie on the side, it was just a matter of holding out a little longer and Tony would come crawling to his wife in more ways than one. She knew her husband too well. A once a month humpfest, even with a beautiful woman like Cam, would never be enough to satisfy him. A man with his prodigious sex drive needed more, much more.

Rose thought about her own yearnings. She didn't understand why her libido had diminished so rapidly over the past couple of years. She suspected it had to do with her ever-increasing resentment toward Tony for refusing to adequately provide for his family.

She shrugged with resignation and mentally outlined her plan of attack: First, when Tony got home she wouldn't greet him at the door, a blatant violation of their longstanding practice: The spouse already home made every effort to greet the one arriving. Next, she would ignore him for the remainder of the day. Finally, once they had retired for the night she would innocently brush her hand against his abundant man tool but refuse his overtures to make love, causing him such maddening frustration he would be unable to sleep for the rest of the night. With a week to go before he and Cam would see each other, Rose knew Tony would be so full of pent up sexual energy he would practically beg Rose to put him out of his misery.

Rose grabbed a pillow, squeezed it and sighed, feelings of loneliness engulfing her like London fog in November. She wasn't one big ball of sexual energy like Tony, but she did crave affection and love. Deep down, she had to admit she longed to feel his strong arms embracing her and his soft lips pressing against her mouth and cheeks. She missed the sound of his booming baritone guffaws at her stories about the foolish customers at Emerald's.

A knock at the door brought her out of her funk. "Come in," she called.

The bedroom door was opened. Zoë stuck her head into the room. "Dad's parking the car out front."

Show time, Rose thought. "Okay...Is that all?"

"Well, I guess so," Zoë replied, with half her body still hidden. She abruptly stood erect as a chess piece and scrunched up her face. "Do you want me to leave this door open?"

"Was it already open?"

"No."

"Well, then?" Rose asked. She heard rapid footsteps behind Zoë in the hall.

Zoë turned her head before returning her attention to Rose. "I guess Adam went to see Dad in."

Rose sighed as if bored. "And you're telling me this...why?"

"Right," Zoë replied with a scowl. "Sorry to have bothered you, Mother."

Rose heard the door being slammed and Zoë's footsteps pounding against the hard wood floor, then the door to the thirteen-year-old girl's room being slammed as well. Rose shook her head. What was going on between her and her only daughter? Didn't the child appreciate how her mother had finagled to buy her that expensive flute over her father's tacit objections? Ungrateful little brat. Naturally, a child wouldn't understand the fierce battle Rose had undertaken trying to upgrade their family's standard of living. If all went according to plan Zoë and Adam would enjoy the kind of lifestyle her own parents had been unable to afford because their grandfather was such a dreamer.

Rose considered how she should present herself when Tony appeared. She grabbed a few magazines and cata- logues from the bottom shelf of the nightstand on her side of the bed and spread them out. After considering her repertoire of facial expressions, she settled for the bored, above it all look. She opened one catalogue in par- ticular and turned to a page before placing it by her feet. Hopefully Tony would notice it immediately. The photo- graphs displayed a pair of twin beds for adults. Rose smirked. That should get his attention, if not scare the hell out of him.

Rose waited...and waited. Ten minutes passed. She heard muffled sounds of voices downstairs; no doubt Tony and the twins swapping stories about their day. She felt a twinge of resentment. Perhaps Tony was trying to turn the children against her. She noticed they did seem to prefer his company to hers lately. What a way to repay the woman who had suffered so to safely carry them in- side her body? She would deal with those two later. One battle at a time; that was another thing her mother had taught her.

A buzzing sound prompted her to reach for the mobile telephone resting on her nightstand and read the caller ID information: J Rivers. Rose rolled her eyes. Flirting with him had been a mistake. She hadn't seen him in al- most three weeks, the day she had been summoned to BIA because the twins had gotten into a fight, the day he had attempted to smother—or slobber—her with kisses. Handsome but needy, he continued to call and text her. Rose frowned. Men were such animals; always thinking with their little heads instead of their big heads. She read the message—"Please call. Please."—and turned off her telephone. Next Friday after Tony got laid and paid she would settle with James and get him out of her life.

She heard Tony's footsteps as he climbed the stairs and felt a slight tingle from anticipation. "About time," she whispered, and positioned herself so her back faced the door. She considered how to play the scene, serving as actor and director: Don't even look up when he enters. She pretended to be absorbed in a magazine showcasing professional women's clothing. She heard the door being opened and closed, and felt one hundred ninety-five pounds being placed behind her knees as Tony sat on the bed. Rose interpreted the gesture as the first sign of surrender. It was almost too easy.

"Rose, I want to talk to you."

She continued staring at her magazine and heard the sound of one shoe being dropped onto the carpet, then the other. "So who's stopping you?"

"Would you give me your undivided attention, please?"

Rose couldn't tell if he had seen the twin bed catalogue but decided to make sure. "Okay, let me gather up my toys." She pointed. "Hand me that one please."

Tony complied. "I want to know..." He stopped mid-sentence.

Rose suppressed the urge to snicker as Tony stared at the catalogue. Nothing like a surprise move to throw one's opponent off his timing. "You want to know what, dear?" She drenched the last word with sarcasm as she shifted her body to face her husband.

Tony reached into his shirt pocket and produced a piece of paper which, unfolded, was about the size of his hand. "I want to know how long you've been racking up thousands of dollars worth of bills and not telling me about it?"

Shit, Rose thought, but she responded with a shrug. "I-I don't know what you're talking about."

Tony glanced at the magazines. "Now why doesn't that answer surprise me?" He ran his index finger over the paper. "Let's see, five hundred dollars owed to Lieberman's Jewelers, down from nearly four thousand back in November. Another thousand to Otra Cosa." He paused. "That's Cam's old place, right?" He didn't wait for an answer. "It was two thousand. A separate diamond credit card I didn't know anything about. You still owe them about three grand, down from about seven grand. A separate platinum credit card I didn't know anything about; three grand to clear that one, formerly sixty-five hundred. A card for some cosmetic company I can't even pronounce."

"There must be some mistake."

"Yeah. You made it," Tony replied. He returned to his list. "Now, where was I? Six hundred dollars for makeup? Talk about vanity. Five grand to some place called Panache that specializes in custom-made jewelry." He scoffed. "I must be the stupidest man in the world not to have noticed all that new jewelry. Well, that will change." He ran his finger over the list to mark where he had left off. "A secret post office box, two credit cards for places that turned out to be women's boutiques." He tossed the paper, which bounced off Rose's left breast and rested on the bed. "You've been busy—and I've been a damn fool."

Rose could feel her heart pounding. She would have to think fast. Better to take the offense. She sat up. "So it's come to this? You've been spying on me?" She pointed at the paper. "I have to look professional for my job. What's the big deal?"

"The big deal is," Tony snarled, "that you've been lying to me, just like you did about that flute for Zoë—for which we still owe a bundle, as well."

"Nobody's been lying to you," Rose declared, raising her voice. "I handle the bills so I don't tell you every little detail. You're so busy correcting papers and going to volleyball games and tending to your precious students that I have to see to this house and the kids."

Tony shook his head. "You amaze me, Rose," he growled, likewise raising his voice. "You're starting to act like a politician who believes her own bullshit."

Rose rolled over and stood so that the king-sized bed separated them. She grabbed the pile of magazines and threw them onto the bottom shelf of the nightstand on Tony's side of the bed. She pushed her hair away from her eyes, pointed at him and exclaimed, "I don't like the idea of my own husband snooping on me. It's unseemly. Whatcha do? Pay some goon in a trench coat to check up on me, your own wife?"

"No," Tony answered. "A man from Homeland Security gave me a report."

Rose grimaced. "Homeland Security? But you told him to take your name off the list of people considered for that damn commission."

"I did."

"And?"

"He didn't."

"And why not?"

Tony shrugged with exaggeration. "Oh I don't know. Maybe telling him my wife won't let me come out and play wasn't a good enough excuse."

Rose didn't like the direction of the conversation. She had expected Tony to be on the defense, but he had taken the offense. Time to dig into her arsenal. Dig deep. She sauntered around the bed and eased forward until literally bumping into Tony. She spoke in a sultry, hushed tone. "I've been a naughty girl, haven't I?" To complete the transformation she nuzzled Tony's chin with her nose. "I'm going to have to be punished, I suppose." She hooked her arms under Tony's, then kissed his cheek a couple of times and pulled on his ear with her teeth. "Don't be too hard on me," she whispered, "—or better yet, be as hard as you want." She traced the inseam of his pants with her index finger.

"Where are the bills, Rose?"

She blinked. "What bills?"

Tony gently nudged Rose backward until she stood at arm's length. He pointed. "The bills on that paper."

Rose could see the smoldering anger in Tony's eyes and stuttered a reply while looking away. "I-I-I don't know." She closed in on Tony again, took his face in her hands and kissed him softly on the mouth. "Let's talk about that later," she added and let out a long sigh. "Oh baby," she moaned. "I've missed your love. Where are the kids? Lock the door. We don't want them to hear—"

"Where are the goddamn bills, Rose?" Tony snapped loudly.

Rose released him, humiliated and angry. "At work in my desk."

"You're lying."

"How dare you!" Rose shouted. "I'm your wife."

"We'll talk about *that* later," Tony retorted. "Right now, I want to know where the bills are. And I mean *all* of them" He spoke through gritted teeth. "Are you going to tell me or am I going to have to tear this whole house apart looking for them?"

Confused and angry, Rose made a mistake by glancing at her bottom dresser drawer.

Tony arched his eyebrows and approached the dresser. "Are they in here?" He reached for the bottom drawer.

"No! Stop!" Rose shrieked. "Damn you, Tony. I told you they're at work. I'll give them to you on Monday.

What's the hurry? Seriously, what difference does it make if—"

A knock on the door interrupted Rose's protest. Sensing a saving measure of serendipity, she called to Zoë or Adam to enter.

Adam slowly eased open the door. He wore blue jeans and a Boston International Academy sweat shirt. He spoke very tentatively, his voice shaking with apprehension. "Mom, Dad..."

"Go downstairs, Adam," Tony commanded. "Your mother and I have to talk."

"I know," Adam retorted. "We can hear you."

"It's for your mother and me to sort out, son," Tony said, his voice softer. "And we will. Now please, go downstairs and stay there and tell your sister to do the same."

Rather than obey, Adam stepped into the room. "Zoë's gone. She left."

Rose's anger immediately shifted to concern. "What do you mean, she left?"

Adam shrugged. "I mean she left the house about a couple of minutes ago in tears."

Rose pointed at the window. "It's dark out there. And didn't you see the news on TV the other day about some pervert in the neighborhood who's been flashing young girls?" She grabbed Adam by the shoulders and shook him. "And you just let her leave?"

"Rose!" Tony called, and stepped between his wife and son.

Adam lowered his head. "I tried to stop her," he whined, "but I couldn't. She said she couldn't stand it anymore and just stormed out."

Tony turned to face Adam. "On foot?"

"She rode off on her bike."

"Does she have her phone with her?" Rose asked.

Adam nodded. "I think so, I've called but she doesn't answer."

Rose grabbed Tony's arm. "We have to go get her!" she whimpered.

Tony shook his head. "Not we. You stay here in case she comes back. Keep calling her." He sat on the bed and put his shoes back on.

"I'll go with you," Adam insisted.

"No, stay here with your mother," Tony said and stood.

Adam cut him off at the door. "I've never disobeyed you, Dad, but if you don't let me go with you, the minute you leave I'll get my bike and go look for her myself."

Tony gritted his teeth. "Adam, do what I tell you."

Adam's eyes filled with water. "Please, Dad."

Rose stared at her son and recognized the boy was wracked with guilt from being unable to prevent Zoë from leaving. "Maybe he should go with you, Tony," she suggested. Besides, it would be easier to find a hiding place for her bills if she were alone in the house.

"Okay," Tony agreed and placed his hand on Adam's shoulder. "We'll find her together." He nodded to Rose. "We'll find her," he declared and raced out the door with Adam behind him.

Rose fell back onto the bed and pushed her hair away from her face with both hands. "Lord Jesus," she prayed, "please bring my little girl home."

TWENTY-TWO: CAM TO THE RESCUE

Cam glided through the moderate Friday evening traffic on Highway 128 but her mind wasn't completely on her driving. She changed from the right lane into the middle one to pass a slow moving pickup truck and noted the eight thirty time displayed on her dashboard GPS. She would be home in less than thirty minutes but in five minutes she would pass the Boston community of Hyde Park, where her beloved Tony lived. Although eager to get home, that feeling of emptiness since Tony kissed her goodbye three weeks earlier suddenly plagued her again. She would have to wait one more week before their scheduled meeting, a wait she found almost unbearable.

Cam attempted to distract herself by recalling the events of the past few hours. She had spent an exhilarating afternoon in the town of Canton riding a majestic Arabian filly at an exclusive equestrian club. A wealthy British mother and her mousy daughter had been her hostesses. They had persuaded Cam to design the latter's wedding dress at the last minute—at double her usual fee—after some kind of "row" with the mother's previous choice.

Cam attempted to assuage her loneliness further by remembering the shift in the conversation during dinner at a fancy country club after the mother had consumed her third martini. The attractive woman had inquired, "If you don't mind me asking, darling, who did your work?" She had followed up her query by placing her hands under her own ample bosom, pushing up and divulging, "I went to Dr. Buscemi in Sudbury. A real artist." It had taken a few seconds before Cam had understood the question. "Oh no, no," she had replied before pointing her thumbs at her chest. "These honkers are mine." Rather than be embarrassed by Cam's revelation the mother had roared with laughter and exclaimed, "You lucky, lucky angel, you!"

Cam refocused on her driving. In a few minutes she would pass the exit taking her to the Monroe house. She pressed a button on the steering wheel of her BMW sedan to turn up the radio's volume, then pressed it again, turning the sound back down when she heard a commercial for Masters Motors. Cam reflected on how fate changes life's outcomes. Had Rose chosen Phil Masters for her husband, Tony could have been hers. A young man with long black hair driving a black Dodge Charger bolted in front of her, causing her to refocus on her driving.

Cam sighed. The month of May had crept along so slowly. She longed to be with Tony right now, preferably in bed underneath him, kissing him, holding him, loving him, making love to him. A slight fear tempered her longing. She had allowed him to believe the idea for the arrangement had originated from her. Would he be angry with her? Would he be indignant enough to call off the remainder of the contract?

A ringtone of the famous allegro to Beethoven's Fifth Symphony diverted her attention. Cam grabbed her telephone headset and clipped it to her ear, then pressed a button on her steering wheel to answer the call. She read the caller ID information on her dashboard's monitor. Someone calling from a Holiday Inn? "Hello."

"Aunt Cam. This is Zoë. I'm in trouble."

Cam recognized the sound of distress in the girl's voice. "Zoë? What's the matter, doll?"

"I left the house without permission."

Well, Cam thought, it could be something much worse. "Alone?"

"Yes."

"Why honey? What happened?"

Zoë's voice broke as she explained. "Mom and Dad were arguing and I couldn't take it anymore, so I jumped on my bike and rode off."

Cam checked the time on the dashboard GPS again. "Sweetie, it's after eight thirty. You shouldn't be out alone. Now you get yourself home right now. Where are you?"

"I'm using the phone at a hotel," Zoë answered. "There were these teenage boys in an old beat up car following me, so I came in here. The desk clerk said I could use the phone. I forgot to charge mine so I can't make any calls."

Cam swallowed. "But why didn't you call your mom or dad to come get you?"

"I can't," Zoë whimpered. "They're going to be so mad at me, especially Mom."

"Well, you have to call them," Cam insisted. "They're going to be worried." Silence ensued. Cam waited a few seconds before speaking. "Zoë, are you there?"

"Yes, Aunt Cam. I was wondering if...if..."

"Yes?"

"...you'd call them for me and tell them where I am."
Cam frowned. "Oh Zoë..."

"Please, please, Aunt Cam," the girl begged. "Please. If I call home and Mom answers I'll just die."

Cam shrugged. She recognized the importance of getting Zoë home as soon as possible. "Okay. Give me the address." She pressed another button on her steering wheel and repeated the address aloud. After glancing again at her dashboard GPS she announced, "You know, I'm just about ten minutes away from where you are."

"Oh thank you, Jesus! Thank you, Jesus!" Zoë cried. "Would you take me home?"

Cam shook her head. "No, doll, but I will call your father and tell him where you are, then I'm going to call your mother."

"Would you at least wait here with me until they get here?"

Cam twisted her mouth from side to side. "It's against my better judgment, but okay." She endured a cascade of profuse thank-yous from Zoë before ending the call, slicing through the traffic into the right lane and exiting the highway.

*

Cam huddled with Zoë on a firmly padded sofa in the lobby of the hotel. They absently watched a flat screen television placed atop a stand perched on a mantle above a fake fireplace. Zoë's bicycle rested behind them leaning against the back of the sofa. A matching, empty loveseat next to them and an assortment of small tables and chairs also occupied the brightly lit, wall-to-wall carpeted area. A jovial, middle-aged female chef on television regaled an audience about the secrets to making tastier meat loaf.

Cam turned her head to the left when she heard the separating pair of glass automatic front doors. A distinguished looking older couple strolled by holding hands as if they were on their honeymoon. The sight of them made Cam joyful and sad. Would that ever be her and her man some day? Perhaps. Unfortunately, that man wouldn't be Tony.

"I'm sorry for being such a bother, Aunt Cam," Zoë whined.

"Shhh," Cam whispered, and kissed the girl on the forehead. Zoë placed her head on Cam's shoulder.

The desk clerk, a woman barely in her twenties with elaborately painted fingernails wearing a white shirt and navy blue vest, bode the elderly couple good evening as they passed her, then returned to texting on her mobile telephone.

A minute later the doors parted again, followed by the appearance of Tony and Adam. Cam and Zoë stood in unison.

Zoë lowered her head and took a couple of steps forward. She cried as Tony and Adam hugged her. "I'm sorry Daddy. I'm sorry Adam. Please don't be mad at me."

Tony squeezed his only daughter and smiled. "Oh, you little muskrat." His voice sounded reassuring. "Nobody's mad at you."

"Mom's real mad, isn't she?" Zoë asked.

"She's worried," Tony replied. "Like your brother and I have been, but right now the important thing is that you're alright."

Adam hugged his sister, then tapped her lightly on the head with his knuckles. "You're such a pest, Sis. You know you're making me miss the NBA playoff game?" He laughed.

Cam took a step back, not wanting to intrude on the family reunion. She admired the twins' closeness. Zoë even wore the same BIA sweatshirt and jeans as her brother.

After a few seconds, Tony released Adam and Zoë. "Okay, let's get you home," he commanded gently. "Adam, take your sister's bike, put it in the trunk of the car, then both of you wait for me in the car." He handed Adam the keys. "Be careful. Don't scratch the finish." He snickered before making eye contact with Cam. "I have to talk to your aunt for a minute." He approached Cam but turned to watch the twins leave before speaking. "I don't know how to thank you. I'm sorry you got dragged into our family drama." He inspected Cam, who wore a black caped jacket over a short, satiny purple dress. "You look lovely."

"Thank you," Cam said, and actually blushed. She immediately sought to assure him she had not been out on a date. "I had dinner with two charming women. I'm designing a wedding dress for the daughter." She wanted to throw her arms around his neck and kiss him but knew such a move would be inappropriate. "I'm glad I could help." She pointed. "Are you okay yourself?"

Tony nodded. "I am now. Things are...well, shaky at home."

"You know you can talk to me," Cam whispered, "about anything, anything at all, my love." She felt her heart fluttering.

Tony nodded again. "I know—and thank you again." He turned to glance at the door. "I better get my little brood home."

Cam sighed. "Can I at least get a hug?"

"If I take you in my arms, baby," Tony whispered, "I won't ever want to let go."

Cam felt disappointed but relieved. Apparently he wouldn't hold the sin of omission conspired with Rose against her. "I understand. I feel the same way. So I'll see you exactly one week from tonight." She glanced at her watch. "I rode a beautiful horse today, but that's nothing compared to how I'm going to ride you." She forcefully pulled Tony by the lapel of his jacket and whispered in his ear. "Like a fucking stallion."

Tony smiled. "Big talk."

"And I can back it up, too," Cam retorted. "Just you wait and see." The two said goodbye and Cam walked a few feet behind Tony. As she passed the desk clerk she dropped a fifty dollar bill on the counter. "Thanks for helping out my niece."

The clerk widened her eyes and picked up the bill. "Whoa!" she exclaimed. "Thank you!"

*

A week later Cam lay in bed on her side, exhausted, while holding onto Tony, who lay on his back. The love they had shared for the past hour had exceeded her expectations. Male and female bodily fluids—the product of their passion—slowly oozed out of her body. The slow moving ceiling fan fought the pungent scent of sweat and musk that saturated the area, meagerly lit by a pair of dimmed nightstand lamps. Sated for the time being, the two paramours snuggled closely and now would talk. Cam usually spoke first.

For several minutes they talked about the twins, especially Zoë; Tony had persuaded Rose not to severely punish the girl for running off. "We're as much to blame for upsetting the child," he had insisted. They eventually switched to the topic of work and their families. Cam hugged Tony and shuddered with apprehension, for she had decided to break their tacit agreement and bring up a touchy subject.

"Baby," she opened, "you know I don't usually do this, but if you want to talk about you and Rose, I'll listen." She mashed her lips together and waited.

After several seconds Tony finally replied. "It's not good. She's been lying to me probably for years. Secret credit cards, shopping sprees, a post office box." He shook his head and relayed the story about his dinner with Robert Kwan. "On Monday she gave me the bills. I don't know if she gave me all of them. I'll never be able to trust her again."

Cam considered asking why would he want to stay married to a woman whom he no longer trusted but recognized the self-serving nature of such an inquiry. Instead she asked, "So what are you going to do?"

Tony shrugged. "I don't know. We sleep in the same bed but don't go near each other. In fact, we've developed this unspoken rule to never go to bed at the same time."

Cam felt elation at that revelation but said nothing.

Tony continued. "We go to church together. We eat dinner with the kids." He sighed. "She's the mother of my children, and it would hurt them if we split up, so I guess we join the throng of married couples who stay together for the sake of the children."

"But," Cam interjected, "one day the children are going to leave home. Then what?"

"I don't know," Tony replied. "That's in five years."

"What about marriage counseling? Maybe with the pastor of your church."

"I suggested it," Tony said, "but Rose said no. She's pissed off at me. She deceives me and somehow I'm the villain. Can you freaking believe it?"

Actually, Cam thought, she could believe it, and for the first time ever she seriously considered whether Rose was the kind of person she wanted to have as a friend. They had known each other for years, but people change. Rose had always been self-absorbed and shallow—but when had she become this manipulative, lying bitch? She didn't deserve a wonderful man like Tony. Cam closed her eyes. Perhaps her fervent love for him clouded her judgment. She opened her eyes and hugged Tony again. "I'm sorry you're hurt over this, my sweet," she said. "Is there anything I can do?"

Tony hugged her back. "You're doing it right now. Thank you." He rubbed her arm quickly as if to erase the morose mood. "Enough about that. Let's get back to talking about more pleasant things."

Cam agreed, and the two perked up and moved on to the NBA playoffs and a new political scandal in Washington D.C. Eventually they talked themselves out, kissed, exchanged goodnights and fell silent. Tony turned over on his side and Cam held onto him. She felt something she had never felt before—a sliver of hope. She pondered the possibility this man whom she loved with all her heart might possibly be free eventually, which would leave the door wide open for her to walk through and claim him for herself. She kissed his back. "How much do you love me?" she whispered.

"Very much," Tony replied.

His words caused Cam to tingle all over as she drifted off to sleep.

*

Cam dreamt she twirled and danced in a garden surrounded by beautiful flowers while wearing a long-flowing, white gown. The animals in the garden likewise danced with her. Squirrels, rabbits, chipmunks, hedgehogs—even skunks—sang with her while an assortment of birds flew overhead fluttering their wings before descending to join in the chorus of a song without words.

She was awakened by Tony kneading her breast with his left hand. The two lay spoon fashion with Tony behind her.

"Dearest Cam," he whispered.

"What is it?" she asked. "Is something wrong? "What time is it?"

"It's nearly midnight," Tony answered. "And nothing's wrong. I hate waking you but you're so beautiful and sexy that..." He paused to kiss and nibble her shoulder. "...I need to have you some more. I promise I won't take long."

Cam felt as if she would cry from loving a man so much. "Take me, my darling, and take as long as you want. What's your pleasure? Oh, I know." She smiled and got on all fours. "You just love it like this, don't you?" A night light plugged into the wall near the door provided enough light for her to feel intrigued by the encounter. She felt a slight chill from discarding the sheet and blanket, and from the cool breeze of the ceiling fan. She felt Tony's hands on her buttocks as he positioned himself behind her. Lustful excitement replaced intrigue.

Tony panted an answer to her question. "You know how much I love this." He pulled her hair and eased himself inside, then grabbed her by the wrists to hold her arms behind her.

Cam closed her eyes and squealed with ecstasy. This was far better than a garden full of flowers and singing animals.

*

The ringing telephone on the nightstand caused Cam to open her eyes. Although she couldn't see Tony due to the darkness, she was aware he lay beside her. She raised her head to check the clock radio on the other nightstand. Who would be calling at 3:13 in the morning? She picked up the telephone and read the caller ID information but didn't understand the abbreviations. Fed something. "Hello?"

"Camellia, my dove, this is Vincent."

Cam grimaced as if she had just tasted a sour lemon. "Vincent, do you know what time it is? You've really messed up now. You're violating the harassment prevention order I took out on your ass, so you're going to jail."

"That's where I am, dear Camellia. I need your help."

Cam sat up. The rotating ceiling fan made her feel uncomfortably cool so she pulled the sheet over her naked breasts. She heard the desperation in her ex-husband's voice but didn't trust him. "What? Don't play games with me, Vincent."

"I'm not," he replied. "I'm in a federal prison in California, but I assure you it's all a big misunderstanding."

Cam scoffed. "I'm sure it is. Why don't you call your parents—or your girlfriend, the dainty little thing who called me a few months ago and told me to leave you alone?"

"I can't get a hold of my parents—and Danielle? That bitch won't help me."

No doubt she wised up sooner than I did, Cam thought. Assuming the call had awakened Tony, she placed her hand over the telephone and whispered, "It's Vincent."

"Are you going to help me, Camellia, for old time's sake?" Vincent pleaded. "I can't stay here. I'll go mad."

Cam thought for a few seconds, then retrieved a remote under her pillow to slightly bring up the lights before grabbing a small pad of paper and pen from her nightstand. "Tell me exactly where you are and I'll see what I can do."

TWENTY-THREE: UPPER HAND

Rose sipped iced tea from a can while sitting on a blanket spread over very dry grass. It was almost two o'clock, according to her watch. The event would start shortly. Cam sat next to her on her right. Adam sat next to Cam oblivious to either woman or the estimated seven thousand people who surrounded them. He fixed his attention on the multiple dueling space ships inside his hand-held video game. Rose fanned herself with the program she had been given that described the free concert at the Hatch Memorial Shell—or simply the Hatch Shell, an outdoor concert facility that bordered the Charles River Esplanade near downtown Boston. The venue featured a shell-style stage for performers and a 90,000 square feet lawn for spectators.

Only Zoë's appearance would prompt Rose to bake under a hot sun in ninety degree weather watching an outdoor concert. She felt proud Zoë had been selected, along with two dozen other teenage musical phenoms, to perform a couple of numbers with the world famous Boston Pops Orchestra. The theme of the day for the eighty-minute, late July concert: "Show Tunes: Music from the Stage and Screen." To Zoë's disappointment, Tony couldn't attend his daughter's event. He was finishing the last of a two-day, all-day summer school course, the last needed to renew his teaching certificate. Rose actually felt relieved he wasn't there, given their relationship had been reduced to politeness in the presence of the children or in public, and pointed indifference when alone.

"Hot today," Cam said, and likewise fanned herself with a program.

Rose nodded and pushed her large sunglasses closer to her face. She wore an oversized, sleeveless, flower-printed summer dress over a pair of short leggings. "If Zoë wasn't performing," she declared, "I'd be indoors on a day like this." She worried privately about her relationship with Zoë, wondering why they couldn't seem to get on the same page. Perhaps they were, as the saying goes, too much alike. Zoë could be headstrong and given to sulking and pouting, just like her mother. Rose refocused on Cam. "So what's the latest on that no good ex of yours? How long has it been since he called, begging for your help?"

Cam, hiding underneath a wide-brimmed hat, a pair of sunglasses and gobs of sunscreen, sipped her iced tea and thought for a few seconds. "Over two months."

Rose scoffed. "I don't understand why you helped that asshole."

"I didn't do much," Cam replied. "I just located his parents and told them where he was. They and Vincent are estranged, so they didn't bother to tell him they were traveling abroad. They were in Paris."

Rose cackled. "Estranged from Vincent? Really? I wonder why."

Cam cocked her head to one side and ran her fingers under her chin. "Maybe because he's a no good, lying, cheating, conniving bum who's sitting in federal prison waiting to be tried on multiple counts of credit card fraud, identity theft and conspiracy."

Rose placed her hand on Cam's shoulder and made a lugubrious face. "You poor dear. You miss him desperately, don't you?"

Cam exaggerated a woeful sigh and pretended to wipe a tear from her eye. "Does it show? I'm trying to be strong."

Rose joined Cam in a hearty laugh before shielding her eyes from the bright sun and trying to catch a glimpse of Zoë. She couldn't locate her daughter among the scores of roaming bodies on or near the stage, about fifty yards away. Rose leaned forward, peering past Cam to see about Adam. The boy sat totally engrossed by his video game. Although he wore ear buds Rose decided to make sure he couldn't hear her. "Adam?" she said in a normal voice. Nothing. She motioned for Cam to scoot closer to her.

Cam scooted as requested. "What is it, doll?"

"Look Cam," Rose opened. "I'm going to just lay my cards on the table."

"Okay."

Rose looked around. The crowd paid them no attention, with the exception of the occasional males gawking at Cam, who paid them no attention. "It's like this. I've been playing by Tony's rules for the last couple of months because he kinda had me over a barrel after he found out about...well, you know. I told you about it already."

"Yeah," Cam said. "I know."

"Well," Rose continued, "we're virtually roommates now." She put her hand over her chest. "It's killing me, but what can I do? Tony's being totally unreasonable. He's checking bank statements, going over the bills, acting all suspicious and stuff. You know he said we've got to cut back on how often we eat out? It's no way to live, trust me."

"Oh," Cam said and touched Rose's hand. "I'm so sorry to hear that."

Rose arched her eyebrows. Just for a second she thought Cam was actually making fun of her. She dismissed her suspicion as derived from nerves due to stress.

"Mom," Adam said.

"What is it, honey?"

Adam pointed. "I see some friends from school. Can I go sit with them?"

Rose scanned an area about twenty yards away parallel to Adam. Two young teenage boys, wearing short-sleeved BIA T-shirts similar to Adam's, waved. The boys sat with a half-dozen other teenage boys and girls. Rose recognized the faces of one boy and Jia-Li. After getting a couple of names from Adam and his assurance he would stay within her sight, Rose allowed him to leave. She shrugged. "He's at that age where he'd rather hang out with his friends than sit with his mother." She blinked a couple of times and pretended she had lost her train of thought. "Where were we?"

"Something about it's no way to live," Cam replied.

"Yeah," Rose said. "Anyway, I can't live like this, watching every penny, being spied on by my own husband. It's driving me crazy. You know what I'm saying?"

Cam nodded meekly. "I guess so."

"What I'm saying is," Rose whispered, "remember when at the end of April we were talking and Tony came home a little earlier than we thought he would?"

Cam chuckled. "Yeah. We both looked like a couple of kids who just got caught smoking in the girls' bathroom at school."

Rose rolled her eyes. "Talk about awkward. Anyway, remember you said you'd be willing to maybe chip in a little extra if I needed it, but I never asked you for it." Rose paused and stared at Cam, trying to read her facial expression. Her best friend said nothing. "I wouldn't ask if it wasn't absolutely necessary."

After several seconds of silence, Cam lowered her head. "How much do you need?"

Bingo! Rose thought, but she would have to proceed with caution. "Tell you what, we've only got..." She counted with her fingers. "...August, September and October left." She studied Cam's face again and noticed the woman's tightening jaw. Rose interpreted the woman's body language as an indication of mild distress; her eyes also gave her away. The thought of the arrangement ending soon obviously produced some anguish.

"Yes, just three more months," Cam agreed, trying unsuccessfully to sound nonchalant.

Rose suddenly felt intense jealousy. She inspected Cam's modest attire: a sleeveless off white cotton blouse and denim Capri slacks. Nothing showy, but it didn't matter. The former bikini model who worked out five days a week would look sexy and gorgeous wearing a potato sack. Men stared only at her; five years earlier they would have stared at both of them.

"You were saying, Rose?" Cam asked.

Rose gritted her teeth. She felt herself sliding into the zone of resentment caused by the image in her mind of her husband on top of Cam, both naked, stuffing his huge penis—formerly reserved only for his wife—inside her, putting his tongue in her mouth, moaning in her ear. Hadn't she, Rose, made a tremendous sacrifice for the sake of her family? Why shouldn't she seek a little something for herself? She had legal rights to a commodity of value, for which someone who had plenty of money was willing to rent. Well, sometimes rent goes up. She checked on Adam and grimaced. "Shit," she whispered.

"What?" Cam asked. "What's wrong?" She turned. "Is Adam still there?"

"He's there," Rose said. "He better be. But I see someone else, too."

Cam continued to face Rose. "Someone you know?"

Someone she knew alright. About fifteen yards farther than Adam and his friends, Rose spotted a man sitting on a blanket with a shapely, dark haired woman who looked to be in her late twenties. James Rivers and the woman giggled and caressed each other like a pair of high school sweethearts, a shameful way for a married man to carry on in public, if anyone wanted Rose's opinion on the subject. "It's that damn bill collector I told you about, the one who was pestering me. He's here with some bimbo."

"Oh," Cam said. "Where?" She started to turn. "Should we move?"

"Don't look, dumb ass," Rose half joked. "With that big hat of yours I don't think he can see me. And how about we go tell Adam that Mommy's former stalker is here so we have to move?"

Cam nodded again. "You make a good point. Has he stopped bothering you?"

"Yeah," Rose said. "I hadn't heard from him in over two months. Looks like he found another victim."

"Good riddance, I say."

Right," Rose agreed, but the sight of Rivers intensified her resolve to carry out her agenda. Men were fickle, guided only by their prurient interests. A woman had to look out for herself. She returned to negotiations. "Back to what we were talking about: You know me, I'm not greedy. I just need a little extra something to tide me over, you know."

Cam frowned. "But keeping secrets from Tony again. I don't like it."

Rose leaned closer. Her face contorted with indignity. "Oh, well then, fuck me." She shook her head. "Not really, since my husband hasn't touched me in months. At least you're getting your hot box stretched from time to time. Here I am making the ultimate sacrifice for my family and..." She straightened up. "Never mind. Forget I said anything."

Cam touched Rose's forearm. "I'm sorry, doll. Please forgive me. I didn't mean to be insensitive. Really, how much do you need?"

Rose wiggled her toes in her sandals with delight. Don't smile, she said to herself. "I don't know. I hadn't thought of a number. What do you think you could manage?"

Cam shrugged. "Would another thousand be enough?"

Rose felt like laughing out loud. She had planned to ask for five hundred. "I think so—and we're just talking about for the next three, um, visits. Just slip it in the bag. Tony never even looks at what's inside. Of course, this will be between us."

Cam nodded. "Of course."

A tall man in a white shirt, black pants and a smile the size of the Boston Harbor stepped out into the middle of the stage and grabbed the microphone. "Good afternoon, ladies and gentlemen..."

Rose listened to the introductions and beamed with self-satisfaction. Tony thought he was so damn smart, checking up on her, spying on her. Well, that'll be the day when she couldn't stay one step ahead of him.

*

During the late afternoon on the second Thursday in September, Rose sat at the piano in the living room leisurely playing Franz Schubert's famous "Ständchen," or "Serenade." She was casually, comfortably dressed because she had the day off from Emerald's but would have to work both Saturday and Sunday, which she hated. She played the music from memory while contemplating a risky move with Tony. She didn't see any other choice. She had to do something to force his hand. Summer had come and gone, and they were no closer to resolving their differences. Her thirty-eighth birthday had likewise come and gone, along with their fifteenth wedding anniversary, and neither event had been particularly...well, eventful. She felt stagnated. She had become openly despondent and frustrated, and wanted to do something about it.

She closed her eyes and swayed in rhythm with the music, momentarily lost in its serenity, remembering when she and Zoë had played the selection together the previous week. The felicity faded when she opened her eyes and noted another school year had begun. Tony was now busier than ever, working on lesson plans and grading papers, totally ignoring her dissatisfaction about their standard of living. On top of that he had, against her wishes, spent several days the previous month in Washington, D.C. with a bunch of other education eggheads working on that stupid commission, generating pointless recommendations that would be lucky to make page five in the newspaper and would probably never be implemented.

The twins had likewise been re-engaged in school life and paid their mother little attention. Sporting events, music lessons, science projects, and never-ending texts from friends occupied their little minds; that and a whole laundry list of material items they "needed." Even Cam seemed to have less time for her due to a flurry of business ventures that would no doubt make her even richer; the woman sure had the Midas touch.

Rose hated to admit it but she also felt lonely and empty, which led to her eating more which led to her gaining even more weight. She had considered her options and had reached the conclusion the tactic she had devised was the only way to motivate Tony to quit that stupid job and take care of his family properly. He might initially resent her machinations but after a year of affluence he would eventually realize she had been right all along and they would return to being a loving couple. But she had to be smart about the plan's execution or it could blow up in her face. If Tony called her bluff the results could be disastrous—for her.

She sauntered to the picture window near the front door and peeked past the semi-sheer curtains. Tony was parking his car behind hers. Rose waited for him, listening for his footsteps as he climbed the five stairs on the front porch, then opened the door.

Tony looked surprised. "Um, hello, Rose. Were you going somewhere?" He wore a light blue shirt with a navy blue tie and pants.

"No," she answered. "I was waiting for you."

"Oh?" Tony said as he entered the house carrying a full tote bag in each hand. "Is everything okay? Where are the kids?"

"They're not home from school yet," Rose reported, growing a little annoyed. She didn't even know why. "They're helping the music teacher move some equipment, remember?"

"That's right," Tony said. "They reminded us about that yesterday." He sniffed the air. "Something smells good."

"Adam asked me to make lasagna for dinner, so I did," Rose said. She stopped Tony from saying another word by briskly waving her hands. "Anyway, I've come to a decision."

Tony laid his tote bags on the floor. "A decision about what?"

Rose paused for dramatic effect. Wait until he asked again. Wait...

"Rose?"

Rose took a deep breath and announced, "I think we should separate. I want you to move out."

TWENTY-FOUR: WISDOM

"**I** want you to move out," Tony said. "That's what she told me." He supported his weight by gripping the front of his desk and leaning against it. He and his guest were the only two in his classroom.

"Whoa!" Robert Kwan replied. He leaned against the student desk opposite Tony. "When did all this happen?"

"Four days ago. Last Thursday."

"And what did you say?"

"Not much," Tony answered. "The kids came home so we didn't talk a great deal. Rose had to work Friday, Saturday and yesterday, so we haven't really discussed it." He walked behind his desk and typed on the keyboard to log off his e-mail client. "But she's not working today so I guess today's the day we have it out." He checked the time on the wall clock behind him. "Oh, it's after three thirty. I didn't mean to keep you this long."

"It's fine," Robert said. "I've got the rest of the day off." He shook his head slowly while staring at his shiny, black wingtip shoes. "I'm really sorry, man. I think I made a mistake by giving you that report. You know, I never saw the aftermath of my little mission until now. I realize I've been wrong. I should mind my own business."

Tony exhaled. "This isn't your fault. I bet most of the men you talked to found out about their wives' secret, whatever it was, eventually. Rose and I have been sweeping our problems under the rug for years. You can't do that forever."

Robert opened his arms. "Okay, but why is it coming to a head now?"

Tony considered disclosing his arrangement with and feelings for Cam but held his tongue. This coming Friday he would embrace Cam for the second to the last time, and as always he could hardly wait to see her. "Lots of reasons for it coming to a head now, I guess," he explained, "but they're too complicated to go into."

"Okay," Robert said. "When you're ready, my brother, I'll listen."

Tony smiled. "Thanks for your support. I need all I can get." He liked Robert. They had met a few times with other male friends to play basketball and share a bite to eat. Tony had been less than forthcoming with Rose about his new friendship, advising Robert to call him at work or on his mobile telephone. Tony had decided he didn't need to add another point of contention between him and Rose.

Robert heard a sound behind him and turned. He took a couple of steps toward the door, tugged on the jacket to his gray pinstriped suit and spoke to a pair of female students standing in the hall. The girls wore cheerleading outfits. One was tall and had tied her long, black hair into a pony tail. The shorter one had fashioned her medium length hair into elaborate French braids. "Hello," Robert said. "Are you here to see Mr. Monroe?"

The girls replied by glancing at each other before darting off, giggling and exchanging comments about the two adults inside the classroom.

"Oh my God, they're both so handsome!"

"One for each of us."

Robert laughed and returned to his spot in front of the student desk. He pointed in the direction of the fleeing students. "Kids. Do you get a lot of that?"

"Every now and then," Tony replied. "So, it looks like you really enjoyed yourself today."

"Man, did I!" Robert exclaimed. "I know I've said this more than once but please allow me to say it again: What you do here is nothing short of God's work."

Tony nodded. "If only my wife shared your opinion."

"You mean she doesn't?" Robert asked. "How can she not? I mean, the kids are so terrific. That girl in your sixth period class, the one who sat right here." He patted the top of the desk with both hands. "The one who knew about the Zimmerman Telegram. What was her name? Ebony? Did you see how earnest she was?"

Tony snickered. "I would say smitten was a better word, the way she kept staring at you. And what's with you and my dark sisters anyway?"

"Oh go on," Robert said, waving his hand to playfully dismiss Tony's remark. "Now back to you. You don't have to tell me, but what are you going to do about your home life?"

"I don't know," Tony answered. "I've got to consider what's best for my children."

"True," Robert said. "Have you been praying about this?"

"My friend," Tony replied, "for the past four days that's about all I've been doing."

Their conversation was interrupted again, this time by Monique, who swaggered into the classroom as though she owned the building. Stopping about a yard from Robert, she put her hands on her hips—modeling a gray dress with a V-neck top that displayed her curves—and cranked her neck while addressing Tony. "So I've got to come over here to collect my man, huh?" She huffed. "Don't think this is going to be a habit."

Robert eased over to her and chuckled. "Sorry, babe, but you and I were moving things in your classroom for over an hour and I thought we were finished. I told you I'd be back."

"You said 'in a minute' and that was twenty minutes ago," Monique whined. She straightened Robert's tie and put her hand on his cheek. "You said you were going to go with me to the mall."

Tony intervened. "It's my fault. We got to talking and, well, you know how it is."

Monique glanced at Tony, then returned her attention to Robert, handing him a set of keys. "Honey, would you go to my room? There's a box sitting on a chair next to my desk. Would you take it to my car please? I have to talk shop with Tony for a minute. I won't be long." She placed her arms akimbo again. "I know what a minute is."

Robert laughed, took the keys and waved at Tony. "We still meeting at Sam Parker's place this Sunday to watch the Patriots?"

"Of course," Tony declared. "We're gonna walk all over those Dolphins!"

"They won't know what hit them!" Robert exclaimed. "What kind of sissy name is Dolphins for a football team anyway?"

Monique stepped between the two men and nudged Robert. "Please honey, go."

Robert laughed again and backpedalled. "I'll wait for you by your car."

"Go Patriots!" Tony called. Robert replied in kind on his way out the door. Tony turned off his computer. "So what did you want to talk to me about?"

Monique leaned against the same desk Robert had vacated. "Nothing really. I just wanted to thank you for introducing us; me and Robert. He's a good man. He knows who he is and what he wants. No games, no bullshi—um, no BS." She grimaced. "I promised him I'd clean up my mouth."

"He is a very good man," Tony said. "And you deserve a good man, Monique."

"He's smart and he loves history, just like we do."

"Yes he does," Tony said. "You should have seen the kids during each of my classes today. They hung onto his every word."

Monique continued her litany of praise. "He has that law degree from Northeastern, but he's not all full of himself. He listens. He's interested in what I have to say."

"That's because you have a lot of interesting things to say."

"And he's so full of passion," she gushed, "and stamina. In bed that man can go all night."

"Um, too much information."

Monique cackled. "Sorry." She glanced at the door and stepped closer to Tony. "What I wanted to ask is, have you told Robert about how I..." She paused, obviously embarrassed. "...you know, made a fool of myself when I tried to get you to..."

"No, of course not," Tony assured her. "It's already forgotten. I'm glad you two have hit it off. Robert's had it tough but now he's happy." He pointed at the door. "But you better get downstairs before one of those coquettish seniors tries to run off with him."

Monique stomped her feet with mock indignation. "You let 'em try." She smiled. "Thank you, Tony. You have the wisdom of Solomon."

Tony watched Monique scamper away before grabbing his tote bag and briefcase. "Well," he said aloud, "let's see if I can apply some of that wisdom at home."

*

"Okay, Rose," Tony said, standing in front of the bedroom door he had just closed. He wore a pair of sweatpants and a short-sleeved T-shirt. "It's almost six o'clock. We've eaten dinner and cleaned up. The kids are in their rooms, so as I was saying to...well, as I was thinking earlier, I suppose this is the day we have it out and discuss our future."

"I've already made my wishes known," Rose replied. Dressed similarly as Tony, she sat on the loveseat at the corner of the room with her legs dangling over its arm. "This house isn't big enough for both of us, so one of us should leave." She pointed. "I vote you."

"So you've said," Tony acknowledged. "But you haven't told me why."

"Because I feel like a prisoner in my own house," Rose declared. "Because you don't trust me, looking over my shoulder all damn day long. I can't live like this. That's why."

"That's not what I've been doing," Tony said. "But under the circumstances you can understand why I feel a need to, as they said during the Reagan years, trust but verify."

"Yeah, yeah, yeah," Rose said. She placed her legs on the floor. "Okay, so I made some mistakes. Are you going to punish me for the rest of my life?"

Tony sat at the foot of the bed. "Rose, you lied to me."

"I never lied to you, Tony."

He held up his hands. "You kept me in the dark about things you shouldn't have."

"I said I was sorry."

"Not really."

Rose shrugged. "I'm sorry. Okay? Sometimes I go a little overboard. I wanted Zoë to have a quality instrument of her own, not some cheap school hand-me-down."

"I understand your intentions," Tony said, "but it was a decision we should have made together."

"But look how it turned out," Rose pleaded. "Our daughter is obviously some kind of child prodigy. She keeps that flute on her lips for hours every day. And Dasha, that grad student at the New England Conservatory who Zoë goes to for her private music lessons, she told me after Zoë graduates from BIA, being admitted into the Conservatory is a *fait accompli*." She pounded a fist into her hand. "But we're shooting for Julliard."

"That's not the point, Rose," Tony countered. "It was a decision we should have made together."

"You kept saying maybe," Rose said. "Someone had to step up to the plate."

Tony shook his head. "Going solo creates more problems than it solves."

"But that's not the main issue anyway," Rose added. "It's your job."

Tony stood, sighed and rolled his eyes. "I don't want to practice law. Why is that so hard for you to accept?"

"That's not what you told me before we got married," Rose declared. "You're the one who lied."

"That's not true and you know it," Tony retorted. "People change."

Rose stood and closed the distance between them. "But honey, if you just gave it a chance you might see you were born for corporate law. Face it, a teacher's salary isn't going to pay for the things we need—and after this Friday we've only got one more...extra income payment." She returned to the loveseat. "And I want to talk about that too."

"No, Rose," Tony insisted. "I don't want to give corporate law a chance. I interned at a corporate law office and hated it. As far as the other thing goes, I'll trust you to handle the family finances again. No looking over your shoulder from me, okay?"

Rose smiled slightly. "Well, that would help."

The telephone rang. Tony picked it up and said hello.

"Tony, this is Vincent Moreau."

Tony widened his eyes. "Vincent?" He pointed at the telephone in his hand while facing Rose. "I thought you were in prison—where I'm sure you belong."

"They finally let me out on bail," Vincent reported, "thanks to my parents, but they took my passport and I have to wear this damn ankle bracelet like some low life thug."

"You are a low life thug, Vincent," Tony rejoined. "What do you want?"

"I want you to give me ten thousand dollars," Vincent demanded. "I have to rent an apartment out here and good lawyers don't come cheap."

Tony laughed. "And why would I give you a penny?"

"Because if you don't," Vincent growled, "I'll call back when you're not home and tell Rose you've been fucking Camellia, her best friend."

"Vincent, you are a fool," Tony hissed. He handed the telephone to Rose. "Vincent wants to talk to you." He watched with amusement.

Rose made no attempt to hide her disdain for the man. "Vincent, if you move up a few million years in evolution you'd get to be a snake...Tony and Cam are what?...She pressed the back of her hand against her forehead. "Oh dear me. I'm so destroyed." She ground her teeth as she spoke. "Well, you can't blame her after dealing with your three inch limp dick. I've got better things to do than talk to an idiot like you—and one more thing: If you ever call my house again I'm going to notify the U.S. attorney in California and see what he or she thinks about extortion." She handed the telephone back to Tony.

Tony spoke with a mocking tone. "You still there, Vincent?"

"Um, yeah," the man replied softly.

"My wife said her piece," Tony said. "Now I'll say mine. If I ever see you on the street I'm going to beat the shit out of you. So be afraid, asshole. Be very afraid." He pressed a button to end the call and placed the telephone back on the nightstand. "It's not my place to question the good Lord but I can't imagine His reason for putting someone like that on this earth."

"To show us what the devil looks like," Rose suggested. She approached Tony again. "Before that wretched excuse for a worm interrupted us, you said you'll trust me again?"

Tony nodded. "Yeah. Don't make me sorry."

Rose placed her hands on Tony's chest. "And what about being a lawyer? Don't you see it would be the answer to all our problems?"

Tony gently removed her hands. "Trying to be something I'm not isn't going to solve any problem."

Rose took two steps back and pushed her hair away from her face. "I don't understand why you won't do this for us, for your family."

Tony shook his head. "You wouldn't care if I did what you asked and was miserable for the rest of my life, would you?"

"Who said you'd be miserable?" Rose asked. "How do you know if you don't even try? You wouldn't have to quit your job right away. You could take a leave of absence and—"

"The answer is no," Tony interrupted. "No to corporate law, and for our children's sake, no to moving out. If you want to separate that badly, you move out—which I don't want because it would hurt the children." A long silence ensued. "Well, what's it gonna be?"

Rose shrugged. "I guess we can wait and see how time affects all of this."

Tony nodded, then opened his dresser drawer and searched for underwear and socks to place on the chair; he always laid his clothes out so he wouldn't turn on the light in the morning while Rose still slept. "Wait a second." He turned around. "Something you said earlier, something about our so-called extra income ending next month."

Rose approached Tony yet again. "I was thinking...well, perhaps we could persuade Cam to continue until the end of the year. I bet she would."

Tony stared into Rose's eyes. Who was this woman whom fifteen years earlier had pledged to love, honor and cherish him for the rest of her life?

Rose opened her hands. "What do you think?"

Several seconds passed before Tony finally answered. "You're insane," he whispered. He slammed his dresser drawer closed, walked to the door, opened it and stepped across the threshold before muttering, "I've got some work to do. I'll be in my office."

TWENTY-FIVE: COSTLY ACQUISITION

Rose stopped at the red light a few blocks from her home, flipped down her vehicle's sun visor and examined her reflection in the mirror. She turned her head slightly left and right, and nodded with satisfaction. Nothing like getting one's hair de-grayed and styled on a Saturday morning to make a woman feel like a million bucks. While waiting for the light to change she also inspected the leaves on the nearby trees and admired their natural incipient change in color from green to red and orange. Finally the light changed, prompting her to step on the gas pedal. Speaking of bucks, Rose thought, it being nearly ten thirty on the third Saturday in September Tony should be home by now with her—their money.

After obeying a stop sign she turned right and noted a year had passed since she had first approached Tony with the idea of the arrangement. Rose furled her perfectly pruned eyebrows and grimaced, struggling with jealousy about Tony making love to Cam, but her tense features softened and her hurt feelings assuaged somewhat upon remembering she would personally net an extra thousand dollars for her sacrifice.

The mellow jazz music on her radio faded, replaced by a smooth talking Phil Masters touting the value of his higher end automobiles. Rose sighed. Had she been smart and chosen Phil over Tony she wouldn't have to share her husband with her best friend. How she wished she could go back in time and choose differently. "Too late now," she lamented and changed the station.

She turned left and searched for street parking on her block. To her surprise Tony's automobile was nowhere in sight. Rose felt a touch of trepidation. God forbid he had arrived earlier, carried his duffel bag to their bedroom and examined its contents himself. Her imagination expanded the scenario. Perhaps he had counted the extra cash, called Cam and she had revealed the truth, prompting him to return the money—all of it. Rose quickly parked her SUV in front of the house, jumped out and raced up the stairs under the partly cloudy skies. She pushed open the front door and was greeted by Zoë, holding her flute.

"What's wrong, Mom?" the girl asked. "Why'd you come flying through the door like that?"

"Where's your father?" Rose demanded to know.

"He's not home yet."

"You mean he hasn't come home from his other job?"

Zoë shook her head. "No. Isn't that all right?"

Rose felt relieved, but resentment replaced her anxiety. Tony had been coming home from Cam's later and later each month. Well, Rose thought, as long as he walked through the door bearing the fruits of his labor. She comforted herself by remembering Cam had delivered the extra payment last month as agreed and Tony had not been the wiser, so Rose assumed he would bring eleven thousand dollars home any minute.

A backpack lying next to the piano bench caught Rose's attention. "Whose is this?"

"It's Jia-Li's," Zoë replied. "You said she could come over to practice with me."

"So where is she?"

Zoë hesitated before answering. "I think she went to the bathroom upstairs."

Rose pointed to the back of the house. "Why not the powder room down here?"

Zoë stuttered a reply. "I-I-I don't know."

Rose frowned. "Uh-hum." She quietly walked a straight line to the bottom of the stairs and climbed the first three. Turning to check on Zoë she noticed the girl hunched over with her back to her. She raced back to Zoë, put her hand on the girl's shoulder and spun her around. "What have you got there?" Not waiting for an answer, she snatched Zoë's mobile telephone out of her hand and read the unfinished, unsent message.

moms hom

Rose squinted. "Texting your brother, huh?" She stuffed the telephone into the pocket of her sweater and placed her hand on Zoë's shoulder, guiding the girl onto the piano bench. "I'll deal with you later, young lady." Zoë responded by abruptly standing up. Rose returned the girl to the bench with a more forceful nudge. "You'd be making a big mistake to believe because you're taller than me now, you can defy me. Don't you move unless the house is on fire, you hear me?"

Zoë lowered her head and answered softly. "Yes, Mother."

Rose kicked off her shoes and crept upstairs. After reaching the second floor she paused for a few seconds outside Adam's room. Placing her ear to the closed door yielded little intelligence, not even the sound of voices. "The hell with this," she muttered and slowly pushed the door open. She saw a neat, well-kept room brightly lit by natural sunlight from two large windows. She also saw Adam and Jia-Li sitting at the foot of his bed with their arms around each other, kissing passionately. The two teens stood and separated quickly, both looking guilty and embarrassed.

"Hello Mom," Adam opened with a soft, diffident voice.

"I see you've been diligently practicing your music, Jia-Li," Rose said.

Jia-Li, a cute, short girl wearing short hair and glasses, put her hands over the bottom half of her face. Her eyes expressed dismay. She removed her hands. "Mrs. Monroe, I was just, um..."

"Just being terribly inappropriate in my house," Rose declared. "That's what you were doing."

"It's not her fault, Mom," Adam asserted and pointed at himself. "If you want to blame someone, blame me."

"That's very noble of you, Adam," Rose said. "So how long has this been going on?"

"Jia-Li and I are together, Mom," Adam replied. "She's my girlfriend."

Rose glanced at Jia-Li, then stared at Adam. "Oh, is that right?" She returned her gaze to Jia-Li. "So if I tell your mother and father about this they'd say fine, right?"

Jia-Li staggered closer to Rose. "Oh please, Mrs. Monroe, please, don't tell my parents. They wouldn't understand." She touched Rose's arm but jerked her hand back. "Forgive me for being so forward," she pleaded and began sobbing loudly.

"Your parents wouldn't understand what, Jia-Li?" Rose inquired. "The fact that you've got a boyfriend or the fact that you've got a black boyfriend?" Rose shook her finger. "I trusted you and treated you practically like a member of the family and you go and pull something like this? Shame on you."

Jia-Li covered her face with her hands and wailed. "Please don't tell them! Please!"

Adam put his arm around the girl and glared at his mother. "God, Mom, why'd you have to say something like that to her? It's not her fault. We care for each other. What's so terrible about that?"

Her son's word stirred some feelings of regret in Rose. "Well, I just don't want you two getting yourselves in over your heads, that's all."

"Now what the hell's going on?"

All three turned to see Tony standing at the threshold of the door with Zoë behind him. He was casually dressed in blue jeans, just as the other four.

"Come on in Tony," Rose insisted with a wave of her hand. "I'm sorry about all this. I know you're tired from a hard night's work." She glanced at Zoë, looking smug from her father's ostensible protection. Sneaky brat.

Tony stepped inside and approached Jia-Li, who was still crying. "What's the matter, honey?" Receiving no answer, he opened his hands and addressed the other adult in the room. "Rose, what's going on here?"

Rose pointed at the teenage couple. "I came home obviously sooner than expected and found your son and Jia-Li in bed with their lips locked together."

Tony remained where he stood but took a few seconds to visually inspect the made bed. "Okay," he said, "but that doesn't explain why the poor thing is crying her eyes out."

"Mom was mean to her, Dad," Adam whined. "She made her feel like—"

"Hush boy," Tony ordered but with a gentle tone. "Grown folks are talking."

"I'm sorry Dad," Adam said. "But we weren't in bed. We were just sitting—"

"Quiet," Tony said. "Let your mother and me handle this." He put his hand on Jia-Li's shoulder. "It's okay, doll." He motioned for Zoë to enter the room. "Sweetie, take Jia-Li downstairs and give her something to drink." He gestured to Adam with his thumb. "Go with them." After a few seconds he addressed Rose over the sound of three pairs of footsteps thumping against the stairs. "I'll take Jia-Li home after she calms down."

Rose put her hands on her hips. "That's it? I catch Adam up here alone with some girl and you're just going to take her home?"

"What else should I do?" Tony asked. "It appears you've done everything else. Besides," he added, "it wasn't some girl. It's Jia-Li. We've known her since she was knee high to a grasshopper. She's a good kid. Her parents keep her on a short leash."

"Obviously not short enough."

"They're just kids with a crush," Tony said. "Remember that other girl last spring you were all bent out of shape about? What was her name? Lucy?"

Rose scoffed. "Well, I'd like to see Jia-Li's parents when she tells them she's got a black boyfriend. How do you say 'No niggers' in Chinese?"

"While you jump to conclusions about that," Tony said, "I'll take Jia-Li home."

Rose inspected the room. "Where's your duffel bag?"

Tony pointed. "Don't worry. It's right outside the door."

Rose scurried into the hall and picked up the bag. "I'll take care of this." She heard Tony's footsteps behind her as he passed by, then his voice as he descended the stairs.

"I'll take everyone with me so you two can be alone."

Rose responded with one word. "Fine."

*

Later that same day Rose stepped outside and heard a clicking sound behind her as a thin, middle-aged woman locked the front door that now separated them. The woman, who wore a little too much makeup in Rose's opinion, owned a respected jewelry store located just off Washington Street in downtown Boston. The store normally closed at five o'clock but due to a sale had remained open until six. Rose's business had taken a few minutes past six. She felt certain the handsome proprietress didn't mind. After all, the last customer to leave had just paid cash for a six hundred dollar sterling silver cuff bracelet.

Rose inspected her surroundings. Both automobile and foot traffic had already begun to thin because most shops in the area closed by four or five o'clock. The descending sun, which would not set for another half-hour, still shone through a few patchy clouds but the temperature had begun to drop slightly, probably low to mid sixties. Rose buttoned her sweater and beamed with pride at her recent acquisition. It would go perfectly with the gray suit she had bought the previous month. She clutched her purse, which held the bracelet along with an additional four hundred fifty dollars, and briskly walked toward the tiny lot three blocks away where she had parked her vehicle.

She passed several closed shops and reflected on the events that had taken place at her home earlier. She regretted having caused Jia-Li such distress. When she got home she would assure Adam the incident would not be relayed to Jia-Li's parents, a message Adam would certainly forward to his "girlfriend." Rose didn't have anything against Jia-Li personally. In fact she was quite fond of the well-mannered, soft spoken child who struggled to merge Chinese and American culture, but as an African American mother she had to ensure Zoë and Adam married people of their own race someday.

Rose strolled down a narrow side street and slowed her pace to admire a parked black Rolls Royce with a silver trim, but her ringing telephone cut her sightseeing short. She retrieved the item from her back pocket and said hello.

"Where are you, Rose?" Tony asked. "When are you coming home?"

"I'm in the parking lot at Emerald's," Rose lied while still walking. "I left you a note saying I'd be out shopping. I guess I lost track of time." She could hear Tony chuckling.

"That three hundred fifty dollars is burning a hole in your pocket, huh?" he joked.

Try one thousand, three hundred fifty dollars, Rose thought.

Tony made another inquiry. "Should we wait for you before we eat? When we got home we spent all day sprucing up the yard. After a little hard work the kids acted like they've been on a deserted island without food for days, so we bought Chinese."

"No, go ahead and eat," Rose replied. "I'll be home before dark. And Tony."

"Yes?"

Rose sighed. "How's Jia-Li? I really didn't mean to upset her."

"I know," Tony said. "She's okay. Adam said she can be quite delicate at times."

"Yeah," Rose said. "Well, I'll see you...when I get home." She and Tony said goodbye with little fanfare. Eventually she reached the outer edge of the formerly full parking lot, located behind a men's clothing store; it only covered enough space for two dozen vehicles. Currently the area was half-populated by automobiles but no people were in sight. While about six feet from her SUV Rose pressed a button on her remote to unlock the door but before she could reach for the door handle her path was suddenly intercepted by a young man.

"Okay, lady," the man said. He appeared to be barely twenty years old. He wore sunglasses and a black jacket with a hood over his head. "Don't lose your head and you won't lose your head." He took his hand out of his jacket pocket and produced a small caliber revolver.

Terror gripped Rose like cold air in January. She glanced left and right but could spot no one from whom she could summon help. The corner of the parking lot in which she stood faced two walls twelve feet away and a large van had parked next to her SUV, which prevented passers-by from seeing her predicament. "What do you want?"

"Give me your purse," the man demanded. "Hurry up!" He reached for the purse.

"Without thinking, Rose clutched the purse closer to her chest. "No," she moaned.

"I ain't gonna tell you again, lady," the man said, and cocked the hammer of the gun.

Rose spoke while gasping for air. "There are cameras all over."

The man grabbed for the purse again. "That's my problem."

Rose released the purse with one hand but due to her tenseness inadvertently pressed the button to her SUV's remote with her other hand, setting off the alarm. "Oh Jesus!" she whimpered, her eyes growing as large as egg yolks. "It was an accident," she cried to the assailant over the high-pitched screeching of the alarm.

"Fucking bitch," the man growled and fired one shot.

TWENTY-SIX: MOVING ON

Seven months later

Cam waited while curled up on the sofa in Tony's living room. She had volunteered to stay with the twins until he arrived home from his appearance at the Suffolk County Courthouse. It was after seven p.m. according to the clock sitting on the fake fireplace mantel; about a half-hour of daylight still remained in the late April evening, six weeks into daylight saving time.

Cam had assumed Zoë and Adam would need moral support. She anticipated spending the evening distracting them from the topic of Tony's court appearance and had arrived bearing items necessary toward that endeavor. She had filled a tote bag with unpopped popcorn, books, movies and board games. Perhaps, she imagined, they would just sit together and talk about life—and death.

Her good intentions notwithstanding, after eating dinner together and cleaning up the kitchen, the fourteen-year-olds had raced upstairs to their rooms, Zoë to practice her flute and Adam to participate in a video conference with a bunch of teen science geeks scattered across the country. Adam had excitedly explained the nature of the conference but Cam hadn't understood much of it.

Now she sat by herself under a floor lamp with her shoes off reading a romantic suspense novel on her tablet. She felt comfortable and warm in black jeans and a long-sleeved sweater top, although every few minutes she raised her head upon hearing an approaching automobile.

After about twenty minutes she dropped the tablet into her lap and stared at the baby grand piano a few feet away. She had taken piano lessons in middle and high school but had all but abandoned the pastime after becoming interested in clothing design. She considered trying her hand at the keyboard but dismissed the idea and returned to her book. A passage in her novel reminded her Mother's Day would arrive in less than three weeks. She worried about how the twins would react to the observance.

Footsteps on the front porch stairs caused her to bounce out of her seat and scamper to the bottom of the stairs inside the house. "Zoë, Adam, your father's home!" she called while looking up at the second floor. Her anticipation as she opened the front door reminded her of the times she had met Tony at her home during their arrangement.

Unused door key in hand, Tony smiled. The porch light on his face along with the orange and purple twilight sky gave him an almost ghostly appearance. He wore a shirt and tie, and to guard against the spring evening chill, his leather jacket. "Hello, Cam," he said and stepped inside. "Where are the kids?"

She rolled her eyes playfully and pointed. "They're in their rooms. I haven't seen or heard from them since dinner."

Tony chuckled. "Welcome to my world." He took off his jacket.

Cam grabbed it from him. "I'll hang it in the closet."

"Don't trouble yourself."

"Let me do it," Cam insisted. She opened the closet door located a few feet from the front door, hung up the jacket and returned. "Have you eaten? We had curried chicken, brown rice, broccoli with cheese and carrot cake. I can fix you a plate."

"No, thanks. I already ate," Tony said.

"Do you want me to get you something to drink?"

"I'm fine, really," Tony informed her. "I want to talk to the children."

Cam nodded. "I understand. You want to be alone with them. I'll go on home." She reached for the door-knob to the closet door again to get her jacket.

Tony covered her hand with his. "I want you to stay."

Cam felt her body quiver at his touch.

Zoë, followed by Adam, both clad in jeans and a sweatshirt, reached the first floor and gathered around Tony. After a few exchanges of greetings and reports about each eighth grader's school day, Tony gestured for everyone to gather in the great room. Zoë and Adam sat on the sofa.

Cam felt somewhat conflicted about where to sit. She assumed Tony would sit on the loveseat, perpendicular to the sofa, and wanted to be next to him but given the upcoming topic feared it would be inappropriate.

Tony addressed the seating issue. "Adam, are you sitting while a lady stands?"

Adam got on his feet. "Um, sorry Dad. I was just about to suggest that Aunt Cam sit with Zoë and me." He gestured. Cam sat in the middle of the sofa. Adam found a spot at one end so that Cam sat between the brother and sister.

Cam felt comfortable being included in their family gathering, even more so when Zoë rested her head on her shoulder. She held the girl's hand.

Tony sat on the loveseat as expected, placing him closest to Zoë. "Well, it's all over. Your mother's family and I were there. Because of some procedural thing it was late afternoon before it got started." He paused as if struggling for words. "As you know, he had already pleaded guilty last month to second degree felony murder. He was sentenced to life in prison but he'll be eligible for parole in fifteen years."

Cam felt saddened because she missed Rose. She considered expressing her sentiments but thought it better to remain silent and wait for a Monroe family member to speak.

"Was that assistant district attorney there?" Zoë asked and sat up. "You know, that woman who practically accused you of having something to do with what happened to Mom because of her life insurance?" She scowled. "Witch."

Tony shrugged, opened his arms and looked at Cam.

Cam recognized his tacit solicitation for her intervention. "She had to rule him out, sweetheart," she said. "The surviving spouse is always the prime suspect at first. She didn't know your dad is this wonderful man who would never hurt his family."

"And," Tony added, "once she investigated and discovered that both your mother and I had identical policies we took out over six years ago, she lightened up."

"I didn't like her," Zoë moaned and hugged Cam.

Cam hugged her back. "Well, fortunately you won't have to deal with her anymore."

"Before he was sentenced," Adam said, "did he say he was sorry or anything?"

"Yes," Tony said. "He claimed he didn't mean to...shoot."

"Did you believe him?" Adam asked.

"Yes," Tony answered.

Cam remembered Tony expressing a contrary opinion privately about the man's remorse but appreciated his desire to spare his children any further pain.

"Well," Tony said, "that's about it—unless you have more questions."

"I don't know why we couldn't be there," Zoë said.

Tony sighed. "It was grown folks business for grown folks to handle."

Cam disagreed with Tony's decision about excluding the children but said nothing.

"How's Grandmother?" Zoë asked.

Tony laughed. "Okay. She insisted I eat dinner at her house. You know your grandmother. She asked the ADA when we were going to get the bracelet your mom had bought."

Cam smiled. Tony's report changed the mood. Everyone laughed.

Tony stood. "Well, I'm going to talk to your Aunt Cam for a few minutes and see her to her car, then get out of these clothes."

I'd like to get you out of those clothes, all right, Cam thought. She couldn't get over how handsome Tony looked. She winced and berated herself. Oh my goodness, Cam, you are a shameless, wanton hussy, harboring such thoughts at a time like this.

Everyone stood. Zoë and Adam hugged Tony and Cam, then went back upstairs.

Cam approached Tony and wrapped her arms around him. "Seriously, how are you?" The feel of him returning her embrace sent a cascade of goose pimples across her arms. They had not been truly alone since their eleventh rendezvous back in September. Since then they had only shared compassionate hugs. She wanted to hold him and comfort him but didn't want to appear presumptuous.

Tony flashed a sad smile. "I'm okay. I'm very glad this part is over." He sighed. "I confess I do have one regret." He released Cam, and they sat on the sofa.

"What's that?"

He cocked his head to one side before answering. "I'm sorry I didn't tell Rose about the bar exam class I was taking last year or that I was actually taking the bar exam last July when you and she and Adam went to hear Zoë play with the Boston Pops."

"You're a teacher who now also happens to be a lawyer," Cam declared. "You wanted it to be a surprise. You told me that back in January."

"Yeah," Tony acknowledged, "but I also didn't think Rose would understand I wanted to continue being a teacher. I wanted to pass the bar, not to become a corporate lawyer, but for me."

"I for one am very proud of you," Cam declared. The silence between them prompted her to broach a subject she had been afraid to bring up. She closed her eyes. "Tony, you've never said anything about, you know, the money. Are you angry at me? Do you blame me for what happened to Rose?" Her heart pounded furiously as she awaited Tony's answer.

He reached for her hand and squeezed it. "Of course not."

Cam opened her eyes and put her hand over her mouth. "If I hadn't agreed to give her the extra money she wouldn't have been at that jewelry store and—"

"Now you stop that," Tony insisted. "Rose was at the wrong place at the wrong time, but the only person at fault is that man, and he's where he belongs."

Cam stared into Tony's eyes. "So you don't blame me?" She thought about how ironic life could be even in a terribly tragic death: Rose's $300,000 life insurance policy had wiped out all her family's debt and would secure her children's college education.

Tony squeezed Cam's hand again. "You've been carrying this around for the past seven months?" He scratched his head. "Now you put that out of your mind this second." His face remained stoic. "Actually, it's kind of flattering to think someone valued me so much. An extra thousand, huh?"

Cam squeezed Tony's hand. "An extra thousand? I would have paid that and more to keep seeing you, darling." Now that the subject of her feelings for him had also surfaced, Cam couldn't hold them back. "Don't you know I would trade everything I have to be with you?" She put her hand over her mouth again. "I'm sorry to be talking like this after what you've been through. Forgive me." She stood. "It's time for me to go home." She grabbed her tablet and crammed it into her bag.

Tony tapped her bag as they walked to the door. "What's all this?"

"Don't ask," Cam joked. She slipped on her shoes.

"Thanks for being with the kids."

"Yeah," Cam replied with a laugh. "They didn't need me at all."

"Having you here," Tony said, "is a comfort to all three of us, believe me."

They walked outside and stood next to her car, obviously not knowing how to say goodbye.

"Cam," Tony said as he held her door open. "I've got no right to ask you to wait, but..."

"I'll wait," Cam insisted. She kissed Tony on the mouth. The first time she had done so in seven months. "I love you. I'll wait." She got into her car and drove away.

*

Nine weeks later, on the last Friday evening in June, Cam opened her front door and smiled. As a single woman living alone she never opened her windows so she enjoyed the warm outdoor air caressing her face. "Hello, handsome," she said. She wore casual clothes, her hair down and very little makeup. "Come in." It marked the first time Tony had visited her home in over nine months.

He stepped across the threshold into the centrally air-conditioned home carrying an overnight bag in his right hand. "Good evening, beautiful."

Cam inspected Tony from top to bottom and felt her body warming at the sight of him in his short-sleeved shirt that revealed his muscular arms. He had also shaved his head bald, much to her delight. "My oh my," she cooed and ran her fingers over his smooth pate. "You are looking so sexy." She stared at Tony's left hand, in which he usually carried his duffel bag. He wiggled the empty hand and snickered. Cam mashed her lips together to suppress a giggle. "Forget something?"

Tony laughed out loud. "I've got direct deposit now." He set his bag on the floor and took Cam in his arms. "I've missed you."

After a few seconds of passionate kissing, Cam buried her face in his chest. "Tony, if this is a dream please don't wake me up."

Tony kissed her on the forehead. "It's not a dream, dearest Cam. It's me. The kids will be in Providence all weekend visiting their great-grandmother and I'm here with you."

"Are you sure about this?" Cam asked. "About you being here?"

"Very sure," Tony answered. "How else would I get to see Elvira?"

Cam punched him lightly in the stomach.

Tony opened his arms and dropped them at his side. "We have the whole weekend. So, what would you like to do? Do you want to sit on the sofa for a while?"

Cam shook her head. "No," she panted and embraced Tony. "Don't make me wait any longer." She ran her fingernails against his back. "I'm on fire. I want to go upstairs."

*

The following afternoon Cam laughed as she and Tony entered her kitchen via the garage with Cam in the lead. They were bathed with sunlight from three large windows. She spoke in a high-pitched, teasing voice. "So you're afraid of skunks."

"Shoot," Tony said. "Who isn't? I suppose out here you see all kinds of little critters."

Cam nodded. "Skunks, pheasants, deer, possums, wood chucks, wild turkeys, rabbits, field mice, snakes—eating the field mice, thank goodness—squirrels, chipmunks...you name them, they're out here."

Tony grinned and playfully scoffed. "I didn't expect one of your little friends to cut me off in broad daylight while I was getting out of your car to grab your mail. He handed Cam her mail. "I faced unspeakable dangers in order to deliver this to my lady love."

Cam kissed Tony on the cheek and clasped her hands together. "My hero!"

Tony chuckled. "Anyway, thanks for lunch. Good food."

Cam took Tony by the hand as they drifted into the living room. "You know, that was the first time we've ever been out together. It was our first date."

Tony took Cam in his arms. "I enjoyed every minute and hope there'll be many more." He kissed her. "You're okay with going to church with me tomorrow?"

Cam nodded. "Yes, baby. I'd go anywhere with you but..."

"But what?"

"I've got something on my mind," Cam whispered.

"Uh-oh," Tony said. "This doesn't sound good."

Cam pointed at the sofa. "Sit down, honey." Tony did. Cam kicked off her shoes and plopped down next to him. "I've been meaning to ask you something since last night but we were kinda busy."

"I'll say."

She felt her heartbeat racing and took Tony's hand. "I love you Tony. I've been waiting for a man like you my entire life. You're the real deal. I want...I mean..." She squeezed Tony's hand and stared into his eyes. "I don't want to wait any longer. I want to be with you forever and be a good stepmother for Zoë and Adam—and I swear I will be. They need me. You need me, and I need you." She held her breath and waited, fearing she had moved too soon. For God's sake, Cam, she thought, the man just buried his wife nine months ago. She tried to read Tony's facial expression and began second guessing the wisdom of placing her cards on the table.

Tony smiled and nodded. "I love you too, dearest Cam. You must know that by now."

"You don't understand, my love, my life," Cam said. "I'm asking you to marry me."

TWENTY-SEVEN: A FAMILY

Eleven months later

Tony drove his SUV in the drizzling rain, pleased he would arrive at his destination in a few minutes. He hoped the pesky early May showers, now appearing for the third straight afternoon, would end soon. He turned on the defroster to keep his windshield clear. The ubiquitous jazz music on the stereo drowned out the steady, leisurely beat of the flapping windshield wipers. "Yeah, smoke that saxophone," he whispered and snapped his fingers. His was in a good mood in spite of the rain, gray skies and unseasonably cool temperature. His work day had gone well; his students had been attentive and respectful.

He turned onto his street, which ran two football fields long. Only three other houses had been built on it, for a total of two on each side. His home rested at the end of the street on the left. He enjoyed noticing subtle changes in the trees he passed; some bore leaves while others still flaunted spring flowers. He had met his neighbors—a neurosurgeon, a corporate lawyer and a relief pitcher for the Boston Red Sox—and had found them to be quite friendly. While impressed with Cam, to his surprise they had expressed unreserved awe of him, a high school teacher.

Tony turned left and crept across his driveway that would easily accommodate sixteen automobiles; two abreast and eight parked end to end. Eventually he eased his SUV into the three-car garage between Cam's two vehicles, glad he would not have to get wet before entering the home he and Cam—mostly Cam—had bought in Milton, Massachusetts, a town bordering the southern boundary of Boston. Population: less than thirty thousand.

Tony shut off the engine and recalled Cam's plan to add an additional two-car garage onto their three acres of land. She had explained: "After Zoë and Adam get their driver's licenses they'll need a place to park their cars." The twins had ecstatically seconded the idea. Tony had insisted they not put the cart before the horse, or garage before the auto.

He got out of his SUV while clutching his tote bag and briefcase, and walked sideways like a crab past the narrow open space in front of Cam's sedan. He twisted the doorknob leading into the kitchen and grunted with satisfaction. His repeated pleas to lock each door inside the garage—the one leading into the kitchen and the one leading into the living room—had finally bore fruit. He retrieved his keys from the pocket of his three-quarter length raincoat but the kitchen door was opened for him by a short, plump woman in her mid-forties with jet black hair.

"Good afternoon, Mr. Tony," the lady said. She wore an apron over a short-sleeved shirt and jeans. "You're home early. Not quite four o'clock." She helped him shed his coat, then reached for his tote bag and brief case. "I take these."

Tony wiped his feet on the large mat protecting the shiny Brazilian tigerwood flooring. For the past month, every time he entered the five thousand square feet home he still widened his eyes with admiration. "Good afternoon, Isabella," he replied. "I can manage. Thank you anyway." He tugged on his raincoat.

"Ah-ah-ah," Isabella retorted, and gently smacked Tony's hand as if scolding a child. "What for we do this again? You want me out of a job, huh?"

"Okay, okay," Tony conceded, smirking and releasing the raincoat. Isabella exited the kitchen muttering something in Spanish, which freed him to approach the built-in double ovens. After quickly looking over his shoulder, he cracked open the top oven door and inhaled the aroma of the lasagna baking in a large stainless steel roaster. Next, he inspected the contents of the center island, about half as long as the dining table, the latter which seated twelve. Apparently he had interrupted Isabella's preparation of a salad.

Isabella returned. "I hang up the coat and put your things in your office upstairs," she announced in her thickly accented alto voice. She resumed chopping lettuce at the center island while facing three huge cathedral-style windows overlooking a yard with a large patio, swimming pool and an acre of grass and trees. She stopped and raised her head. "You need something else, Mr. Tony?"

"No, thanks," Tony replied. He felt useless in the kitchen but smiled and declared, "Dinner smells good."

"Si," Isabella said. "Lasagna with garlic bread and salad for dinner," she announced with self-satisfaction. "I bake apple pie, too." She pointed at the built-in refrigerator-freezer. "There French vanilla ice cream for the pie. I keep it simple like you say."

"*Bueno*," Tony responded. "*Muy bueno*." He walked toward the edge of the kitchen but turned around and returned. "Isabella, I appreciate what you do here but I don't want you and Miss Cam spoiling the children. It's fine that you do their laundry and all, but I want Zoë and Adam to clean up their own rooms."

Isabella looked hurt. "But Mr. Tony, it's so wonderful to have children in the house and they be so well behaved and have so good manners. Miss Zoë have to practice her music and Mr. Adam have science things. Let me help. No trouble."

"You have enough to do," Tony insisted. "Zoë and Adam are fifteen-year-old ninth graders. They should pick up after themselves and not take advantage of you, okay?"

Isabella nodded and smiled. "Si, Mr. Tony. You so good man."

Tony smiled and turned just in time to meet face-to-face with Adam, who now stood six feet tall. "Hello, son. Another rained out game."

"Hey, dad," replied Adam, who started at third base for Milton High School's baseball team. The two males exchanged reports about their day.

"Where's Zoë and your stepmother?" Tony asked.

Adam pointed. "They're upstairs in Zoë's room. Zoë's not feeling well."

Tony tightened his face and looked upward as if trying to see into the second story. He took three rapid steps forward. "Is she okay?"

Adam stepped in front of his father. "She's fine. She and Edward broke up. She found out he was seeing another girl."

Tony frowned. "Oh." He tilted his head to the side. "I guess I should talk to her."

"Well," Adam said, "that's what Bia is doing right now. It's something a woman, a mother, should talk to her about, don't you agree?"

"Tony blinked three times. "Who's...Bia? Did I say it right? BEE-ah?"

Adam nodded. "Yes, it's what Zoë and I call Aunt Cam now. Zoë discovered the name when she was doing some research at the library. It's an old Shoshone and Paiute word. It means mother, but it was also used for mother's sister."

Tony scratched his hairless head. "Really? That's very interesting."

Adam continued. "We didn't want to keep calling her Aunt Cam or Stepmother. We'll always love Mom and we miss her every day, but we wanted Bia to know how much we've grown to love her." He lowered his voice. "And we bought her a gift for Mother's Day with our own money. This is all okay, isn't it, Dad?"

Tony smiled and placed both hands on his son's shoulders. "It's more than okay, and I couldn't be prouder of you and Zoë."

Adam walked with Tony and stopped at the bottom of the stairs leading to the second floor, located a few feet from the front door. "And one more thing, Dad."

"Yes?"

"Zoë and I want to take Milton Academy up on its offer. Bia's already said it's okay with her. It's expensive but..." Adam grinned, showcasing a smile now absent of braces. "...here's the plus side of having a stepmother who's loaded!" He laughed. "God bless you, Dad, for marrying her."

Tony chuckled. "I'm glad you approve." His children attending a fancy prep school in the fall. Wouldn't Rose be thrilled? He opened his hands. "If that's what you and Zoë want, it's fine with me." He tapped Adam on the shoulder. "But let's talk about it later. I want to go see your sister and, um Bia."

Father and son parted and Tony started to climb the winding stairs. By the time he reached the fourth stair he heard a door being opened on the first floor. Lakshmi, Cam's administrative assistant, exited her tiny office, located before Cam's spacious inner office.

"Good afternoon, Mr. Tony."

Tony stopped. "Hello, Lakshmi."

She pointed upward. "I put a copy of you and Miss Cam's new will in your office." She smiled. "If you don't mind me saying so, sir, I can't tell you how good it is to see Miss Cam so happy."

"I don't mind you saying so at all. Thank you," Tony said. "I've committed my life to making her happy. Well, I'll see you later."

"Very good sir."

Tony waved and continued his ascent. He was still getting used to having so much hired help around the house during the day; people to clean, cook, shovel the snow, mow the lawn, plant flowers, run errands and so forth. The children sure seemed to enjoy it—too much, in his opinion. That's why he had spoken to Isabella about cleaning their rooms. He didn't want his children to become pampered, spoiled brats.

He strolled down the hall past Adam's bedroom and knocked on the door to Zoë's bedroom, one of six in the house, now five since he used one as his office. He heard Cam's voice on the other side bidding him to enter. He did and saw Cam and Zoë, propped up by several pillows, huddled together on Zoë's bed. Zoë had retained the music motif for her room, including a lavender bedspread decorated with black musical notes. A lively but soft classical flute piece played in the background on her stereo. "I don't mean to interrupt," Tony said, "but I wanted to see about my daughter and my bride."

Cam ran to Tony and kissed him. "Hello, darling," she said. "How was work?"

Tony nodded. "Fine. I'm getting used to how they do things at Milton Public Schools. I've been asked to coach junior varsity basketball next year. How was your day?"

"Good," she said, and whispered in his ear, "Vincent took a plea and got three years."

Tony whispered back. "Couldn't happen to a nicer guy." He slowly approached Zoë's bed. "Is it okay if I hug you, sweetie-pie?"

Zoë nodded.

Tony sat in the spot Cam had occupied. "How are you, honey?" He glanced at her desk and admired a photo of Rose playing the piano. A photo of a beaming Cam and Zoë, absent her braces, rested next to it, taken six weeks earlier on the day of the wedding. It had been a small ceremony at Cam's home in Weston just before she had sold it. Zoë had served as maid of honor and Adam as best man. He gestured and Cam responded by sitting at the foot of the bed.

Zoë hugged Tony. "You know about Edward?"

"Yes, sweetie," Tony replied. "Your brother told me. I'm really sorry. You'll be okay?"

Zoë nodded again. "Yes, Daddy. I'll be fine. Bia has been taking good care of me."

Cam smiled with obvious pride. "Bia is a Shoshone-Paiute thing, I'm told."

"I heard," Tony said. "Adam told me that too." His daughter's tear on his wrist saddened him. However, he had taught high school long enough to foresee she would indeed be fine. The proper words to soothe her broken heart escaped him other than those that would always prove meaningful between a parent and child. "I love you," he whispered, and kissed Zoë on the forehead, then stood and gestured for Cam to return to her spot. "I'll let you two talk."

Cam placed her hand on his chest and smiled. "Thank you, Tony dear."

Tony took a couple of steps and turned. "Zoë, you'll be down for dinner?"

Zoë tightened her embrace around Cam and whimpered. "No, Daddy," she whined. "Bia said she'd asked Isabella to bring dinner to my room, just this one time."

Tony and Cam exchanged glances, tacitly agreeing. Tony shrugged. "Okay, but make sure you finish your homework. I'll look in on you later." He made his way to the door and heard the two most important women in his life speaking as if he weren't there.

"I'm never going to fall in love again."

"Don't say that, doll. You're so wonderful there are going to be dozens of boys who are going to fall in love with you. You don't want to disappoint them, do you?"

"You think so? I mean, that other boys will love me?"

"Of course, doll."

"You've always understood me, Bia."

"I'm trying, sweetheart. You know I'm new at this mother thing."

"I love you, Bia."

"And I love you too, sweetheart."

"Will you stay with me a while longer?"

"As long as you want."

Tony heard the smacking sound of kisses and gently closed the door behind him.

Acknowledgments

First of all, I thank my sweet and wonderful wife, Marieta, for her willingness to sacrifice so much of our precious time together, which enabled me to complete this novel. As my initial reader and critic, her contributions have been extremely valuable throughout the process of writing this book.

I thank Gayle Hince and Tamara Young, who served as beta readers.

I thank my family for their continued support throughout my life, especially my brother Melvin. I also thank friends Ken, Hugh and Barry for their friendship and encouragement in all my endeavors.

I thank two mentors who are no longer with us: my high school English teacher Arvid Goplen, who encouraged me to keep writing; and writing coach D. Mark Rider, who challenged me to become a better writer. I'm still working on that.

Finally, I thank attorney Joseph Hill in Madison, Wisconsin, whose generosity years ago helped me to finish graduate school.